A Scot promises
to captivate, deceive…
and utterly seduce.

When a Scot Ties
the Knot

Maddie felt dizzy, as though she were standing on the edge of a precipice. She took a deep breath, gathered her nerve . . . then jumped.

"Very well, I accept. We can be married as soon as it's practicable."

"Practicable?" He laughed. "This is Scotland, lass. There's no need to wait for banns or be married in a kirk."

"But you promised no one would suspect the truth. That means you must appear to be fond of me, at least at first. I think if you were truly *my* Captain MacKenzie, and we'd waited all these years to be together, you would want me to have a proper wedding."

"Lass, if I were truly *your* Captain MacKenzie, and I'd spent years at war, yearning for the woman I wanted to hold more than life itself . . . ? I wouldna wait another night."

She swallowed hard. "Truly?"

"Aye, truly. And I would have done this an hour ago."

His head tipped to the side, gaze dropping to her lips. And then his mouth did the strangest thing.

It started drawing closer to hers.

By Tessa Dare

Castles Ever After

ROMANCING THE DUKE
SAY YES TO THE MARQUESS
WHEN A SCOT TIES THE KNOT

Spindle Cove

A NIGHT TO SURRENDER
A WEEK TO BE WICKED
A LADY BY MIDNIGHT
THE SCANDALOUS, DISSOLUTE,
NO-GOOD MR. WRIGHT (novella)
ANY DUCHESS WILL DO
BEAUTY AND THE BLACKSMITH (novella)

Stud Club Trilogy

ONE DANCE WITH A DUKE
TWICE TEMPTED BY A ROGUE
THREE NIGHTS WITH A SCOUNDREL

The Wanton Dairymaid Trilogy

GODDESS OF THE HUNT
SURRENDER OF A SIREN
A LADY OF PERSUASION

Tessa Dare

When a Scot Ties the Knot

Castles Ever After

AVONBOOKS

An Imprint of HarperCollins*Publishers*

AVON BOOKS
An Imprint of HarperCollins*Publishers*
195 Broadway
New York, New York 10007

Copyright © 2015 by Eve Ortega
ISBN 978-0-06-234902-6
www.avonromance.com

First Avon Books mass market printing: September 2015

Avon Trademark Reg. U.S. Pat. Off. and in Other Countries, Marca Registrada, Hecho en U.S.A.
HarperCollins® is a registered trademark of HarperCollins Publishers.

Printed in the U.S.A.

10 9 8 7 6 5 4 3 2 1

For Bren
Because one does not simply write a novel.
Your friendship is precious to me.

Acknowledgments

As always, I owe tremendous debts of gratitude to my long-suffering editor, Tessa Woodward; her fearless assistant, Elle Keck; my fantastic agent, Steve Axelrod; publicist extraordinaire Jessie Edwards, and everyone at Avon Books, including but not limited to: Erika Tsang, Pam Spengler-Jaffee, and Tom Egner, who gave this book its beautiful cover.

Lindsey Faber, you are amazing and brilliant. Thank you.

Brenna Aubrey, Carey Baldwin, Courtney Milan, and Leigh LaValle are the best friends a writer could hope to have. To Zoe, Nico, and Bree—thank you for virtual hand-holding and hugs when I needed them.

Much love to Mr. Dare and the entire Dare family (kitties included) for their unending patience and the comforts of the cuddle puddle.

Lastly, but never least—thank you so much to all my readers.

Prologue

September 21, 1808

Dear Captain Logan MacKenzie,

There is but one consolation in writing this absurd letter. And that is that you, my dear delusion, do not exist to read it.

But I run ahead of myself. Introductions first.

I am Madeline Eloise Gracechurch. The greatest ninny to ever draw breath in England. This will come as a shock, I fear, but you fell deeply in love with me when we did not cross paths in Brighton. And now we are engaged.

Maddie could not remember the first time she'd held a drawing pencil. She only knew she could not recall a time she'd been without one.

In fact, she usually carried two or three. She kept them tucked in her apron pockets and speared in her upswept dark hair, and sometimes—when she needed all her limbs for climbing a tree or vaulting a fence rail—clenched in her teeth.

And she wore them down to nubs. She sketched songbirds when she was supposed to be minding her lessons, and she sketched church mice when she was meant to be at prayer. When she had time to ramble out of doors, anything in Nature was fair game—from the shoots of clover between her toes to any cloud that meandered overhead.

She loved to draw *anything*.

Well, almost anything.

She hated drawing attention to herself.

And thus, at sixteen years old, she found herself staring down her first London season with approximately as much joy as one might anticipate a dose of purgative.

After many years as a widower, Papa had taken a new wife. One a mere eight years older than Maddie herself. Anne was cheerful, elegant, lively. Everything her new stepdaughter was not.

Oh, to be Cinderella in all her soot-smeared, rag-clad misery. Maddie would have been thrilled to have a wicked stepmother lock her in the tower while everyone else went to the ball. Instead, she was stuck with a very different sort of stepmother— one eager to dress her in silks, send her to dances, and thrust her into the arms of an unsuspecting prince.

Figuratively, of course.

At best, Maddie was expected to fetch a third son with aspirations to the Church, or perhaps an insolvent baronet.

At worst . . .

Maddie didn't do well in crowds. More to the point, she didn't do *anything* in crowds. In any large gathering—be it a market, a theater, a ballroom— she had a tendency to freeze, almost literally. An arctic sense of terror took hold of her, and the crush of bodies rendered her solid and stupid as a block of ice.

The mere thought of a London season made her shudder.

And yet, she had no choice.

While Papa and Anne (she could not bring herself to address a twenty-four-year-old as Mama) enjoyed their honeymoon, Maddie was sent to a ladies' rooming house in Brighton. The sea air and society were meant to coax her out of her shell before her season commenced.

It didn't quite work that way.

Instead, Maddie spent most of those weeks *with* shells. Collecting them on the beach, sketching them in her notebook, and trying not to think about parties or balls or gentlemen.

On the morning she returned, Anne greeted her with a pointed question. "There now. Are you all ready to meet your special someone?"

That was when Maddie panicked. And lied. On the spur of the moment, she concocted an outrageous falsehood that would, for better and worse, determine the rest of her life.

"I've met him already."

The look of astonishment on her stepmother's face was immensely satisfying. But within seconds, Maddie realized how stupid she'd been. She ought to have known that her little statement wouldn't put paid to the matter. Of course it only launched a hundred other questions.

When is he coming here?

Oh, er . . . He can't. He wanted to, but he had to leave the country at once.

Whatever for?

Because he's in the army. An officer.

What of his family? We at least should meet them.

But you can't. He's from too far away. All the way in Scotland. And also, they're dead.

At least tell us his name.

MacKenzie. His name is Logan MacKenzie.

Logan MacKenzie. Suddenly her not-real suitor had a name. By the end of the afternoon, he had hair (brown), eyes (blue), a voice (deep, with a Highland burr), a rank (captain), and a personality (firm, but intelligent and kind).

And that evening, at her family's urging, Maddie sat down to write him a letter.

. . . Right this moment, they think I am writing a letter to my secret kilted betrothed, and I am filling a page with nonsense instead, just praying no one looks over my shoulder. Worst of all, I shall have no choice but to post the thing when I'm done. It will end up in some military dead letter office. I hope. Or it will be read and passed around whole regiments for ridicule, which I would richly deserve.

Stupid, stupid, stupid. Now the clock is ticking, and when it strikes doom I will have to confess. I will firstly be compelled to explain that I lied about attracting a handsome Scottish officer while staying in Brighton. Then, when I do, I shall have no further excuse to avoid the actual rejection of countless English gentlemen come spring.

My dear imaginary Captain MacKenzie, you are not real and never will be. I, however, am a true and eternal fool.

Here, have a drawing of a snail.

October 5, 1808

Dear not-really-a-Captain MacKenzie,

On second thought, perhaps I won't have to explain it this year. I might be able to stretch this for a whole season. I must admit, it's rather convenient. And my family looks at me in a whole new light. I am now a woman who inspired at least one headlong tumble into everlasting love, and really—isn't one enough?

Because, you see, you are mad for me. Utterly consumed with passion after just a few chance meetings and walks along the shore. You made me a great many promises. I was reluctant to accept them, knowing how our nascent love would be tested by distance and war. But you assured me that your heart is true, and I . . .

And I have read too many novels, I think.

November 10, 1808

Dear Captain MacWhimsy,

Is there anything more mortifying than bearing witness to one's own father's love affair? Ugh. We all knew he needed to remarry and produce an heir. To take a young, fertile wife made the most sense. I just didn't expect him to enjoy it so much, or with so few nods to dignity. Curse this endless war and its effect of hampering proper months-long honeymoons. They disappear together every afternoon, and then I and the servants must all pretend to not know what they are doing. I shudder.

I know I should be happy to see them both happy, and I am. Rather. But until this heir-making project takes root, I think I shall be writing you fewer letters and taking a great many walks.

December 18, 1808

Dear Captain MacFantasy,

I have a new accomplice. My aunt Thea has come to stay. In her youth she was a scandalous demimondaine, ruined at court in France by a wicked comte, but she's frail and harmless now.

Aunt Thea adores the idea that I'm suffering with love and anxiety for my endangered Scottish officer. I scarcely have to lie at all. "Of course Madeline doesn't wish to attend parties and balls in London! Can't you see, the poor dear is eaten with worry for her Captain MacKenzie."

Truly, it's a bit frightening how much she cherishes my misery. She has even convinced my father that I should be served breakfasts in my room now, like a married lady or an invalid. I am excused from anything resembling public merriment, I am permitted to spend as much time as I please sketching in peace. Chocolate and toast are delivered to my bedside every morning, and I read the newspaper even before Papa has his turn.

I am starting to believe you were a stroke of brilliance.

June 26, 1809

Dear Captain Imaginary MacFigment,

O happy day! Ring the bells, sound the trumpets. Swab the floors with lemon oil. My father's bride is vomiting profusely every morning, and most every afternoon, as well. The signs are plain. A noisy, smelly, writhing thing will push its way into the world in some six or seven months' time. Their joy is complete, and I am pushed further and further to the margins of it.

No matter. We have the rest of the world, you and I. Aunt Thea helps me chart the routes of your campaign. She tells me stories about the French countryside so that I might imagine the sights that will greet you as *you drive Napoleon to the other side of the Pyrenees. When you smell lavender, she says, victory is near.*

I must remind myself to appear sad from time to time, as though I'm worried for you. Sometimes, oddly enough, it's quite an easy thing to pretend.

Stay well and whole, my captain.

December 9, 1809

Oh, my dear captain,

You will be put out with me. I know I swore my heart to be true, but I must confess. I have fallen in love. Lost my heart to another, irrevocably. His name is Henry Edward Gracechurch. He weighs just a half stone, he's pink and wrinkled all over . . . and he is perfect. I don't know how I ever called him a thing. A more beautiful, charming angel never existed.

Now that Papa has an heir, our estate shall never pass to The Dreaded American, and I will never be thrown into genteel poverty. This means I do not have to marry, and I no longer need a fictional Scottish suitor to explain it.

I could claim that we've grown apart, put an end to all these silly letters and lies. But Aunt Thea is ever so fond of you by now, and I am ever so fond of her. Besides, I would miss writing.

It's the oddest thing. I do not understand myself. But sometimes I fancy that you do.

November 9, 1810

Dear Logan,

(Surely we can claim a Christian-name familiarity by now.)

What follows is an exercise in pure mortification. I can't even believe I'm going to write it down, but perhaps putting it on paper and sending it away will help rid me of the stupid habit. You see, I have a pillow. It's a fine pillow, all stuffed with goose down. Quite firm and big. Almost a bolster, really. At night I put it on one side of the bed and place a hot brick beneath it to warm it all up. Then I nestle up alongside it, and if I close my eyes and fall into that half-sleep place . . . I can almost believe it's you. Beside me. Keeping me warm and safe. But it's not you, because it is a pillow and you are not even a real person. And I am a bug. But now I've grown so accustomed to the thing, I can't sleep without it. The nights simply stretch too long and lonely.

Wherever you are, I hope you are sleeping well. Sweet dreams, Captain MacPillow.

July 17, 1811

My dear Highland laird and captain,

You have pulled off quite a trick for a man who is no more than a pillow stuffed with lies and embroidered with a hint of personality. You are going to be a land-owner. Aunt Thea has convinced my godfather, the Earl of Lynforth, to leave me a little something in his will. That "little something" being a castle in the Scottish Highlands. Lannair Castle, it's called. It is meant to be our home when you return from war. That is the perfect ending to this masterpiece of absurdity, isn't it?

Dear Lord. A castle.

March 16, 1813

Dear captain of my heart's true folly,

Little Master Henry and Miss Emma are growing like reeds. I've enclosed a sketch. Thanks to their doting mama, they have learnt to say their nightly prayers. And every night—my heart twists to write it—they pray for you. "God bless and keep our brave Captain MacKenzie." Well, the way Emma says it, it sounds more like "Cap'n Macaroni." And each time they pray for you, I feel my own soul sliding ever closer to brimstone. This has all gone too far, and yet—if I were to reveal my lie, they would despise me. And mourn you. After all, it's been almost five years since we did not meet in Brighton.

You are part of our family now.

June 20, 1813

My dear, silent friend,

It breaks my heart, but I have to do it. I must. I can't bear the guilt any longer. There's only one way to end this now.

You have to die.

I'm so sorry. You can't know how sorry. I promise, I'll make it a valiant death. You'll save four—no, six—other men in a feat of courage and noble sacrifice. As for me, I'm devastated. These are genuine tears dotting this parchment. The mourning I shall wear for you will be real, as well. It's as though I'm killing off part of myself—the part that had all those romantic, if foolish, hopes. I will settle into life as a spinster now, just as I always knew I would. I will never be married. Or held, or loved. Maybe if I write those things out, I'll get used to the truth of them. It's time to stop lying and put aside dreaming.

My darling, departed Captain MacKenzie . . .
Adieu.

Chapter One

Invernesshire, Scotland
April 1817

*B*lub.
 Blub-blub-blub.
  Maddie's hand jerked.

Ink sputtered from her pen, making great blots on the wing structure she'd been outlining. Her delicate Brazilian dragonfly now resembled a leprous chicken.

Two hours of work, gone in a heartbeat.

But it would be nothing if those bubbles signified what she hoped.

Copulation.

Her heart began to beat faster. She set aside her pen, lifted her head just enough for a clear view of the glass-walled seawater tank, and went still.

Maddie was, by nature, an observer. She knew how to fade into the background, be it drawing-room wallpaper, ballroom wainscoting, or the plastered-over stone of Lannair Castle. And she had a great deal of experience observing the mating rituals of many strange and wondrous creatures, from English aristocrats to cabbage moths.

When it came to courtship, however, lobsters were the most prudish and formal of all.

She'd been waiting months for Fluffy, the female, to molt and declare herself available to mate. So had Rex, the male specimen in the tank. She didn't know which of them was the more frustrated.

Perhaps today would be the day. Maddie peered hard at the tank, breathless with anticipation.

There. From behind a broken chunk of coral, a slender orange antennae waved in the murky gloom.

Hallelujah.

That's it, she silently willed. *Go on, Fluffy. That's a girl. It's been a long, lonely winter under that rock. But you're ready now.*

A blue claw appeared.

Then receded.

Shameless tease.

"Stop being so missish."

At last, the female's full head came into view as she rose from her hiding place.

And then someone rapped at the door. "Miss Gracechurch?"

That was the end of that.

With a *blub-blub-blub*, Fluffy disappeared as quickly as she'd emerged. Back under her rock.

Drat.

"What is it, Becky?" Maddie called. "Is my aunt ill?"

If she'd been disturbed in her studio, *someone* must be ill. The servants knew not to interrupt her when she was working.

"No one's ill, miss. But there's a caller for you."

"A caller? Now that's a surprise."

For an on-the-shelf Englishwoman residing in the barren wilds of the Scottish Highlands, callers were always a surprise.

"Who is it?" she asked.

"It's a man."

A *man*.

Now Maddie was more than surprised. She was positively shocked.

She pushed aside her ruined dragonfly illustration and stood to peer out the window. No luck. She'd chosen this tower room for its breathtaking view of the rugged green hills and the glassy loch settled like a mirror shard between them. It offered no useful vantage of the gate or entryway.

"Oh, Miss Gracechurch." Becky sounded nervous. "He's ever so big."

"Goodness. And does this big man have a name?"

"No. I mean, he must *have* a name, mustn't he?

But he didn't say. Not yet. Your aunt thought you had best come and see for yourself."

Well. This grew more and more mysterious.

"I'll be there in a moment. Ask Cook to prepare some tea, if you will."

Maddie untied her smock. After pulling the apron over her head and hanging it on a nearby peg, she took a quick inventory of her appearance. Her slate-gray frock wasn't too wrinkled, but her hands were stained with ink and her hair was a travesty—loose and disheveled. There was no time for a proper coiffure. No hairpins to be found, either. She gathered the dark locks in her hands and twisted them into a loose knot at the back of her head, securing the chignon with a nearby pencil. The best she could do under the circumstances.

Whoever this unexpected, nameless, ever-so-big man was, he wasn't likely to be impressed with her.

But then, men seldom were.

She took her time descending the spiraling stairs, wondering who this visitor might be. Most likely a land agent from a neighboring estate. Lord Varleigh wasn't due until tomorrow, and Becky would have known his name.

When Maddie finally reached the bottom, Aunt Thea joined her.

Her aunt touched a hand to her turban with dramatic flair. "Oh, Madling. At last."

"Where is our mysterious caller? In the hall?"

"The parlor." Her aunt took her arm, and together they moved down the corridor. "Now, my dear. You must be calm."

"I *am* calm. Or at least, I *was* calm until you said that." She studied her aunt's face for clues. "What on earth is going on?"

"There may be a shock. But don't you worry. Once it's over, I'll make a posset to set you straight."

A posset.

Oh, dear. Aunt Thea fancied herself something of an amateur apothecary. The trouble was, her "cures" were usually worse than the disease.

"It's only a caller. I'm sure a posset won't be necessary."

Maddie resolved to maintain squared shoulders and an air of good health when she greeted this big, nameless man.

When they stepped into the parlor, her resolve was tested.

This wasn't just a man.

This was a *man*.

A tall, commanding figure of a Scotsman, dressed in what appeared to be military uniform: a kilt of dark green-and-blue plaid, paired with the traditional redcoat.

His hair was overlong (mostly brown, with hints of ginger), and his squared jaw sported several days' growth of whiskers (mostly ginger, with hints of brown). Broad shoulders tapered to a trim torso. A simple black sporran was slung low around his waist, and a sheathed dirk rode his hip. Below the fall of his kilt, muscled, hairy legs disappeared into white hose and scuffed black boots.

Maddie pleaded with herself not to stare.

It was a losing campaign.

Taken altogether, his appearance was a veritable assault of virility.

"Good afternoon." She managed an awkward curtsy.

He did not answer or bow. Wordlessly, he approached her.

And at the point where a well-mannered gentleman would stop, he drew closer still.

She shifted her weight from one foot to the other, anxious. At least he'd solved her staring problem. She could scarcely bear to look at him now.

He stopped close enough for Maddie to breathe in the scents of whisky and wood smoke, and to glimpse a wide, devilish mouth slashing through his light growth of beard. After long seconds, she coaxed herself into meeting his gaze.

His eyes were a breathtaking blue. And not in a good way.

They were the sort of blue that gave one the feeling of being launched into the sky or plunged into icy water. Flung into a void with no hope of return. It wasn't a pleasant sensation.

"Miss Madeline Gracechurch?"

Oh, his voice was the worst part of all. Deep, with that Highland burr that scraped and hollowed words out, forcing them to hold more meaning.

She nodded.

He said, "I'm come home to you."

"H-home . . . to *me*?"

"I knew it," Aunt Thea said. "It's him."

The strange man nodded. "It's me."

"It's who?" Maddie blurted out.

She didn't mean to be rude, but she'd never laid eyes on this man in her life. She was quite sure of it. His wasn't a face or figure she'd be likely to forget. He made quite an impression. More than an impression. She felt flattened by him.

"Don't you know me, *mo chridhe*?"

She shook her head. She'd had enough of this game, thank you. "Tell me your name."

The corner of his mouth tipped in a small, roguish smile. "Captain Logan MacKenzie."

No.

The world became a violent swirl of colors: green and red and that stark, dangerous blue.

"Did you . . ." Maddie faltered. "Surely you didn't say Cap—"

That was as far as she got. Her tongue gave up.

And then her knees gave out.

She didn't swoon or crumple. She simply sat

down, hard. Her backside hit the settee, and the air was forced from her lungs. *"Oof."*

The Scotsman stared down at her, looking faintly amused. "Are ye well?"

"No," she said honestly. "I'm seeing things. This can't be happening."

This really, truly, could *not* be happening.

Captain Logan MacKenzie could not be alive. He could not be dead, either.

He didn't exist.

To be sure, for nigh on a decade now, everyone had believed her to be first pining after, then mourning for, the man who was nothing but fiction.

Maddie had spent countless afternoons writing him letters—missives that had actually just been pages of nonsense or sketches of moths and snails. She'd declined to attend parties and balls, citing her devotion to the Highland hero of her dreams—but really because she'd preferred to stay home with a book.

Her godfather, the Earl of Lynforth, had even left her Lannair Castle in his will so that she might be nearer her beloved's home. Quite thoughtful of the old dear.

And when the deceit began to weigh on her conscience, Maddie had given her Scottish officer a brave, honorable, and entirely fictional death. She'd worn black for a full year, then gray thereafter. Everyone believed her to be disconsolate, but black and gray suited her. They hid the smudges of ink and charcoal that came from her work.

Thanks to Captain MacKenzie, she had a home, an income, work she enjoyed—and no pressure to move in London society. She'd never intended to deceive her family for so many years, but no one had been hurt. It all seemed to have worked for the best.

Until now.

Now something had gone terribly wrong.

Maddie turned her head by slow degrees, Miss Muffet fashion, forcing herself to look at the Highlander who'd sat down beside her. Her heart thumped in her chest.

If her Captain MacKenzie didn't exist, who was this man? And what did he want from her?

"You aren't real." She briefly closed her eyes and pinched herself, hoping to waken from this horrid dream. "You. Aren't. Real."

Aunt Thea pressed a hand to her throat. With the other, she fanned herself vigorously. "Surely it must be a miracle. To think, we were told you were—"

"Dead?" The officer's gaze never left Maddie's. A hint of irony sharpened his voice. "I'm not dead. Touch and see for yourself."

Touch?

Oh, no. Touching him was out of the question. There would not be any touching.

But before Maddie knew what was happening,

he'd caught her ungloved hand and drawn it inside his unbuttoned coat, pressing it to his chest.

And they were touching.

Intimately.

A stupid, instinctive thrill shot through her. She'd never held hands with any man. Never felt a man's skin pressed against her own. Curiosity clamored louder than her objections.

His hand was large and strong. Roughened with calluses, marked with scars and powder burns. Those marks revealed his life to be one of battle and strife, just as surely as her pale, ink-stained fingers told hers to be a life of scribbling . . . and no adventure at all.

He flattened her palm against the well-worn lawn of his shirt. Beneath it, he was impressively solid. Warm.

Real.

"I'm no ghost, *mo chridhe*. Just a man. Flesh and bone."

Mo chridhe.

He kept using those words. She wasn't fluent in Gaelic, but over the years she'd gathered a few bits here and there. She knew *mo chridhe* meant "my heart."

The words were a lover's endearment, but there was no tenderness in his voice. Only a low, simmering anger. He spoke the words like a man who'd cut out his own heart long ago and left it buried in the cold, dark ground.

With their joined hands, he eased aside one lapel of his coat. The gesture revealed a corner of yellowed paper tucked inside his breast pocket. She recognized the handwriting on the envelope.

It was her own.

"I received your letters, lass. Every last one."

God help her. He knew.

He knew she'd lied. He knew everything.

And he was here to make her pay.

"Aunt Thea," she whispered, "I believe I'll be needing that posset after all."

So, Logan thought. *This is the girl.*

At last he had her in his grasp. Madeline Eloise Gracechurch. In her own words, the greatest ninny to ever draw breath in England.

The lass wasn't in England now. And pale as she'd grown in the past few seconds, he suspected she might not be breathing, either.

He gave her hand a little squeeze, and she drew in a gasp. Color flooded her cheeks.

There, that was better.

To be truthful, Logan needed a moment to locate his own composure. She'd knocked the breath from him, too.

He'd spent a great deal of time wondering how she looked. Too much time over the years. Of course she'd sent him sketches of every blessed mushroom, moth, and blossom in existence—but never any likenesses of herself.

By the gods, she was bonny. Far prettier than her letters had led him to imagine. Also smaller, more delicate.

"So . . ." she said, "this means . . . you . . . I . . . gack."

Much less articulate, too.

Logan's gaze slid to her aunt, who was somehow *exactly* as he'd always pictured her. Frail shoulders, busy eyes, saffron-yellow turban.

"Perhaps you'll permit us a few minutes alone, Aunt Thea. May I call you Aunt Thea?"

"But . . . certainly you may."

"No," his betrothed moaned. "Please, don't."

Logan patted her slender shoulder. "There, there."

Aunt Thea hurried to excuse her niece. "You must forgive her, Captain. We believed you dead for years. She's worn mourning ever since. To have you back again . . . well, it's such a shock. She's overwrought."

"That's understandable," he said.

And it was.

Logan would be surprised, too, if a person he'd invented from thin air, then cravenly lied about for close to a decade, appeared on his doorstep one afternoon.

Surprised, shocked . . . perhaps even frightened.

Madeline Gracechurch appeared to be no less than terrified.

"What was it you mentioned wanting, *mo chridhe*? A poultice?"

"A posset," Aunt Thea said. "I'll heat one at once."

As soon as her aunt had left the room, Logan tightened his grip around Madeline's slender wrist, drawing her to her feet.

The motion seemed to help her find her tongue.

"Who are you?" she whispered.

"I thought we covered that already."

"Have you no conscience, coming in here as an imposter and frightening my aunt?"

"Imposter?" He made an amused sound. "I'm no imposter, lass. But I'll admit—I am entirely without conscience."

She wet her lips with a nervous flick of her tongue, drawing his gaze to a small, kiss-shaped mouth that might otherwise have escaped his attention.

Wondering what else he might have missed, he let his eyes wander down her figure, from the untidy knot of dark hair atop her head to . . . whatever sort of body might be hiding under that high-necked gray shroud.

It didn't matter, he told himself. He hadn't come for the carnal attractions.

He was here to collect what he was owed.

Logan inhaled deep. The air hovering about her carried a familiar scent.

When you smell lavender, victory is near.

Her hand went to her brow. "I can't understand what's happening."

"Can't you? Is it so hard to believe that the name and rank you plucked from the air might belong to an actual man somewhere? MacKenzie's not an uncommon name. The British Army's a vast pool of candidates."

"Yes, but I never properly addressed anything. I specifically wrote the number of a regiment that doesn't exist. Never indicated any location. I just tossed them into the post."

"Well, somehow—"

"Somehow they found their way to you." She swallowed audibly. "And you . . . Oh, no. And you *read* them?"

He opened his mouth to reply.

"Of course you read them," she said, cutting him off. "You couldn't be here if you hadn't."

Logan didn't know whether to be annoyed or grateful that she kept completing his side of the conversation. He supposed it was habit on her part. She'd conducted a one-sided correspondence with him for years.

And then, once he'd served his purpose, she'd had the nerve to kill him off.

This canny little English heiress thought she'd come up with the perfect scheme to avoid being pressured into marriage.

She was about to learn she'd been wrong.

Verra wrong.

"Oh, dear," she muttered. "I think I'll be sick."

"I must say, this is a fine welcome home."

"This isn't your home."

It will be, lass. It will be.

Logan decided to give her a moment to compose herself. He made a slow circle of the room. The castle itself was remarkable. A classic fortified tower house, kept in a fair state of repair. This chamber they currently occupied was hung with ancient tapestries but was otherwise furnished in what he assumed to be typical English style.

But he didn't care about carpets and settees.

He paused at the window. It was the surrounding land that interested him. This glen was ideal. A wide, green ribbon of fertile land stretched alongside the clear loch. Beyond it lay open hills for grazing.

These were the Highlands his soldiers had known in their youths. The Highlands that had all but disappeared by the time they'd returned from war. Stolen by greedy English landlords—and the occasional fanciful spinster.

This would be home for them now. Here, in the shadow of Lannair Castle, his men could regain what had been taken from them. There was space enough in this glen to raise cottages, plant crops, start families.

Rebuild a life.

Logan would stop at nothing to give them that

chance. He owed his men that much. He owed them far more.

"You," she announced, "have to leave."

"Leave? Not a chance, *mo chridhe*."

"You have to leave. Now."

She took him by the sleeve and tried tugging him toward the door. Unsuccessfully.

Then she gave up on the tugging and started pushing at him instead.

That wasn't any help, either. Except, perhaps, as an aid to Logan's amusement.

He was a lot of man, and she was a mere slip of a lass. He couldn't help but laugh. But her efforts weren't entirely ineffectual. The press of her tiny hands on his arms and chest stirred him in dangerous places.

He'd gone a long time without a woman's touch.

Far too long.

At length, she gave up on the pulling and pushing, and went straight to her last resort.

Pleading. Big, brown calf's eyes implored him for mercy. Little did she know, this was the least likely tactic to work. Logan wasn't a man to be moved by tender emotion.

However, he was a man—and he wasn't unmoved by a pretty face. What with all her exertions, he was starting to see a flush of color on her cheeks. And an intriguing spark of mystery behind those wide, dark eyes.

This lass didn't belong in gray. With that dark hair and those rosy lips, she belonged in vibrant color. Deep Highland greens or sapphire blue.

His own smile took him by surprise.

She was going to look bonny wearing his plaid.

"Just go," she said. "If you leave now, I can convince my aunt this was all a mistake. Because it *was* a mistake. You must know that. I never meant to bother you with my silly ramblings."

"Perhaps you didna mean to. But involve me you did."

"Is it an apology you want, then? I'm sorry. So very, very sorry. Please, if you'll just give me the letters back and be on your way, I'll be most generous. I'd be glad to pay you for your troubles."

Logan shook his head. She thought a bribe would appease him? "I'm not leaving, lass. Not for all the pin money in your wee silk reticule."

"Then what *do* you want?"

"That's simple. I want what your letters said. What you've been telling your family for years. I'm Captain Logan MacKenzie. I received every last one of your missives, and despite your best attempts to kill me, I am verra much alive."

He propped a finger under her chin, tilting her face to his. So she would be certain to hear and believe his words.

"Madeline Eloise Gracechurch . . . I've come here to marry you."

Chapter Two

*A*unt Thea sat across from Maddie at the tea table. "Well, my dear. I must say, this has been a most surprising afternoon."

Maddie could not dispute it. She dipped her spoon in the posset and traced figure eights in the pale, lumpy brew.

The entire encounter with Captain MacKenzie had left her reeling.

I've come here to marry you, he'd said.

And in return, what had she said? Had she given him a scathing, witty refusal? Shredded his smirk to ribbons with her rapier wit? Sent him riding into the sunset, sworn to never again pester an unsuspecting Englishwoman in her home?

Hah. No, of course not. She'd merely stood there,

still as a stone and twice as dumb, until her aunt had returned, posset in hand.

I've come here to marry you.

Maddie blamed her upbringing. Every gentleman's daughter was raised to believe that those words—when spoken by a reasonably attractive, well-intentioned gentleman—were her key to bliss. Marriage, she'd been taught over the course of a thousand dollhouse tea parties, should be her desire, her goal . . . her very reason for existing.

So ingrained was this lesson that Maddie had actually felt a foolish *zing* of exhilaration when he'd declared this preposterous intent. A little voice inside her had kept standing up to cheer. *You've finally made the grade! At last, a man wants to marry you.*

Sit down, she'd told it. *And be still.*

She refused to define her personal worth on the basis of a marriage proposal. Much less this one. Which was not a true proposal but a threat—delivered by a man who was *not* a gentleman, *not* well intentioned, and attractive to an *un*reasonable degree.

"I never dreamed that this was possible." Maddie circled her spoon in the bowl again and again. "I can't imagine how it occurred."

"To be sure, I'm stunned as well. The back-from-the-dead part is quite a shock, of course. Even more than that . . ." Her aunt propped her chin on the back of her hand and stared out the window looking onto the courtyard. "Just look at that man."

Maddie followed her aunt's gaze.

Captain MacKenzie stood in the center of the grassy space, giving directions to the small band of soldiers in his command. His men had brought their horses inside the castle walls to be fed and watered and stabled for the night. After that, they'd expressed an intent to make camp.

They were practically taking up residence.

Dear heaven. How had this happened?

The same way all of it had happened, Maddie told herself.

It was her fault.

She'd made one mistake years ago, in much the same way a child made a snowball. It had been a small, manageable, innocent-looking thing at first. It had fit in the palm of her hand.

Then the snowball had rolled away from her and taken a wild bounce down a hill. From there, everything escaped her control. The lies built on themselves, growing ever larger and gaining furious speed. And no matter how long and hard she chased after it, she never quite managed to get the snowball back.

"To think that my little Madling—at the tender age of sixteen—snagged that glorious specimen. And here I thought you only collected seashells." Aunt Thea toyed with her cuff bracelet. "I know you told us a great deal of your captain, but I assumed you were overstating his qualities. It would seem you were being humble instead. Were I thirty years younger, I'd—"

"Aunt Thea, please."

"Now I understand why you resisted marrying elsewhere all this time. A man like that will ruin a woman for all others. I know it well. It was just the same between me and the Comte de Montclair. Ah, to relive that springtime at Versailles." She looked over at Maddie again. "You haven't touched your posset."

Maddie peered at the lumpy, aromatic mess before her. "It smells . . . adventurous."

"It's just the usual. Hot milk, curdled with ale. A bit of sugar, anise, clove."

"Are you certain that's all?" Maddie gathered a spoonful. "No special ingredients?"

"Oh, yes. I did add a dram of Dr. Hargreaves' Elixir. And a pinch of pickling spice to clear the phlegm." She nodded at the bowl. "Go on. Be a good girl and eat it up. We've hours yet before dinner. I told your captain to bring his men in for the evening meal once they've settled."

"We're going to feed them?" Everyone knew that once you fed a pack of wandering beasts, they'd never leave. "Cook will quit in protest."

"They're soldiers. They'll only want simple fare.

Bread, beef, puddings. No need for a lavish menu."
Aunt Thea raised a silver brow. "Unless you're offering up a pair of lobsters?"

Maddie looked up, horrified. "Fluffy and Rex? How could you even suggest it?"

"What I'm suggesting, my dear, is that your time as a shellfish voyeur may be drawing to a close."

"But I've been commissioned by Mr. Orkney to draw a series illustrating the lobster's life cycle. Mating is only one part of it. They can live for decades."

The lobsters were only one of a few small projects she had underway. With a bit of luck—and Lord Varleigh's assistance—she hoped to have larger undertakings soon.

"You have a life cycle of your own to get on with." Aunt Thea placed her hands atop Maddie's. "Now that the captain has returned, you can be married soon. That is, assuming you still *want* to marry him. Do you not?"

Maddie met her aunt's gaze.

This was it. Her chance to give that ever-growing snowball a swift kick of truth. Break it apart once and for all.

Actually, Aunt Thea, I don't wish to marry him. You see, I didn't manage *to snag that glorious specimen of man. I'd never seen him before today. There never was any Captain MacKenzie at all. I told a silly, panicked lie to avoid a season of disappointment. I deceived everyone for years, and I'm sorry for it. So very sorry and ashamed.*

Maddie bit her lip. "Aunt Thea, I . . ."

"Hold that thought," her aunt said, rising from the table and moving toward the cabinet. "First, I'm pouring myself some brandy to celebrate. I know this is *your* miraculous day. *Your* sweetheart, come home. But in a way, it is my triumph as well. After all those times I went to battle with your Papa, when he wanted to force you back into the *ton* . . . I'm just so happy for you. And happy for myself, as well. I'm vindicated. The past ten years of my life have meaning now." She brought her glass of brandy back to the table. "Well? What is it you have to say?"

Maddie's heart pinched. "You do know how grateful I am. And how much I adore you."

"But of course I do. I'm rather easy to adore."

"Then I hope you can find it in your heart to forgive me."

"Forgive you?" Her aunt laughed. "Whatever for, my Madling?"

Maddie's head began to throb at the temples. She gripped the spoon until her knuckles ached.

"For not eating the posset." She gave her aunt a sheepish smile. "I'm feeling better. Might I have a brandy, too?"

She just couldn't do it. Aunt Thea must not be made to suffer for Maddie's mistakes. The old dear had no fortune of her own. She depended on Maddie for financial support, and Maddie depended on her aunt for everything else. To tell the truth now would hurt them both too deeply.

This predicament was one of her own making.

That intimidating Highlander in the courtyard was her problem.

And Maddie knew, then and there—it was up to her to solve him.

By the time Logan emerged from the castle, his men were anxiously awaiting news. And judging from the looks on their faces, they expected the news to be bad.

"So . . . ?" Callum prompted. "How did it go?"

"As well as could be expected," Logan replied.

Better than he'd expected, in some ways. Logan had anticipated arriving to find a woman plagued with pockmarks or afflicted with a harelip. At the least, he'd told himself, she would be plain. Why else would a gently-bred heiress feel compelled to invent a sweetheart?

But Madeline wasn't afflicted in any visible way, and she certainly wasn't plain. She was lovely.

A lovely little liar.

He wasn't yet certain whether that made things better or worse.

"If that's so," Rabbie asked, "why are you out here with us?"

"She'd believed I was dead," he said. "Our return came as a shock to her. I'm giving her a moment to recover."

"Well, at least she's still here," Callum said. "That means you fared better than I did."

Munro, the field surgeon, joined them. "Still no news about your lass, Callum?"

Callum shrugged. "There's news. My uncle in Glasgow checked the records of the ship what sailed for Nova Scotia. There was no Miss Mairi Aileen Fraser on the passenger list."

"But that's good," Munro said. "Means she's still here in Scotland."

The round-faced soldier shook his head. "I said there was no Mairi Aileen Fraser on the list. There was, however, a Mrs. Mairi Aileen MacTavish. So much for my returning hero's welcome."

The older man clapped Callum on the back. "Sorry to hear it, lad. If she didna wait, she didna deserve you."

"I canna blame her." Callum patted his chest with the stump of his left forearm—the one missing a hand Munro had amputated in the field. "Have a look at me. Who'd wait on this?"

"A great"—Fyfe hiccupped—"many lasses, surely."

Logan pulled a flask of whisky from his sporran, uncapped it, and passed it to Callum. Sympathetic words were never his strong point, but he was always ready to pour the next round.

It wasn't supposed to be this way. When the regiment had landed at Dover last autumn, they'd been greeted as triumphant heroes in London. Then they'd marched north. Home, to the Highlands. And he'd watched his men's lives and dreams fall apart at the seams, one by one.

Callum wasn't the only one. The men gathered around him represented the last of his discharged soldiers, and the worst off: the homeless, the wounded, the left behind.

They'd fought bravely, survived battle, won the war for England on the promise of coming home to their families and sweethearts—only to find their families, homes, and sweethearts gone. Pushed off the lands they'd inhabited for centuries by the same greedy English landlords who'd asked them to fight.

And Logan couldn't do a damned thing about it. Until today.

Today, he took it all back.

The hulking man at the edge of their group startled. "What's this, then? Where is this place?"

"Easy, Grant."

Grant's was the saddest tale of the lot. A mortar had landed too close at Quatre-Bras, tossing the giant of a man twenty feet through the air. He'd survived his injuries, but now he couldn't remember a blessed thing for more than an hour or so. He had a perfect recollection of everything in his life up until that battle. Anything new slipped through his grasp like so much sand.

"We're at Lannair Castle," Munro explained. The grizzled field surgeon had more patience than the rest of them put together. "The war is over. We're home in Scotland."

"Are we? Well, that's bonny."

No one had the heart to dispute it.

"Say, Captain," the big man said. "Will we be making our way to Ross-shire soon? I'm keen to see my nan and the wee ones."

Logan nodded tightly. "Tomorrow, if you like."

They weren't going anywhere near Ross-shire tomorrow, but Grant would forget the promise anyhow. Most days, Logan couldn't bear to tell him they'd been to Ross-shire months ago. Grant's nan was dead of old age, the wee ones had perished of typhus, and their family cottage was a burned-out shell of ash.

"Tomorrow would be fine." After a pause, Grant chuckled to himself and added, "Did I tell ye the one about the pig, the whore, and the bagpipes?"

The rest of the men groaned.

Logan silenced them with a look. At Corunna,

Grant had held off an entire line of *voltiguers,* giving their company time to fall back. He'd saved their lives. The least they could do was listen to his bawdy joke one more time.

Logan said, "Let's hear it, then. I could do with a joke today."

The telling of it lasted a while, what with several starts, stops, and pauses for Grant to collect his thoughts.

When he finally came to the end, all the men joined him in a bored tone: " 'Squeal louder, lass. Squeal louder.' "

Grant laughed heartily and slapped Logan on the back. "A good one, isn't it? Can't wait to tell it back home."

Home. This place was as close to a home as Grant could have now.

Logan raised his voice. "Have a look around the glen, lads. Start choosing your sites for cottages."

"They'll never let us have this," Rabbie said. "Are ye daft? It's been more than eight years since you kissed her good-bye. This land's in English hands now. That lass of yours has a father or a brother somewhere who'll show his face to chase us off, and we'll be on the next ship to Australia."

Callum shifted his weight. "Perhaps we should wait to be certain she'll marry you, Captain."

Logan squared his shoulders. "Have no worry on that score. I'll be making certain of it. Tonight."

Chapter Three

Once she'd reached her decision, Maddie washed her face, sipped some brandy, and readied herself to go out and confront Captain Logan MacKenzie.

She got as far as the doorway—where he appeared, looking for her.

His gaze swept her up and down, leaving her painted with gooseflesh.

"You look as though you could use some air, *mo chridhe*. Let's take a stroll and talk, the two of us."

"Very well," she agreed, a bit dismayed that it wasn't her idea now. She wanted to be in control. Or at the very least, holding her own.

But how could she ever hold her own with a man like this?

Maddie struggled to keep up with him as they walked out of the castle and through the arched stone gateway. His long, easy strides translated to a brisk pace for her.

They emerged from the castle's shadow into the afternoon sun and walked out toward the loch's edge. The weather was deceptively cheery—sunny and warm for April, with a gentle freshness in the breeze. The sky and water seemed to be having a contest to out-blue one another.

Captain MacKenzie's eyes bested them both.

"What a bonny afternoon to walk along the waterfront," he said. "Just like old times, in Brighton."

"You can stop teasing me. I'm well aware that I was a fool at sixteen. But I didn't stop maturing when I stopped writing you letters. I've grown into a woman."

"Oh, have you now?"

"Yes. An independent woman. One who manages her own household and affairs. So let us be direct."

They came to a halt on a small spit of land that extended into the loch like a gnarled green finger.

Heavens, he was so tall. Maddie realized that she was going to have an ache in her neck from staring up at him. She stepped onto a large, flat rock, closing their height difference to a more manageable amount.

Unfortunately, closing that distance only brought her closer to his handsome features and breathtaking eyes.

His attractiveness didn't matter, she reminded herself. This was *not* a long-abandoned dream miraculously come true. This man was *not* the heroic Captain MacKenzie she'd invented. He was just a soldier who happened to share the same name.

And he certainly wasn't in love with her.

No, this man wanted something, and that something wasn't Maddie. If she could learn what his goal was, perhaps she could convince him to go away.

"You said you don't want money. What is it you're after?"

"I'm after this, lass." He nodded toward the loch. "The castle. The land. And I'm prepared to do anything to get it. Even marrying a deceitful English minx."

At last, here was an explanation she found credible.

Unfortunately, she also found it terrible.

"You can't force me to wed you."

"I willna need to force you. You'll wed me eagerly enough. As you say, you're an independent woman now. 'Twould be a shame for these letters"—he pulled the yellowed paper from his breast pocket—"to fall into the wrong hands."

He cleared his throat and began to read. "'My Dear Captain MacWhimsy. This morning, the dreadful Miss Price came to call. Lavinia is always prodding me for stories about you. Today she asked if we had kissed. I said of course we had. And then of course she had to ask me what the kiss was like.'"

As he read, Maddie felt her face growing hotter. The edges of her vision turned a pulsing shade of red. "That's enough, thank you."

He went on reading. " 'I should have said something insipid, like *sweet* or *nice*. Or better yet, nothing at all. Instead . . .' "

"Captain MacKenzie, please."

" 'Instead,' " he continued, " 'this silly, boastful word tripped off my tongue. I'm not certain where it came from. But once it was out there, I couldn't take it back. Oh, my captain. I told Miss Price our kiss was—' "

She dove for the paper. He raised his hand overhead, removing it from her reach. Despite herself, she hopped in a futile attempt to grab it. He chuckled at her attempt, and she felt the loss of dignity keenly.

" 'I told Miss Price our kiss was *incendiary*,' " he finished.

Oh, Lord.

He folded the paper and returned it to his breast pocket. "This one isna so bad, really. There are more. Many more. You may recall, they grew quite personal."

Yes. She recalled.

For young Maddie, those letters had served as a diary of sorts. She would write down the things she didn't dare speak aloud. All her petty complaints, all her most uncharitable thoughts born of adolescent moods and disappointments. Her ill-informed dreams about what love *could* be between a woman and a man. She'd sent those letters to Captain Mac-Kenzie precisely because she'd never wanted anyone who knew her to read them.

And now he threatened to expose them to the world.

A sense of despair churned in her belly. She felt as though she'd spent her youth stuffing heartfelt wishes into bottles and tossing them into the ocean—and suddenly, years later, they'd all been returned.

By a sea monster.

"What if I refuse to marry you?" she asked.

"Then I think I'll forward your letters on to someone else. Someone who'd be verra interested."

She winced. "I suppose you mean my father."

"No, I was thinking of the London scandal sheets. Most likely I'd go to both and see which one will offer me more money."

"I can't believe anyone would be that heartless."

Chuckling, he touched the folded letter to her cheek. "We're just getting acquainted, *mo chridhe*. But believe me when I tell you I'm nothing you ever wanted and worse than you could have dreamed."

Of course he would be.

This was a perfect example of Maddie's luck. Of all the ranks in the army, all the names in Christendom, and all the clans in the Highlands . . . she had to randomly choose his.

If this had only been a matter of some mortification, Maddie would have taken that punishment, and gladly. However, if those letters became public, it would mean more than simple embarrassment.

People laughed at a fool; they hated a fraud. Perhaps she hadn't set out to deceive all of England, but she'd made no objections to stirring her family's sympathy and her peers' jealousy. Years later, after the captain's supposed death, she'd accepted their condolences.

She'd even accepted a *castle*.

All of her acquaintances would know that Maddie had deceived them, and for the silliest of reasons. The gossip would haunt her family for years. And who would commission scientific illustrations from a woman infamous for lies? She could find herself all alone with no means of support.

Her sense of panic only grew.

"Let's discuss this rationally," she said. "You're proposing to blackmail me with letters I wrote when I was sixteen years old. Didn't you do anything rash and foolish when you were sixteen years old?"

"I most certainly did."

"Good," Maddie said eagerly. Perhaps she could convince him to be sympathetic. He would agree that no one should be forced to pay a lifelong price for youthful folly. "And what was your foolish choice?"

"I joined the army," he said. "More than ten years

later, I'm not through paying for that choice. Most of
my friends paid with their lives."

She bit her lip. When he put it that way . . .

"Please try to understand. If you read my letters, you must believe I took no pleasure in lying.
It simply mushroomed beyond my control. I've
wished so many times that I'd never said anything."

"You'd take it all back?"

"*Yes.* In a heartbeat."

She thought he flinched a little at her eagerness,
but maybe it was just her imagination. She had a
well-established surfeit of imagination. Particularly
when it came to men in kilts.

"If you want to take back your lies," he said, "then
you should marry me."

"How do you reason that?"

"Think on it. You wrote letters to your Scottish
intended. I received them. Those are the plain facts,
are they not?"

"I suppose."

"Once you marry me, none of it is a lie," he
pointed out. "It will be exactly as though you've told
the truth all these years."

"Except for the part where we love each other."

He shrugged. "That's a minor detail. Love is just
a lie people tell themselves."

Maddie wanted to disagree with that statement,

but she wasn't sure she could make a convincing case. Not from personal experience, at any rate.

And despite herself, she was growing intrigued. "What kind of arrangement are you suggesting?"

"A simple one. We marry for our own reasons, as a mutually beneficial arrangement. I get the property. You'll get your letters back."

"What about . . ." Her cheeks warmed with a blush. "You know."

"I'm not sure I do know."

He knew what she meant, the rogue. He just wanted the amusement of making her say it.

She forced the words out. "What about marital relations?"

"Do I mean to ravish you, you mean?" He lifted a brow. "The marriage must be consummated. But I'm not interested in children."

"Oh. I'm not interested in children, either."

That wasn't precisely true. Maddie loved babies. But for one reason and another, she'd long given up on the idea of motherhood for herself. It wouldn't be much sacrifice to jettison the last raft of hope now.

"So just one night of consummation?" she asked. "And no emotional involvement whatsoever."

He nodded. "We'll only need to live together for a few months. Long enough for me to establish ownership of the place. I'll build some cottages, put crops in the ground. Then you're free to do as you please."

"You mean leave? What would I tell my family?"

"That we're like any other couple who married in haste and then found themselves reconsidering, wanting to live apart. It's not uncommon."

"No," Maddie admitted. "It isn't uncommon. In fact, that wouldn't even be a lie."

Her head was spinning.

The idea of marriage had sounded preposterous at first. But maybe this *was* the next-best thing to going back in time. Perhaps she really *could* take it back—this ridiculous, impetuous tale that had taken over her life.

And, oh—her heart pinched.

For the first time in years, she could visit her family without feeling like a fraud. This web of lies she'd spun had made it impossible for her to confide in anyone. She didn't dare let anyone too close.

The loneliness had worn on her. Most dreadfully.

And when she wasn't visiting friends or family, she could stay in the castle and continue her work in peace. Captain MacKenzie would be busy managing the lands. She only needed to share a bed with him the once.

She stole a glance at his bare legs.

Perhaps that bedding part wouldn't be entirely terrible. At the least, she would have the chance to satisfy a few matters of curiosity. She spent her days waiting on lobsters to have intercourse. Naturally, she'd wondered about the human equivalent from time to time.

"I need your choice, lass," he said. "Will you be marrying me, or will I be forwarding all these letters to the London scandal sheets?"

She closed her eyes for a moment. "Do you promise me that no one will ever know the truth?"

"I swear they willna know it from me."

"And I will be free to continue my own interests and pursuits."

He nodded. "You have your life, and I'll have mine."

Maddie felt dizzy, as though she were standing on the edge of a precipice. She took a deep breath, gathered her nerve . . . then jumped.

"Very well, I accept. We can be married as soon as it's practicable."

"Practicable?" He laughed. "This is Scotland, lass. There's no need to wait for banns or be married in a kirk."

"But you promised no one would suspect the truth. That means you must appear to be fond of me, at least at first. I think if you were truly *my* Captain MacKenzie, and we'd waited all these years to be together, you would want me to have a proper wedding."

He closed the distance between them.

"Lass, if I were truly *your* Captain MacKenzie, and I'd spent years at war, yearning for the one woman I wanted to hold more than life itself . . . ?" He touched a lock of her hair. "I wouldna wait another night."

She swallowed hard. "Truly?"

"Aye, truly. And I would have done this an hour ago."

His head tipped to the side. His gaze dropped to her lips. And then his mouth did the strangest thing.

It started drawing closer to hers.

He couldn't be—

Oh, Lord. He was. He was going to kiss her.

"Wait." Panicked, Maddie put both hands on his chest, holding him off. "Your men, my servants . . . they could be watching us."

"I'm certain they're watching us. That's why we're going to kiss."

"But I don't know how. You know I don't know how."

His lips quirked. "I know how."

Those three little words, spoken in that low, devastating Scottish burr, did absolutely nothing to ease Maddie's concerns.

Thankfully, she had a reprieve. He pulled back and peered at her hair. He looked like a boy marveling at clockwork, wondering how it all worked. After a few moments, she felt him grasp the pencil holding her chignon.

With one long, slow tug, he eased it loose and cast it aside.

It landed in the loch with a splash.

His fingers sifted through her hair, teasing the locks free of their haphazard knot and arranging them about her shoulders. Tenderly. Like she'd always imagined a lover would. Sparks of sensation danced from her scalp to her toes.

"That was my best drawing pencil," she said.

"It's just a pencil."

"It came from London. I have a limited supply."

His thumb caressed her cheek. "It almost put out my eye. I've a limited supply of those, too. And it's better this way."

"But—" Her breath caught. "Oh."

He bracketed her cheeks with his hands, tilting her face to his.

Her pulse thundered in her ears. She stared at his mouth. A wave of inevitability washed over her.

She whispered, "This is really happening, isn't it?"

In answer, he pressed his lips to hers.

And Maddie went still. The lightning bolt of sensual expertise she'd been hoping for didn't arrive. She was glued to his face, staring at his cheekbone. She had no idea what she was supposed to do.

Close your eyes, ninny.

Maybe, if she was very still and paid close attention, her idiocy wouldn't be obvious. Perhaps he could teach her to kiss, in the same way the sky taught the loch to be blue.

It was a stupid risk, kissing her this soon.

Logan realized it the moment his lips met hers

and she went rigid in response. Bloody hell. If this embrace went wrong, he could scare her off and his grand plans would be over before they began.

That meant his challenge was plain.

He had to make sure this kiss went right.

"Hush, *mo chridhe*. Softly now."

He brushed his lips over hers in brief passes, with all the patience and tenderness a man like him could muster—which wasn't a great deal. But before long she was responding in a shy, sweet way. Her lips brushed his, too.

The same hands that had flattened against his chest to hold him back now clutched at his lapels, drawing him closer. Her lips parted beneath his, and he swept his tongue between them. A small sigh eased from the back of her throat, encouraging and sweet. He explored her mouth with slow, languid strokes.

And then his patience was rewarded, when her tongue touched lightly to his.

Holy God. His knees almost buckled.

Yes. That's the way of it.

She had the idea now, his clever little minx. When he explored, she yielded. When he took, she gave. And she did the same in return.

Logan could have stood by that mirror-finish loch and kissed her for hours. Days. Weeks and months, perhaps, while the seasons changed around them.

There was something different to her. A taste he couldn't quite name, except to decide he'd never known it in a kiss before. A bit of spice, a bit of sweet, and all of it warm.

Whatever it was, that teasing essence had him wanting to kiss harder, probe deeper to chase it. As if he could bring it into himself and make it his own.

But he didn't want to frighten her. After one last, lingering brush of his lips to hers, he lifted his head.

He'd forgotten that she was still standing on tiptoe, balanced on that rock. As he released her and stepped back, she swayed toward him. Their bodies collided with a dull *unf*. Softness meeting strength.

Acting on instinct, he caught her in his arms.

He felt all of her against all of him. Warm and curved and feminine and so alive beneath that gray mourning frock.

Then she looked up at him—with those big brown calf's eyes, fringed with sooty lashes, and her kiss-plumped lips slightly parted.

Holy God. His knees really did waver this time.

Logan believed what he'd told her, with everything he had in that place where a heart ought to be. Love was nothing but a lie people told themselves.

But lust?

Lust was real, and he was feeling it. Feeling it to his core. As he held her to him, his blood pounded with the fiercest, most primal kind of need. One that spoke of possession and claiming and *mine*.

She made him wild.

Surely it was simply because he'd gone so long without female company. Madeline wasn't even his usual sort. Given his choice, he would have said he favored a bonny Scots lass with fiery hair and a knowing gleam in her eye. Not a shy, proper English gentlewoman just learning the taste of her first kiss.

But beneath the shyness and reserve, she possessed a natural, earthy sensuality. He couldn't help but think of what that might mean in bed—when all the rules and corsets were shed, and the dark freed her from propriety.

Damn. He was wondering about her again.

He was weary of that, the wondering. He'd been wondering about this woman for far too long. Day after bloody day, and night after freezing night. For years. It had driven him mad.

He needed to see her. Search her. Taste her. Everywhere. Hear the little noises she made in pleasure. Just once. Then the wondering would be replaced with knowledge, and he wouldn't be haunted by her anymore.

He lifted her down from the rock and set her on her feet.

"Captain MacKenzie," she said dreamily, "I wi—"

"Logan," he corrected. "I believe it's better to call me Logan now."

"Yes. I suppose it is. Logan."

"What was it you meant to say?"

She shook her head. "I've no idea."

He'd take that as a good sign.

"I'd best go clean myself up and gather the men," he said. "You can start preparing for the ceremony."

"I suppose a week ought to be sufficient time," she said. "Though I'd rather have two."

He shook his head. "I'm not waiting a week."

"A few days, then. At least give me that much. I . . . I've nothing suitable to wear."

"I dinna care about the color of your frock, lass. I'm only going to take it off you again."

She blinked. "Oh."

Logan knew he had to make this happen soon. If he gave her time to think about it, she might decide she wouldn't go through with it at all.

He cast a glance at the sun, fast sinking toward the green horizon. "You have three hours. We're marrying tonight."

Chapter Four

Maddie had always been different from other girls, and she had always known it. For example, she was certain she was the only bride to ever write the following to-do list on her wedding day:

- Bath
- Coiffure
- Dress
- Lobsters

Three hours later, she was bathed, coiffed, and dressed—and sadly for both her and Rex, there was still no sign of Fluffy molting.

Now she stood in the gallery, overlooking the scene that was to be her Highland wedding.

It was a stark tableau. There weren't any special decorations. Too early in the year for flowers, no ribbons on hand, and there hadn't been time for anything else.

Outside, a spring thunderstorm had broken. Wind and rain howled, lashing the castle walls. In the high hall, candles blazed in every available holder. The flames danced and flickered, looking as anxious as she felt.

Servants lined one side of the hall. Captain Mac-Kenzie's men lined the other. Both groups were waiting on her.

And she wanted nothing more than to stay exactly where she was, forever. Or go hide with Fluffy under the rocks.

"Ready, lass?"

She jumped, startled. Logan had joined her in the gallery, sneaking up on her with his catlike steps.

Sneaking up on her with his gorgeousness, too.

Mercy.

He, too, had bathed. And shaved. Most of his brown hair had been tamed with a comb, but a few incorrigible locks fell over his brow in rakish fashion. Someone had brushed out his redcoat and polished the buttons. The gold braid and brass gleamed in the candlelight.

He'd been ruggedly attractive earlier today. Now he was magnificent.

Maddie felt unequal to him. Becky had done her

best with the hair, but Maddie had no choice but to wear one of her usual dark-gray frocks. She hadn't had anything else made in years. What would be the point? She never went anywhere, never entertained.

She certainly hadn't been prepared for a wedding.

"I don't feel ready for this," she said.

He swept her with a quick, perfunctory gaze. "You look ready enough."

Hardly what a bride dreamed of hearing on her wedding day. Not *You look beautiful.* Not *You look lovely.*

You look ready enough.

She glanced down at the half dozen soldiers lining the hall. "What do your men think is happening here tonight?"

"They think I'm marrying you."

"So they know about the letters?"

"Aye, they know I received them. But they never read them."

Maddie would have liked to believe he was telling the truth, but she doubted it. To a soldier in grim circumstances, the ramblings of an undersexed, overimaginative English chit must have been high entertainment. Why would he have kept them to himself? It seemed far more likely that her letters had been passed around the campfire for amusement on dreary nights.

"It's just so many people," she said. "And such a large space."

It had started to feel far too much like a crowd.

Maddie didn't do well in crowds.

"You must know from my letters that I can't abide social gatherings like these. My shyness is the reason I invented you in the first place."

"Invented me? Lass, you didna invent me."

"No, you're right. I invented someone understanding and kind." She crossed her arms and hugged herself. No one else seemed likely to do it. "Have you never heard the phrase *painfully shy*? The attention of a roomful of people . . . for me, it's an icy blast in the dead of winter. First my skin starts to prickle all over. Then I go numb. And then I freeze."

"Look around you."

He swiveled her to face the hall, then stood behind her, placing his hands on the railing and bracketing her between his arms. His solid chest met her back, and his chin pressed against her temple. The pose was intimate and oddly comforting.

He indicated his men one by one. "On the end there, Callum lost his hand. Rabbie has a leg full of shrapnel. Fyfe wakes screaming every night, and Munro can scarcely sleep at all. Then there's Grant. He can't hold onto a memory since Quatre-Bras. Even if he noticed something amiss with you, he'd forget about it in an hour. There's not a soul in this hall without his own burdens."

Not a soul?

She craned her neck to look up at him—all six perfectly formed feet of him. "What burden do you have?"

"The burden of duty." His voice lowered to an intense whisper. "I led those men into battle. When they were weary and chilled and sick with fear, I pushed them on. I promised they'd see the day when they'd come home to their wives, their sweethearts, their bairns, their lands. Instead, they came home to nothing."

His anger was palpable, drawing the small hairs on the back of Maddie's neck tall.

"Tonight," he said, "I'm taking their future back."

"So that's why you want this land? For them?"

He nodded. "I've made it clear I'll not stop at lying, blackmail, or thievery. But just in case it needs underscoring, *mo chridhe*, you're going down there if I have to sling you over my back and carry you like a sack of oats."

"That won't be necessary."

He released the railing, took a step back, and offered his arm.

Maddie accepted it. She couldn't delay any longer.

Arm in arm, they descended the stairs. She was aware of the dozens of eyes on her, chilling her like a wintry wind—but at least she had a tall, braw Highlander to offer some shelter.

Aunt Thea gave her a warm smile as she passed. That helped, too.

They made their way toward the center of the room. Along the way, Logan paused to introduce her to his men. Each soldier bowed to her. Between the graveness of their manner and the stormy, candlelit setting, Maddie felt transported back to another time. She might have been a medieval bride, accepting the fealty of her laird's clansmen.

It was a comfort to know he was doing this out of loyalty to his men and not simple greed. Even if he despised her, at least she knew he was capable of caring for someone.

"Here's Grant," Logan said as they reached a large, hulking man at the end of the line. "You're going to meet him several times."

"What's all this, Captain?" Uneasy, the big man rubbed his shaved head with one palm and looked around. "Where are we now?"

Logan reached out and placed a firm hand on Grant's shoulder. "Be easy. We're back in Scotland, *mo charaid*. The war's over, and we're at Lannair Castle in Invernesshire."

The big man's eyes turned to Maddie. He looked at her as though he were struggling to focus. "Who's this lass?"

Maddie offered her hand. "I'm Madeline."

"This is your sweetheart?" Grant asked Logan. "The one what sent all the letters?"

Logan nodded. "I'm marrying her. Right now, as a matter of fact."

"Are ye?" The man stared at her for a moment, and then a low chuckle rumbled from his chest. Grinning, he dug his elbow into Logan's side. "You lucky bastard."

In that moment, Maddie knew one thing.

Private Malcolm Allan Grant was her new favorite person.

He'd made her feel pretty on her wedding day. So long as she lived, she would never forget it.

"Say, can we go to Ross-shire soon, Captain?" Grant asked. "I'm keen to see my nan and the wee ones."

"Tomorrow," Logan said. "We'll go tomorrow."

"That will be fine."

That settled, Logan steered her to the center of the room. "We'd better get on with it."

"Who's going to officiate?"

"Munro will do the honors, but we dinna need anyone to officiate. There aren't any rings to bless. We'll keep this traditional, like the Highland ways of old. 'Twill be a simple handfasting."

"A handfasting? I thought those only last for a year and a day."

"In novels, perhaps. But the kirk put a stop to temporary unions some centuries ago. That doesna stop brides and grooms from exchanging vows in the old way. We clasp hands, like so." He took her by the wrist, gripping her right forearm with his right hand. "Now take hold of me."

She did as he asked, curling her fingers around his forearm as best she could.

"And the other," he prompted.

He claimed her left wrist in the same manner, and she held onto his. Their linked hands now formed a cross between them. It looked something like a cat's cradle or a children's game.

Logan nodded at Munro.

The man stepped forward and wound a length of plaid around their linked wrists, tying them together. Maddie watched, transfixed, as the strip of fabric wound over her wrist and under his, lashing them together.

Her heart began to beat faster. Her breathing, too. Her brain began to feel as light and misty as a cloud.

He must have been able to tell. His grip tightened on her wrist.

"Can we not do this in private?" she whispered.

"There must be witnesses, lass."

"Yes, but this many? It's only that . . ."

She couldn't finish her plea. The numbness had closed in on her, just as it always did. The cold found her, no matter how well she hid. And the ice encased her from toes to tongue, forbidding her to speak or move. Her pulse beat dully in her ears and time's progress slowed to a glacial creep.

"Look at me," he commanded.

When she did, she found him staring down at her. His eyes were intent, captivating.

"Dinna worry about the others. It's only me and you now."

His low words of assurance did something strange to her. Something she would have thought impossible. They heated her blood from the inside out and made her forget everyone else in the room. He'd erected a shield against that beam of attention.

It truly was just the two of them now.

Suddenly, the rain, the dark, the candles, the primal symbolism of being tied to another human being . . . It all seemed magical. And more romantic than she could bear.

She was visited by the strange, unshakeable sensation that this was everything she'd dreamed of since she was sixteen years old.

Don't, she pleaded with herself. *Don't imagine this to be more than it is. That's how all your trouble starts.*

"Now ye repeat the words as I say them," Logan said.

He murmured something in Gaelic, and she repeated the words aloud as best she could.

"Good," he praised.

Again, she warmed inside. Foolishly.

When she'd finished her part, he said something similar in return. She heard her name in the mix of Gaelic.

Then Munro stepped forward and unwound the cloth.

"What now?" Maddie asked.

"Just this." He bent his head and pressed a quick kiss to her lips. "That's all. It's done."

The men all gave a rousing cheer.

It was done. She was married.

Did she feel different? *Should* she feel different?

"I wouldna expect you to wear a full arisaid," her groom said. "But now that you're Mrs. MacKenzie, you should never be without these."

One of the men handed him a length of green-and-blue tartan. Logan draped it from one shoulder to her waist, like a sash.

From his sporran, he pulled something small that flashed in the candlelight. He used it to pin the plaid together in front.

"Oh, that's lovely," Aunt Thea said. "What is it?"

"It's called a luckenbooth," a soldier—the one named Callum—explained. "It's tradition in the Highlands for a man to give such a brooch to his betrothed."

"Then you should have given it to her in Brighton years ago," Aunt Thea said.

"I should have done. I suppose I forgot." With that, he gave Maddie a sly glance.

A realization struck her like a lightning bolt. She now had a confidant. A conspirator. Someone who knew everything. All her secrets. He didn't love her for them, but he hadn't run screaming from her, either.

This ruthless, kilted stranger she'd married might

be the closest thing on earth Maddie had to a true friend.

Thunder boomed somewhere, quite nearby. The candle flames ducked and cowered. The storm must be passing directly overhead.

"What's this?" Grant asked, looking more confused than he had before the ceremony began. "We're drawing fire, Captain. We need to take cover."

Maddie could see now what Logan had meant about the big soldier's memory. The poor man.

Logan reached out to his friend again. Explained, again, that they were safe in Scotland. Promised, again, to take him to Ross-shire tomorrow to see his wee ones and his nan.

How many times must he have made those same assurances, Maddie wondered. Hundreds? Perhaps thousands? He must have the patience of a saint.

"And who's she?" Grant nodded at Maddie.

"I'm Madeline." She held out her hand.

"You're the sweetheart what wrote him all those letters?"

"Aye," Logan said. "And now she's my wife."

Grant chuckled and dug his elbow into Logan's side. "You lucky bastard."

Yes, Maddie thought. Grant was still her new favorite person. Faulty memory or no, she was going to enjoy having him around.

In fact, she was contemplating giving him a kiss

on the cheek, when the hall flashed white, then dark. The entire castle shook with a mighty—

Crash.

"Madeline, get down."

When the lightning struck, Logan's heart took a jolt. And for the first time in years, his initial impulse wasn't to soothe Grant or protect his men.

His attention went solely to his bride.

He wrapped his arms around her, tucking her to his chest and pulling her toward the floor, lest something above them shake loose and fall.

Once the chandeliers had stopped swaying and the danger had passed, he leaned close to speak to her. "Are ye well?"

"Yes, of course. The crash only startled me."

She was still trembling.

And Logan didn't think it was only because of the storm. Through the entire ceremony, her unease had been palpable. She'd grown more and more pale, and by the time they'd spoken their vows, her eyes had refused to focus on his.

She hadn't been exaggerating when she'd said she disliked social gatherings. And this was a mere dozen people in a castle in the remotest part of the Highlands. How much worse would it have been for her in a crowded London ballroom?

He had been accustomed to thinking of her as spoiled or petulant for inventing a sweetheart the way she had. But now he was starting to wonder if there hadn't been something more to it.

Damn. He was wondering about her again.

The wondering ended tonight.

And it didn't matter if she'd had motives of self-preservation. The task of preserving her was his now. He'd just pledged as much before his men and God, and despite this marriage being a convenient arrangement, he wasn't one to take those vows lightly.

He helped her to her feet, acutely aware of how small she was, how delicate. Every wash of pink on her cheeks or labored breath was suddenly a matter for his concern.

Which didn't make a bit of sense, considering he was the villain in her life. He'd just forced her into a marriage she didn't want, and now he was obsessed with protecting her? It was laughable.

But no less real.

As he helped her to her feet, he asked, "Are you well?"

"Just a bit shaky. Perhaps from standing so long."

The men would be expecting a celebration. Music, food, dancing. Logan had asked the castle's cook for a feast and wine. "Come along, I'll take you upstairs."

"Just go slowly, if you will," she whispered to him. "So I can keep pace."

"That won't be necessary. I mean to carry you."

"Like a sack of oats?"

"Nay, lass. Like a bride."

He hefted her into his arms and carried her out of the hall, to his men's cheers and her aunt's evident delight.

Once they'd made it out of the hall, however, Logan realized he had no idea where he was going. "How do I get to your rooms?"

She gave him directions. The directions involved a great many stairs.

"You walk up all of these steps each evening?" he asked, trying to hide the fact that he'd grown a bit winded.

"Usually multiple times a day."

That was the problem with Scottish tower houses, he supposed. They were built tall and narrow for greatest protection from siege—and inside, they were all stairs.

"The original lairds would have housed the servants all the way up here. Why don't you use a room on one of the lower floors?"

She shrugged. "I like the view."

Her bedchamber, once they reached it, was warmly furnished and cozy. The spaces under the sloping gabled ceilings were filled with rows of books and small curiosities. It wasn't at all the way he would have expected an English heiress's room to be—but having read Maddie's letters, he could recognize it as entirely *her*.

His eye was drawn to a pair of miniatures on the dressing table, depicting two fair-haired children, one boy and one girl. Logan knew them at once.

"That's Henry and Emma," he said.

"Yes. How did you know?"

He shrugged. "Maybe I recognized them from your letters."

The truth was, not only did he recognize the children but he also recognized Maddie's hand at work in the miniatures.

A strange sense of intimacy overtook him.

Fast on its heels came an inconvenient wave of guilt.

He set her down.

"Thank you for carrying me."

"You weigh less than a bird. It was nothing."

"It was distressingly romantic, is what it was. Would you try to be a bit less dashing? This is meant to be a convenient arrangement."

"As you like, *mo chridhe*."

She was right. Romance was not in their bargain. Now that he had her upstairs, in a bedchamber, he was eager to get on with the parts they did agree to.

The two of them, in a bed.

He nodded to her as he left the room. "I'll give you a half hour to make ready. And then I'll return."

Chapter Five

I'll give you a half hour to make ready.

A half hour?

Maddie tried not to panic. What was a half hour to prepare for becoming a wife? A mere blink, surely. Thirty minutes were nowhere near enough time to make herself ready.

Thirty *years* might not be enough time to feel ready. There was simply too much to absorb.

She was married. She was about to lose her virginity. And worst of all, she was feeling stupidly infatuated with her new husband.

At this very moment, her heart was throbbing with a sweet, tender ache.

So absurd.

For heaven's sake, she'd only known him half a day,

and he'd been terrible for most of it. Her brain argued back and forth with her foolish, sentimental heart.

He blackmailed you into marriage.

And then kissed me by the loch.

His behavior to you was detestable.

But his loyalty to his men is admirable.

He threatened to carry you like a sack of oats.

And swept me off my feet instead.

Maddie, you are impossible.

She sighed and muttered, "No argument there."

She decided against calling in the maid to help her prepare.

As she removed her plaid sash and gown, she sternly reminded herself that this Captain Logan MacKenzie was not the hero she'd spent her girlhood dreaming of. When he returned to this room in—she checked the clock—nineteen minutes' time, it would not be with the intent of sparking romance; he would come to complete a transaction.

But, but, but . . .

Lightning flashed outside. She froze in the act of unrolling her stockings, suddenly awash with the memory. His arm, wrapping tight around her when the thunder crashed. He'd looked so handsome by candlelight. Not to mention, rather thrilling when he'd whisked her up the stairs.

Oh, she was in so much trouble.

As she pulled a brush through her unbound hair,

shivers of anticipation coursed through her. They played a naughty game of tag as they chased from one secret part of her body to the next. Her skin felt warm and tingly. Willing.

Ready.

She closed her eyes and drew a deep, slow breath. She should not be looking forward to this. She should not be imagining this encounter to mean things that it didn't. That kind of foolishness could only lead to getting hurt.

Love is just a lie we tell ourselves.

And Maddie was all too practiced at lying.

She took another glimpse at the clock. Eight minutes left.

As she replaced the hairbrush on her dressing table, her gaze landed on the small heart-shaped brooch he'd given her at the close of the ceremony. What was the name Callum had told her?

A luckenbooth.

She lifted it for closer examination. The design was simple, even humble. The outline of a heart shape had been worked in gold, with a few chips of semiprecious stones—green and blue—inset near the crest.

Maddie turned the brooch over in her hands to examine the clasp. As she did, her fingertips caught a rougher patch on the otherwise smooth gold.

Interesting. It was engraved.

She leaned closer to the candlelight, peering hard at the tiny markings. It looked to be a pair of initials.

"L.M."

For Logan MacKenzie, of course.

Goodness, he'd arrived prepared. He seemed to have thought everything through. Then she squinted to make out the second set, expecting to find an "M.G." for Madeline Gracechurch.

There was no "M.G." engraved there.

There was, however, another set of letters.

"'A.D.,'" she read aloud.

Unbelievable.

Apparently Captain Logan "Love's just a lie we tell ourselves" MacKenzie was a liar, too. He must have had some history of romance. One that hadn't ended well, evidently—considering he'd given Maddie the brooch he'd bought for this former lover.

The rogue.

Maddie dropped the brooch on the dressing table. At least her tingling, yearning feelings had dissipated. This was exactly the sharp object she'd needed to separate her heart from the rest of her body. Now she had a foolproof way to remember that this was not a real marriage and she should not imagine him to possess any true feelings. She'd be wearing that luckenbooth every day—a little heart-shaped talisman to remind her that all of this was false.

The door creaked on its hinges.

Oh, Lord. It was time.

Maddie scrambled into the bed and dove beneath the coverlet. Not quite fast enough, unfortunately. He'd seen the entire maneuver, she was sure.

She drew the bed linens up to her chin and peered at him.

He'd removed his coat and uncuffed his shirt, rolling his sleeves to the elbow. He appeared to be barefoot, shed of his socks and boots. He wore only that open-necked shirt and his kilt, loosely belted and slung low on his hips.

"Are you ready?" His voice was darker than the shadows.

"I'm not certain," she answered. "But I don't think I'll grow any readier."

"If you're fatigued, we could wait for the morning."

"No, I . . . I think I should rather have it over with tonight." Given any more time to think and worry, she might lose her nerve entirely.

"Well, then."

He licked his fingertips, then extinguished the candles one by one, until the only light in the room came from the flickering red-and-amber fire in the hearth.

The bed dipped with his weight.

Maddie lay very still beneath the coverlet. Her heart was beating faster than a bird's. She felt hot everywhere.

"There's this." She reached for the jar her aunt had given her. "Aunt Thea gave it to me. It's some sort of cream or salve, I think. She said you'd know what to do with it."

He took the jar, unscrewed the cap, and gave the contents a sniff.

"Aye. I know what to do with it." He capped the jar and flung it away. It rolled into a darkened corner.

"But—"

"I ken better than to let your aunt's remedies anywhere near me," he said. "I remember too well how her sleeping tonic fared. Your letter said you had a blistering rash for weeks."

Maddie bit her lip and drew the coverlet tight about her shoulders. He remembered that? Even she'd forgotten about the sleeping tonic. But he was right, she'd been covered in itchy red bumps for weeks.

It was disconcerting how much he knew *about* her without knowing *her* at all. And when it came to knowing the real Logan MacKenzie, she was completely in the dark. In this situation, every advantage was his. He had knowledge, experience, control.

"Drink this instead." He handed her a small flask.

"Is it medicine?"

"It's Highland medicine. Good Scotch whisky."

She gingerly lifted the flask to her lips.

"Toss it back. The burn is worse if you sip."

Squeezing her eyes shut, she tossed her head back and tipped the flask, sending a bolt of liquid fire down her throat. Coughing, she handed it back.

"If the deed's done right," he said, "there willna be any need for any creams or salves." His hand encircled her calf through the bed linens. "And I mean to do this right. You'll enjoy it."

She swallowed hard. "Oh."

"Even so, it's likely to pinch a bit when I—"

"Right."

"But it will be quick from there, much as it pains my pride to say it. That's the usual way when a man's gone without company for a time."

Without the candles, the firelight cast him in murky silhouette.

She would have felt better if she could see him plain. No doubt he'd intended the darkness to be comforting, but Maddie was used to looking at natural creatures in an unfiltered, direct way. Observing where their pieces joined, learning how they moved and worked. Perhaps if she'd been given the same chance to survey his body—even a furtive glimpse or two as he'd undressed—her racing pulse would have calmed.

But it was too late now. The candles were out. And even if they could be relit, she didn't know to *ask* for such a thing.

To her, he was merely shadow. Shadow with hands and heat and a deep, entrancing baritone.

"Don't be afraid." His hand drifted down her body, blazing a path of unprecedented sensation. "I know you've wondered about this. How a man fits with a woman. How it feels to be joined. I can show you everything. I'll make it good. Verra good."

"I don't know if I can do this," she said.

"You can. There's nothing easier. If this were difficult, humanity would have died out long ago."

"I think you underestimate my capacity for taking normal human interaction and making it awkward."

She inched away, putting space between them.

"Try to understand," she said. "You've been reading my letters for years. You know so much about me, and I don't have even the slightest understanding of you. Where you come from, how you've lived your life . . . to me, you're little more than a stranger."

"I'm your husband now."

"Yes, but we've no history together. No shared memories."

"We have seven years of actual history. And we do have memories."

"Such as . . . ?"

He shrugged. "Remember when we first met and you fell on your arse? Remember when we strolled beside the water and spoke of marriage? Remember the time I kissed you so hard, you felt it in your toes?"

"No," she replied defensively. "I only felt it so far as my ankles."

He gripped her waist. "Well, then. I'll have to try harder this time."

He leaned in.

She put her hand on his chest, holding him back. "Can't we get to know each other first?"

"I dinna see any purpose to further chatter," he said. "We agreed this is an arrangement, not a romance."

"That's just it, you see. I don't *want* a romance. I don't *want* to pretend. But when I close my eyes, it's not you touching me. It's some fictional Captain MacKenzie of my own creation. I'm liable to make too much of this. I don't think you want a silly, clinging wife making demands on your affections."

"You're right on that score. I canna say I do."

"It's like you told me. Love is a lie people tell themselves," she went on. "If that's the case, actual knowledge should be the best antidote. Once I get to know you better, I should have no difficulty finding reasons to despise you."

"Is shameless blackmail not enough?"

"I would have thought it would be. But then you told me about your men's dire circumstances. I saw how loyal you are to them. It all became too sympathetic. I need a new reason to dislike you." She crossed her legs. "Let's begin with the basics. Where were you born?"

"Over toward Lochcarron on the western coast."

A sudden thought occurred to her. "Do you have any family?"

"None."

"Oh. That's good. I mean, it's not good. It's terrible for you, and entirely too sympathetic. But it's con-

venient for our purposes. It matches the lies I told."
She bit her lip, cringing. "I can be a bit absorbed in
my own problems at times. It's one of my worst fail-
ings. But you knew that already."

He nodded. "Oh, aye. I knew that already."

"See? You know all about my flaws. It's easy for you
to remain detached. But I don't know any of yours."

"Here's the first." He reached to encircle her ankle
with his hand. His thumb stroked up and down.
"I'm entirely too good in bed. Have a way of ruining a woman for all others."

She pulled her leg away. "Boastfulness would be
the first flaw, then. That will do for a start. What's
the worst thing you've ever done?"

He pushed his hands through his hair. "I'm beginning to think it was marrying you."

"No, no. Don't show a sense of humor. That ticks
a box in the wrong column."

He reached for her and drew her close, then rolled her
onto her back. The hard, heated weight of him pressed
her body into the mattress. "I can tick all the boxes, lass."

She swallowed hard. "Who's A.D.?"

"What?"

"The brooch you gave me. It has the initials L.M.
and A.D. Who is A.D.?"

His eyes hardened to chips of ice. "No one important to me."

"But—"

He bent his head and kissed her neck. A whisper of heat against her skin. Despite herself, she sighed with pleasure.

He heard that sigh. And was encouraged by it.

His hands ranged over her curves. Not grabbing or taking. Simply learning her shape.

And as he did, Madeline was learning things, too. She was used to examining creatures, cataloging all their parts. The key to creating a good illustration was understanding how the creature functioned. The reason for an antenna. The purpose of a spinneret.

As Logan touched her, she realized something crushing. Over the recent years, she'd reduced herself to a rough sketch of a person. She had hands to draw, eyes to see, and a mouth to occasionally speak. But there was so much more to this body she inhabited—so much more to her—and when she lay beneath him, all of it made sense.

It made her wonder which parts of himself he'd been neglecting. How long he'd gone without a woman to remind him of this small, secret hollow of his throat, the perfect shelter his body made when it curved around hers. The way his hand was made to cup her breast just as capably as it gripped a dagger.

It was all too much.

Maddie squirmed out from under him. "I'm sorry. So sorry. I know this is supposed to be physical. Impersonal. It's only that I keep thinking of lobsters."

He flipped onto his back and lay there, blinking up at the ceiling. "Until just now, I would have said there was nothing remaining that could surprise me in bed. I was wrong."

She sat up, drawing her knees to her chest. "I *am* the girl who made up a Scottish lover, wrote him scores of letters, and kept up an elaborate ruse for years. Does it really surprise you that I'm odd?"

"Maybe not."

"Lobsters court for months before mating. Before the male can mate with her, the female has to feel secure enough to molt out of her shell. If a spiny sea creature is worth months of effort, can't I have just a bit more time? I don't understand the urgency."

With a gruff sigh, he drew a fold of her quilt over his lap. "We had a handfasting, lass. The vows we spoke would be considered a mere betrothal on their own. The consummation is what makes it a marriage."

He had her full attention now. "You mean this could still be undone?"

That was interesting.

Very interesting.

"Dinna get any ideas," he said, looking stern. "Let me remind you that I have dozens of reasons why you don't want that. *Incendiary* reasons."

Yes, Maddie thought to herself. He had dozens of reasons stashed away somewhere.

An idea took hold of her.

If she could hold him off from consummating the marriage, she might be able to find those reasons—and burn them once and for all. Watch them go up in smoke. Then he wouldn't have so much power over her.

"You wanted shared memories, did you not?" he asked.

She nodded.

"Remember how on our wedding night I made wild, naked love to you until you were screaming for more?"

"Actually, I remember us staying up all night talking." Just to vex him, she added, "And cuddling."

He scowled. "I dinna do cuddling."

"That's for the best, I suppose," she said. "You offered to wait until tomorrow to consummate the vows if I wished. Well, I do wish to wait. I'm not ready tonight."

And if she could find another way out of this situation, perhaps she would never need to be.

She laid a row of cushions down the center of the bed, carefully dividing it into two sides:

His, and hers.

"Is that truly supposed to stop me?" He fell back on the bed, on his side—peering over the pillow wall at her with amusement. "I fully intended to have my wicked way with you. But now there's this cushion, so . . ."

She burrowed under the coverlet, drawing it up to her neck.

"Now that you mention it," he went on, "I dinna know how this strategy escaped Napoleon's notice. If only he'd erected a barricade of feathers and fabric, we Highlanders wouldna have known how to get over it."

"I don't expect the pillows to keep you out," she said. "They're merely a guard against anything accidental happening."

"Ah." He drew out the syllable. "We canna have any accidental happenings."

"Exactly. I might roll over in the night, and I know how you feel about cuddling. I should hate to take advantage of you."

"Minx." He sat up in bed and plucked the cushion from between them. "I'm here now. I'm flesh and blood, and I'm your husband. I'll be damned if I'll give up my place to a pillow."

She held her breath. What would he do?

"I'll sleep on the floor," he said.

He took that pillow and the spare quilt from the end of the bed and began to arrange a pallet near the hearth.

Maddie told herself to be happy—it was safer that way.

Instead, she couldn't keep from stupidly worrying about his comfort. The floor would be cold and hard, and he'd been traveling. Physical nearness was one kind of danger, but *caring* about him would be even worse.

"We're adults with an understanding," she said.

"You're welcome to share the bed. No barricade required. I'll stay on my side and you'll stay on yours."

"I'll sleep on the floor. I prefer it."

"You prefer the floor to a bed?"

"At the moment, *mo chridhe*, I prefer the floor to you."

Horrid man.

"You said you want to wait," he went on. "I'd like to think my honor makes a stronger barrier than pillows. But tonight, it wouldna be prudent to put that theory to the test."

After a moment, she said, "I see."

He folded the quilt in half, spreading it on the floor. "It's no matter. I slept on the ground for my first ten years of life. Never once in a bed."

"Ten years of the floor?"

"Ten years of the cowshed or the sheep pasture, most accurately. Before the vicar took me in, I was an orphan raised on the charity of the parish. I stayed with whichever family would keep me—and that meant whoever needed a hand with the sheep or cattle that season. I tended the animals, day and night. In exchange, I had my morning parritch and a crust or two at night."

Oh, no. This entire exchange was one step forward, two steps back. A mild insult—excellent. He abandoned her bed for the floor—better. But now, this tragic tale of orphan woe? It ruined everything.

How was she supposed to remember to dislike him when she was picturing a hungry, lanky boy with reddish-brown hair, shivering on the frosted ground all alone?

Maddie wanted to clap her hands over her ears and tra-la-la to drown out the pounding beat of her heart.

Instead, she punched her pillow a few times to soften it. "Sleep well, Captain MacSurly."

What had she done? Just when it seemed she couldn't pay enough ways for telling one silly lie in her youth . . . this happened. She'd agreed to marry a perfect stranger. One who cared nothing for her, and one she was in danger of caring far too much about.

But she wasn't fully married to him yet.

With a bit of luck, perhaps she never would be.

Chapter Six

*L*ogan hadn't expected to get much sleep on his wedding night.

He hadn't thought he'd be spending it on the floor.

But his rest was disturbed for an entirely different reason. It was distressingly quiet.

Everything he'd told Madeline was true. In boyhood, he'd slept in pastures or byres, surrounded by shaggy Highland cattle or bleating sheep. Since joining up with the Royal Highlanders, he'd been bedding down on a pallet surrounded by his fellow soldiers. It hadn't felt much different from sleeping amid beasts, to be honest. There had been a certain comfort to it, with the nightly symphony of crude snorings and scratchings.

But while he'd passed many hours of pleasure

with female company, he was not accustomed to sleeping near a woman. Cuddling? Never happened.

Maddie's presence in the same room made him strangely uneasy. She was too mysterious, too quiet, too tempting. The sweet scent of lavender kept prodding him awake every time he started drifting off to sleep.

As soon as the first light of dawn seeped through the window, he rose from his makeshift bed, buckled his kilt about his waist, and made his way out of the castle to stand by the loch, watching the new day creep across the blue surface and burn off the mist.

"So, Captain. How are ye feeling this fine morn?"

Logan turned away from his view of the loch. "What?"

Callum and Rabbie stood behind him, peering at him with an unusual degree of interest.

Rabbie propped his forearm on Callum's shoulder. "What do you think, lad?"

Callum cocked his head. "I dinna rightly know. I think it's a yes."

Rabbie laughed. "I think not."

Logan frowned. "What the devil are you on about?"

Rabbie clucked his tongue. "Irritability. That's not a good sign."

"But he doesna look well rested," Callum replied. "That should be a point in my favor."

Logan stopped trying to make sense of them. He was in no humor for their joking this morning.

"If you're awake, we might as well get to work," he said.

After breakfast, they all rode out to scout the glen.

Not far from the loch, they found the remnants of a ruined cattle enclosure. Time, weather, or battles had crumbled the low walls ages ago. There was no use in rebuilding it, but the loosened stone could be put to use in building cottages.

He put his hand on a waist-high bit of wall, and a chunk of stone immediately shook loose. It landed on his boot, crushing his great toe. Logan kicked it aside and ground out a curse.

He turned in time to see Rabbie extending an open palm in Callum's direction. "I'll take my payment now."

Callum resentfully dug a coin from his sporran and placed it in Rabbie's hand.

Logan had had enough of their mysterious chatter. "Explain yourselves."

"I'm just settling a wager with Callum," Rabbie said.

"What kind of bet?" he demanded.

"As to whether you bedded your wee little English bride on the wedding night." Rabbie grinned. "I said no. I won."

Damn. Was his frustration that obvious?

Logan thought of the way he'd just cursed at a rock.

Yes, it probably was.

They'd lived too close with each other for far too long. Logan could tell at a glance when Callum's stump was paining him, and he could sense when Fyfe had a difficult night ahead.

He knew his men, and they knew him, too. It would be plain to them all that he hadn't purged his own lust last night.

Though Rabbie's wagers were crass and stupid, he understood why the men would take more than an idle interest in his amorous activities. In order to ensure Castle Lannair would be their permanent home, he needed to consummate the marriage. There was a lot riding on Logan's . . . riding.

As of this morning, he was letting them down.

He hated that feeling. In battle, he'd been their infallible, loyal officer, leading them into battle without so much as a blink. Not anymore.

Callum, always the peacemaker, tried to apologize. "We're just having a bit o' sport with you, Captain. She must have been weary last night, and you only just came home to her. Was quite a shock, I expect. There's no shame in giving her time to adjust to the idea. I'm certain your lass thinks it sweet."

Sweet?

Curse it all. First cuddling. Now he was sweet?

"That'll be enough," he said. "If I hear of any more wagers like this one, heads will be cracked. You should spend your time on something more worthwhile. Like shoveling out the castle stables this afternoon."

"But Captain . . ." Callum lifted his amputated arm.

"No pity from this quarter."

Until he could put any doubt to rest, he would do what he'd done for the past several years: keep the men working and focused on the future.

They placed stones to mark out sites for building and planting. Then he led the group up the slope to survey the grazing lands from a higher vantage.

"There's no time to be wasted," he said. "If we want to have a harvest this autumn, we need to put crops in the ground by Beltane."

"Let's hope the land's yours by Beltane," Rabbie said.

"It's mine already. I've married her."

"Aye, in word. But the English have a way of breaking their word, up here in the Highlands."

"I'll remind you, that's my wife you're discussing."

Rabbie gave him a doubting look. "Is it?"

"*Yes.*"

Maddie would be his wife. Fully, legally, permanently, and soon. He'd acceded to her requests for a delay last night because of everything Callum said: She'd had a shock and a long, wearying day.

He knew she was curious, and he'd tasted her kiss. There was potential for matters to be good between them—perhaps even incendiary. It would be a crime to squander their agreed-upon night by pressing her too far, too fast.

When Logan bedded his wife, she would not only

be willing. She would want it. She would be *pleading* for him.

And he'd leave her so limp and exhausted with pleasure that she could have no thought of any cuddling afterward.

"Say, Captain." Callum motioned back toward the castle. "Looks as though you have a visitor."

Logan peered into the distance. An elegant coach-and-four had drawn up in front of the castle's entrance. A man alighted from the coach. No sooner had the man's boots met the ground than a small figure in gray emerged from the castle to greet him, as though she'd been expecting him to call.

Maddie.

"On second thought," Rabbie said, "looks as though your lady has a visitor."

An uncomfortable silence fell over the group.

"I expect it's probably some man of business," Munro said. "Don't all English ladies have men of business?"

"Do you see that team of bays?" Fyfe put in. "That's no working man's coach-and-four."

Logan remained quiet. He didn't know who Maddie's visitor might be. But he meant to find out.

"Lord Varleigh." Maddie dropped a curtsy. "Do come in. It's always a pleasure to see you."

"The pleasure is mine, Miss Gracechurch."

Miss Gracechurch.

The words gave Maddie pause. *Was* she still Miss Gracechurch? Should she correct him?

Maddie decided against it. It was too complicated to explain right now, and Lord Varleigh would likely be gone before Logan even noticed he was here.

With any luck, she might never need to change her name to Mrs. MacKenzie at all.

Lord Varleigh cleared his throat. "Might I see the illustrations?"

"Oh. Yes. Yes, of course."

Heavens. Would she never lose this awkwardness? She'd had enough conversations with Lord Varleigh over the past year to know he was an intelligent and thoughtful gentleman, but he was also rather an imposing one. Something about his dark, inquisitive eyes and groomed fingernails always made her a bit nervous.

Focus on the work, Maddie. He's here for the illustrations, not for you.

She gathered the folio and carried it to a wide, flat table to lay it open. "As we originally discussed, there are ink drawings for each species in different perspectives."

She stood to the side as he paged through her work. Methodically and slowly, as any good naturalist would do.

"What's this?" he asked, arriving at a watercolor near the end of the stack.

"Oh, that. I took the liberty of combining some of

the species and doing a few plates in color. I know they can't be printed in the journal, but I thought you might like to have them. If not, I'll keep them. They were mostly for my own amusement."

"I see." He tilted his head as he looked at them.

At last, Maddie could bear the suspense no longer. "Do the sketches not meet with your approval? If you don't like them or they're not right, there's still time. I can make changes."

He let the folio cover drop shut and turned to her. "Miss Gracechurch, the sketches are remarkable. Perfect."

"Oh. Good." Maddie exhaled with relief and just a touch of pride.

For the most part, she illustrated for the love of it, and for the pleasure of contributing to knowledge—not for applause. Not that there were a great many people queuing up to applaud scientific illustrators, anyhow.

But Lord Varleigh's praise meant something to her. It meant a great deal. He made her feel she'd done *something* right, despite spending yesterday dealing with a Highlander determined to punish her for her every youthful folly.

"I'm hosting a gathering at my home next week to unveil the specimens," Lord Varleigh said, packing up her illustrations and the glass-boxed samples she'd worked from. "I've invited all the members of the naturalist society, Orkney included."

"It's to be a salon, then?"

"More of a ball."

"Oh." A cold sense of dread washed over her. "A ball."

"Yes. There will be supper and a bit of dancing. We must provide some amusement for the ladies, you see, or they will boycott the evening altogether."

Maddie smiled. "I'm not much of a lady, then. I'm uninterested in dancing, but I would be fascinated by your display."

"Then I hope you'll attend."

"Me?"

"I have a good friend who'll be visiting. Mr. Dorning. He's a scholar in Edinburgh, and he's compiling an encyclopedia."

"An encyclopedia?"

Lord Varleigh nodded. *"Insects of the British Isles,* in four volumes."

"Be still my heart. I do love a book with multiple volumes."

"Does that mean you're interested?"

"Naturally. I should love to see the work when it's finished."

He smiled. "Miss Gracechurch, we seem to be misunderstanding one another. I'm asking if you'd be interested in meeting my friend so that he might consider engaging your services for the project. As an illustrator."

Maddie was stunned. An encyclopedia. A project

of that size would mean steady, interesting work for months. If not years. "You'd truly do that for me?"

"I'd consider it a favor to him, frankly. The quality of your work is exceptional. If you are able to attend our gathering next week, I should be pleased to make the introduction."

She bit her lip. What a chance this could be for her, but . . .

A ball.

Why did it have to be a ball?

"Could I not pay a call earlier in the afternoon?" she asked. "Or perhaps the following morning. It would seem a shame to interrupt your amusements with talk of work."

"The work is the reason for the gathering. You wouldn't be an interruption." His hand brushed her wrist. "I'll look out for you, I promise. Do say yes."

"I have a question," a deep voice interrupted. "Does this invitation extend to me?"

Oh, Lord.

Logan.

After a brief, assessing pause in the doorway, he moved into the room. He was dressed for physical labor, it would seem, in his kilt and a loose homespun shirt. He must have just come in from the glen.

Lord Varleigh looked faintly horrified, but also intrigued. His glance to Maddie sent an almost scientific question:

Just what kind of wild creature is this?

Without so much as a nod in the direction of manners or propriety, Logan crossed the room in firm, muddy strides. He drew near Maddie, but his gaze never left Lord Varleigh's.

He casually draped his arm about Maddie's waist, then flexed it—yanking her to his side. The brisk morning air clung to his clothing, bringing with it the faintly green scents of heather and moss.

"Good morning, *mo chridhe*. Why don't you introduce me to your friend?"

Maddie's tongue went dry as paper. "B-but of course. Lord Varleigh, may I present Captain Logan MacKenzie."

"Captain MacKenzie?" Lord Varleigh looked to Maddie. "Not *the* Captain MacKenzie. The one you . . ."

"Yes," she managed.

"Your intended?" His gaze darted to Logan. "Forgive me, sir. I was under the impression you were—"

"Dead?" Logan supplied. "A common misconception. As ye can see, I'm verra much alive."

"Extraordinary. I had no idea."

"Well," Logan said smoothly, "now ye do."

"I should have mentioned it earlier," Maddie said. "Captain MacKenzie only returned with his men yesterday. It was quite the shock. I'm afraid I'm still a bit scattered."

"I can only imagine, Miss Gracechurch."

"Miss Gracechurch is Mrs. MacKenzie now." Logan's hand slid to Maddie's shoulder in a gesture as baldly possessive as it was unsubtle.

Mine.

"Actually," Maddie interjected, nudging away, "I'm still Miss Gracechurch at the moment."

"We exchanged vows last night."

"In a traditional handfasting. But that's more of a formal betrothal. It's . . . well, it's complicated."

"I see," said Lord Varleigh, although it was clear he didn't.

Really, who could? This was madness. Any explanations she might attempt would only make it worse.

When he spoke, Lord Varleigh's jaw barely moved. "As I've been telling Miss Gracechurch, there will be a ball at my home next Wednesday. I should be delighted to welcome you both." He collected his portfolio and bowed. "Until then."

Even after Lord Varleigh left, Logan's arm remained on Maddie's shoulder. The room vibrated with quiet tension.

She took a step in retreat.

With unsteady fingers, Maddie gathered her folios and pencils from the table. "I need to return these to my studio."

"Wait," he said. "Dinna move."

Her knees went weak as he drew closer. It was

tempting to blame her reactions on his raw masculine appeal, but Maddie knew better.

He was the first—and likely only—man to pursue her this way.

She was curious. She was a romantic. And above all, she was lonely.

Hunger, after all, was a more potent seasoning than salt.

She waited, breathless, for Logan to make his move. But when he did, it wasn't the move she expected.

His gaze focused on something just behind her left elbow. With lightning speed, he lunged forward and smacked the tabletop.

Thwack.

"There," he declared triumphantly, shaking out his hand.

"What are you doing?"

"Killing that disgusting insect before it jumped on you."

"Killing a . . . ?" Maddie wheeled around. "Oh, no."

There it was, on the carpet. A stag beetle. It must have fallen out of Lord Varleigh's specimen case.

"Oh, what have you done?" She fell on her knees to the carpet.

"What have I *done*? Most lasses like it when a man kills the bugs. Along with reaching high places and giving sexual pleasure, it's one of the few universally popular qualities we have on offer."

She scooped up the remnants of the beetle into her hand. "This particular bug was already dead."

And now it was flattened.

She needed to take it back to her studio and put it under glass at once, lest any further harm befall it.

He followed her down the corridor. "Don't walk away from me. I'd like some answers here. Whose invitation did I just accept, and what does that slimy prig want of you? And why do I come third in your affections behind the slimy prig and a squashed beetle?"

"Lord Varleigh owns an estate in Perthshire. We are professional acquaintances. He's a naturalist."

"A naturalist? You mean one of those people who scorns clothing and runs about the countryside bare-arsed?"

"No," Maddie said calmly. She slowed and turned to face him. "No, those would be naturists. A *naturalist* studies the natural world."

"Well, that one seemed to be mostly interested in studying your breasts."

"What?"

He closed the distance between them and lowered his voice to a growl. "He had his hand on you."

A frisson skipped down her vertebrae, practically unlacing her corset as it went. Just those few words, and she was unraveled. Everything about the night before returned to her. She recalled his breath on her neck. His mouth on her skin.

His hands everywhere.

The wanting hit her with such force, so hot and overwhelming, that it threatened to push her brain out through her ears.

This was terrible.

At last Maddie was on the cusp of a career, amassing accomplishments of her own. Imagine, the chance to illustrate a book.

Not just a book but an entire encyclopedia.

Four whole volumes.

Bliss.

And now this could ruin everything. Couldn't he have waited one more week to come back from the not-truly-dead?

"I can explain it better, but I'll need to show you." She put her hand on the door latch behind her. "Come this way."

Her heartbeat quickened as she opened the door.

She never allowed people in her studio. Especially not male people. It was her sanctuary of curiosities—odd and secret and entirely her. Vulnerable.

Opening this door for Logan felt like throwing her heart on the floor and inviting him to tread on it. But she needed to explain Lord Varleigh somehow, and perhaps this time the sheer strangeness would work in her favor.

It just might cure him of the desire to be married to her at all.

Chapter Seven

*H*oly God.

Logan found himself in a veritable chamber of horrors. The rumors about these old castles were true.

He followed her up a narrow flight of stone stairs. Candles in sconces lit the passageway, but they weren't bright enough to shed light into the corners. It was the corners he worried about. Probably crawling with bats or rats or . . . newts. Maybe dragons.

They emerged into a square room that must have been meant as a cell of some sort. It featured only a single narrow window.

He turned to have a look around, then started in alarm. A stuffed owl sat perched on a shelf, not a foot from his face.

The rest of the chamber wasn't much better. The

room was lined with shelves and tables displaying all manner of seashells, coral, bird nests, shed snakeskins, insects and butterflies pinned to boards, and—worst of all—strange mysteries sealed up in murky jars.

"It's ice-cold up here," he said.

"Yes. It needs to be for Rex and Fluffy."

"Rex? And Fluffy?"

"The lobsters. I thought I mentioned them last night."

"You have lobsters named Rex and Fluffy."

"Just because I lack any normal pets like cats or dogs doesn't mean the pets I have can't have proper names." She smiled. "I do enjoy the way you say 'Fluffy.' It sounds like 'Floofy.' They're in here."

She waved him toward a tank in one corner of the room. The water within it smelled of the sea.

"Are they for dinner?"

"No! They're for observation. I've been commissioned to illustrate the full life cycle. The only problem is, I keep waiting on them to mate. According to the naturalist who hired me, the female—that's Fluffy—first needs to molt. And then the male will impregnate her with his seed. The only question remaining is what, exactly, that will look like. I've drawn up several possibilities."

She moved to a wide, cluttered worktable and rifled through a stack of papers. On each page was a sketch of lobsters coupling in a different position. Logan had never seen anything like it. She'd created a lobster pillow book.

He looked around at her desk—the piles of paper, bottles of ink, rows of pencils at the ready. Here and there a drawing of a thrush's nest or a locust's wing.

Logan lifted a sketch of a damselfly and held it so that the light would shine through, illuminating every inked contour.

She'd been deft with sketching ever since she'd begun writing him. But he'd never seen her produce anything like this in all the margins of her scores of letters.

It was beautiful.

When he lowered the paper, he noticed that she'd been studying him just as closely as he'd been studying the page. Staring, with dark-eyed intensity. He was struck by a sudden feeling of self-consciousness.

"That's only a preliminary sketch," she said, biting her lip. "It needs work yet."

"Looks damn near perfect to me," he said. "Ready to fly off the page."

"You truly think so?"

Her face was so serious and pale. As though she were worried about his opinion. Surely with work of this quality and friends like Lord Varleigh, she didn't need a Highland soldier to tell her she had skill. Nevertheless, the vulnerability in her eyes made him want to try.

He wished he knew something clever to say about art. How to compliment the lines or the shading. But he didn't, so he just said what came to mind.

"It's lovely," he said.

She exhaled, and color rushed back to her cheeks. A small smile curved her mouth.

Logan knew a small, quiet sense of triumph. After years of destruction on the battlefield, it felt good to build something up.

"How do you do it?" he asked, genuinely curious to know. "How do you draw a creature so faithfully?"

"Oddly enough, the trick isn't to draw the creature itself. It's to draw the space around it. The hollows and shadows and empty places. How does it bend the light? What does it displace? When I start to draw an animal—or anything, really—I look carefully and ask myself what's missing."

He thought of her a few moments ago, studying him intently. As though she were wondering about *his* missing elements. "Is that what you're doing, then? When I catch you staring at me?"

"Perhaps."

"I suggest you not waste your time, *mo chridhe*."

She crossed her arms and cocked her head, gazing at him. "I've spent years studying all sorts of creatures. Do you know what I've noticed? The ones that build themselves the toughest, strongest shells for protection . . . inside, they're nothing but squish."

"Squish?"

"Goo. Jelly. Squish."

"You think I'm squish inside."

"Perhaps."

He shook his head, dismissing the notion. "Perhaps there's nothing inside me at all."

He turned his attention to a map of the world mounted on the wall. The continents and countries were littered with stickpins.

"What's this?" he asked.

"I place a pin in the appropriate country for every exotic specimen I'm commissioned to draw. I always wanted to travel myself, but between the wars and my shyness, it never seemed possible. This is my version of the Grand Tour."

Logan tilted his head and looked at the map. He saw a smattering of pins in India, Egypt . . . several in the West Indies. But one particular area had the largest concentration of pins, by a wide margin.

"You've drawn a great many creatures from South America, then."

"Oh, yes. Insects, mostly. That brings us back to Lord Varleigh, you see. He recently returned from an expedition to the Amazon jungle, where he collected nineteen new species of beetles. I did the drawings, and he's going to present the specimens to his colleagues next week."

"So your work for him is concluded, then. Good."

"I didn't say that." She took the sketch from his hands and set it aside. "In fact, I hope to do a great deal more illustrations, and not only for Lord Varleigh."

He shook his head. "I dinna think you'll have the time."

"But you said we would not interfere in each other's interests and occupations. That you would have your life, and I would have mine."

"That was before."

"Before what?"

He waved toward the stairs, in the direction of Lord Varleigh's exit. "Before I knew 'your life' included that jackass."

"You needn't be angry just because he made an invitation. He was only being polite, to start. To continue, I was never going to accept. You already know I dislike social engagements."

"I should have accepted his invitation for us both."

She laughed.

"No, truly. I'd take you to that ball and make certain that Lord Varleigh and every last one of those naturists—"

"Naturalists."

"—every last one of those *insects* knows to keep their feelers off my wife."

She shook her head. "He's a professional acquaintance. Nothing more."

"Oh, he'd like to be more."

"And I'm not your wife yet. Not properly."

His hand slid to the back of her head, tilting her gaze to meet his. "You will be."

"Logan, are you . . ." Her eyes searched his. "Surely you can't be *jealous*?"

"He had his hand on you."

"What if he did, Captain MacEnvy? You gave me a brooch with some other woman's initials on it."

He shook his head, refusing to let her bait him. "If you think I'm harboring feelings for another woman, you have it all wrong. I dinna have any feelings, *mo chridhe.*"

"That's another thing. I wish you'd cease calling me that. If you have no feelings, I don't know why you keep referring to me as 'your heart.' "

"My lack of feelings is precisely why it's easy to call you that. Because my heart means nothing to me at all."

"Be that as it may," she said, "am I to believe that you've lived chaste and hermit-like all your life?"

"No. Certainly not *all* my life. Just the past several years of it. And that's your fault, by the way."

"I fail to see how that's my fault."

"There was a time," he said, "when I enjoyed a great deal of female companionship. But then you put me in a cage with those damned letters of yours."

"I'm not understanding you."

"All the men believed I had a devoted sweetheart. They looked up to me, believed me to be loyal and devoted, too. None of them wanted to see that falter. They chased the camp-followers away from my tent. The other officers went to the brothels and left me to mind the camp. Our chaplain passed more time with fast ladies than I did." Agitated, he pushed a hand through his hair. "I haven't lain with a woman since what feels like Old Testament times."

She smiled a little. "Are you saying you were *faithful* to me?"

He rolled his eyes. "Not on *purpose*. Dinna dress it up as something it's not."

"Believe me, I'm trying very hard not to do that. But I have too much imagination. Now I'm picturing you huddled by a lonesome campfire while all the other officers are out carousing. You're holding one of my letters and caressing it like a lovesick . . ."

No, no, no.

Logan had to put a stop to *that* notion, here and now.

His hands went to her waist and he pulled her close, startling a little gasp from her. Her body met his, soft and warm.

"What I'm saying isna romantic. It's raw, primal, and entirely crude." He lowered his voice to a growl. "You, Madeline Eloise Gracechurch, have been driving me slowly mad with lust. For years."

Maddie couldn't decide whether to laugh hysterically or faint with joy. Her, an unwitting temptress? She had no idea how to respond to the idea.

So, naturally, she said the most juvenile thing possible.

"*Me?*"

In answer, he bent his head toward hers.

"Wait." She ducked away from the kiss. "What are you doing?"

"Nothing unless you want it." His thumb caressed an aching spot on her back. It was maddening, how he could melt her defenses with a single touch. "But I think you do want it. I know you're curious. I know how you responded to me last night."

"That's precisely why I need time. I'm not prepared for this. For what it might mean."

"It's only physical," he murmured, kissing her neck. "It doesna have to mean anything."

"I'm sure it wouldn't, for you. But I haven't yet cultivated that talent. I don't know how to make it not mean anything. I think too much, too hard. I invent meaning where there's none to be found. Soon I'll be telling myself that you're . . ."

"That I'm what?"

That you're in love with me.

That was the danger she had to guard against. She knew, rationally, that Logan was no such thing. But she also knew herself, and her heart was far too imaginative.

"Let's take a moment to think," she said. "What would happen if we didn't consummate the marriage?"

He stopped kissing her. "That is out of the question."

"Then maybe we're asking the wrong question. Perhaps there's another mutually agreeable solution. What if I were to lease the lands to you and your men? For a low rent, indefinitely."

He shook his head. "Not enough. You don't think my men had leases on the lands they already lost? The word of an English landowner is worthless in the Highlands now."

"I'm not just any English landowner. I'm one with a most compelling reason to keep my word. You could trust me."

"Trust *you*. That's something, coming from a woman who's lied to everyone in her acquaintance for years."

"I never lied to you."

His gaze held hers, intense. "Even if I could trust you, I canna trust the world. What if something happens to you?"

"What do you mean? If I were to die?"

"If you married elsewhere."

She laughed at the idea. "Me, marry elsewhere? Death is the more likely event. I'm so far on the shelf now, I've accumulated an inch-thick layer of dust."

"You're a gentlewoman. You come from good family. You're an heiress with property, and you're uncommonly pretty. I canna believe you'd have no prospects."

Maddie wanted to argue back at him, but her

thoughts kept snagging on the fact that he'd called her uncommonly pretty.

He went on, "If you were to marry another—or die trying—the lands would pass to someone else. Then all your intentions and promises would be worthless. So a lease willna be acceptable."

She sighed. "None of this is acceptable."

Becky knocked and called up from the foot of the stairs. "Ma'am, Cook is asking how many for dinner this evening."

"Eight," Logan answered.

"*Eight*?" Maddie asked him.

"You, me, your aunt, and my men. Eight."

She shook her head. "We rarely have a formal dinner. Most evenings, I work late and then take a light repast in my room."

"Well, tonight you and I are going to welcome my men to dinner at a proper table. As husband and wife."

"This was supposed to be an arrangement of convenience. I thought we agreed that you would have your life, and I would have mine."

"And we will, once we're married fully and irrevocably. But as you've pointed out, that isna yet the case." He pulled a folded paper from his pocket. "Perhaps you'd prefer for everyone in England to read about your love affair with a pillow?"

"Logan, this isn't fair."

"I never promised you fairness. I promised you

the letters in exchange for a proper marriage. I'm still waiting on my end of the bargain."

"You are such a rogue."

He gave her a devilish look. "I'm a Highlander, an officer, and a man who knows the meaning of 'incendiary.' I'm exactly what you asked for, *mo chridhe.* You shouldna have any complaint."

Then he left her, disappearing in a series of pounding, unapologetic footfalls. Tromping down the stairs as if he owned Lannair Castle already.

But he didn't, fully. Not quite yet.

Maddie had only one possible route of escape. She must find those letters. If she could find and destroy them, his claim on her would be gone, too. She'd been hoping to search for them this morning, but Lord Varleigh had called. She hadn't had the chance.

But Logan couldn't keep her from searching forever.

In the meantime, she would take inspiration from Fluffy—grow a thick, impenetrable shell around herself and stay inside it just as long as she dared.

Chapter Eight

*L*ogan knew his bride hadn't been counting on hosting a half dozen soldiers at dinner. However, he would offer no apologies for including them. He needed to show them that this marriage was real, regardless of what had—or hadn't—happened in their bedchamber last night.

The castle's dining hall was certainly large enough to accommodate their makeshift clan. Even with five of his men, Maddie, her aunt, and Logan in attendance, they still didn't fill the whole table.

Most of all, the men deserved this—to sit down to a table laid with china and silver, and be served joints of roasted meat, jellied fruits, oysters, rich sauces, and more.

This was the lavish homecoming he'd promised

them on the battlefield. And Logan didn't make promises he couldn't keep.

These men—broken-down and brash as they were—had been the closest thing to family Logan had ever known. He wasn't going to let them down.

For the first two courses, they simply ate in awed silence.

Rabbie, of course, would ruin it as soon as the edge of hunger was gone. "I must say, Mrs. MacKenzie, what the captain told us about you . . . Well, it did not do ye justice."

Maddie cast him a worried glance.

"Oh?" Aunt Thea asked. "What *did* Captain MacKenzie say about her?"

"Verra little, ma'am. But if it were me who'd been so fortunate, every man in the regiment would be sick of hearing my boasting."

Munro snorted. "Every man in the regiment was sick of hearing your boasting anyway."

With a bashful smile, Maddie set down her wine-glass. She touched a fingertip to her collarbone, idly stroking up and down the slender ridge.

She did that when she was nervous, Logan had noticed. Unfortunately, the little gesture that she found soothing did not have a similar effect on him. On the contrary—it inflamed his every base desire.

He swallowed hard, unable to tear his gaze away from that single, delicate fingertip stroking back and forth. And back and forth. It was as though he could feel that gentle, teasing touch on his skin. Or on his—

"So, Captain," Callum said, sawing through a joint of mutton. "Now that we're all together, tell us the full story. Start at the beginning. How did ye woo her?"

Logan gave himself a brisk shake and turned his attention to his plate. "The usual way."

"As I told ye, ma'am," Rabbie said. "He's a man of few words."

"A man of few words?" Aunt Thea said. "But surely you're mistaken. Can this be the same man who wrote our Madling so many beautiful letters?"

"Letters?"

"Oh, yes. He sent our Madling reams of love letters. So eloquent and well expressed."

What the devil was this about? Logan sent a sharply inquiring glance at Maddie. She bit her lip and stared into her wine.

"I'm certain she saved them all. Madling, why don't you bring them down so the Captain can read a few? I always wished we could hear them in that delightful Scots brogue."

"That will not be necessary," Logan said.

"Perhaps not necessary," the older woman said, "but I think it would be sweet."

That word again. *Sweet.*

"No one wants to hear them."

At the far end of the table, Callum grinned. "Oh, I'd like to hear them."

His eager sentiment was seconded by every other man at the table, save Grant.

"Perhaps another time, Aunt Thea," Maddie said. "We're in the middle of a meal. The letters are in my dressing table all the way upstairs. As hostess, I can't leave our guests."

"It's out of the question," Logan agreed.

"Of course it is," Aunt Thea replied. "You stay right here, Madling. I'll go fetch them myself."

With that, the elderly woman was gone from the room before Logan and his men could even rise from their chairs as a mark of respect.

As soon as she was gone, Logan slid closer to his secretive bride. "What is she talking about?"

She murmured her response from behind her wineglass. "Well, I had to make up your side of the correspondence, didn't I? It wouldn't have been believable otherwise."

"And what, exactly, did this version of me say?"

A glint of amusement warmed her brown eyes. "Perhaps you should have made this inquiry *before* you pressured me into a hasty wedding. Whatever is in those letters, you're stuck with it now."

Holy God. Logan shuddered to imagine what utter foolishness a romantic sixteen-year-old chit like Madeline Gracechurch would put into the mouth of a Highland officer.

This could be bad. Verra bad.

"Perhaps we could make a trade," she whispered. "I'll give you back your letters if you give me back mine."

"Those aren't *my* letters in your dressing table."

"The ones I sent weren't *your* letters, either. And yet you claim possession of them. You can't have it both ways."

Her lashes gave a coy flutter. So this was what she turned into, given the smallest scrap of power over him. A saucy flirt.

Damned if he didn't like it. Confidence did more to enhance a woman's beauty than any kohl or rouge could manage. Lights sparkled at him from the depths of her dark eyes.

His appreciation dimmed swiftly when Aunt Thea returned to the dining room.

"Here we are."

She plunked an enormous stack of envelopes on the table. Logan marveled. There must have been at least a hundred of them. They were bound with a red velvet ribbon, which the older woman began to unknot.

Logan groaned inwardly.

This wasn't going to be bad. It was going to be a bloody disaster.

Rabbie rose to his feet and cleared his throat. "I'd be glad to offer my services for a dramatic reading."

Logan was tempted to launch a fork in Rabbie's direction. "That won't be necessary."

"So you'll do it?" Maddie asked.

"Yes."

In point of fact, there were few things on earth that Logan wanted to do *less* than read aloud from that menacing stack of parchment, and nearly all of those things involved spiders or entrails. But he didn't see that he had much choice. He couldn't allow any of his men to examine them too closely, or they would see the letters weren't written in his hand.

Maddie was right. Whatever was written in those missives, he couldn't disclaim it without disclaiming her. And disclaiming her meant giving up the lands his men so desperately needed.

In for a penny, in for a pound.

"Do give them here, Aunt Thea," Maddie said. "I'll choose my favorite one."

"*One*," he told her. "And only one."

After which he would burn the things and see that no one ever mentioned them again. Under penalty of pain.

But judging by the amused smile that tugged her lips as she sifted through the envelopes, Logan began to suspect he'd made a mistake in allowing Maddie to choose.

When she plucked a letter from the stack and handed it to him, grinning?

Logan didn't suspect any longer. He *knew*.

He'd made a grave error indeed.

"Read this one." Her voice lilted with false innocence. "It's one where you wrote me a poem."

Maddie watched his face carefully, awaiting Logan's reaction to this statement with giddy anticipation.

"A *poem*," he echoed.

Amazing. When he spoke the words, his jaw did not even move.

"Oh, yes. Two whole verses." She sipped her wine and savored his panicked expression.

At last, she had a moment of victory. This Highlander might have arrived out of nowhere and backed her into a corner, leaving her without options that didn't adversely affect the remainder of her life . . . but she had this one tiny banner of triumph over him.

And she intended to wave that banner now.

Rabbie laughed around a mouthful of food. "Never knew you were a poet, Captain."

"I'm not."

"Oh, don't be so modest," Aunt Thea said. "Yes, he sent our Madling a number of verses. Some of them were even good."

"This one was my favorite." Maddie smiled.

With a heavy sigh, Logan unfolded the letter. Then he set the paper on the table and reached into his sporran, withdrawing something unexpected.

A pair of spectacles.

When he fitted the unassuming wire frames to his face, the change in his appearance was immediate and profound.

Profoundly arousing, that was.

His features were still every bit as strong and unpolished, as though cut from granite with imprecise tools. As always, his jaw sported the shadowy growth of new whiskers—it seemed he could shave twice a day and never vanquish his inner barbarian. But the spectacles added an element of refinement to his masculine appeal. Not only refinement but civility as well. Humanity.

Strangely, they made her even more acutely aware of his raw animal nature. A lion might be trained to walk upright and wear a tailcoat, but one could never forget that beneath the manners, it was still a dangerous beast.

As Logan scanned the contents of the letter, Maddie imagined she could sense him craving violence.

From the far end of the table, his men began to urge and tease.

"Go on, then, Captain."

"What's the delay?"

"You could pass it here, and we'd read it ourselves."

"I wouldn't mind if they do," Maddie said.

He shot her a glare through those spectacles.

She felt it raise every hair on her arms.

At last, Logan cleared his throat. " 'My dear Madeline,' " he read in a bored, dispassionate tone. " 'The nights spent on campaign are long and cold, but thoughts of you keep me warm.' "

The men drummed the table in approval.

" 'I think often on the charms of your fair face. Your dark eyes. And your soft, creamy . . .' " He tilted the paper to peer at it. Suspense thickened the air like humidity. " ' . . . skin.' "

Rabbie whistled. "I was excited for a moment there."

"Good save, Captain," Callum added.

He pressed on, clearly eager to have it all over with. " 'When this war is over, I shall hold you in my arms and never let go. Until then, my love, I offer this verse.' "

"Well . . . ?"

Maddie had to press a hand to her mouth to keep from laughing aloud. She was ever so glad her talents ran to sketching and not poetry. Every verse she'd penned in adolescence was trite and insipid. As an adult, she would never willingly put her name to the horrid things.

Fortunately, she'd put Logan MacKenzie's name to every last one.

" 'To my truest love,' " he began.

"Go on," she urged. "I remember it precisely, if the ink is smudged. Let me know if you need help."

"I won't."

She leaned forward. "It begins like so. 'Were I a bird . . .' "

He exhaled with a sound of finality. Like a trapped hare with no escape, settling down to await its death.

Then he began to read aloud in that deep, resonant Scots burr.

"Were I a bird, I'd sing for thee.
Were I a bee, I'd sting for thee.
Were I a peak, I'd tower for thee.
Were I a tree, I'd flower for thee.
Were I a flute—"

The reading was interrupted as Callum began to cough with alarming violence. Rabbie slapped him on the back with vigor.

"Do I need to stop?" Logan asked. "Are you dying?"

Callum shook his head.

"Because I wouldna mind it if you *were* dying."

"No, no." At length Callum looked up with a reddened face and choked out, "Dinna mind me. Do go on."

"Were I a flute, I'd play for thee.
Were I a steed, I'd neigh for thee."

Now the coughing was contagious. All the men had succumbed. Even the servants had been afflicted. Maddie was fighting a powerful tickle in her throat, too.

Logan plowed on, no doubt hoping to kill them all dead. Then there would be no witnesses.

"Were I a fire, I'd burn for thee.
But being a man, I yearn for thee."

He flung the paper down on the table and whipped off his spectacles. "All my love and et cetera. That's the end." She thought she heard him mutter bitterly, "The end of all dignity."

Quiet reigned for a long moment.

"I have a most excellent cough remedy in my medicine box," Aunt Thea finally remarked. "Captain, I think several of your men could do with a dose."

Maddie motioned to the servants to clear the plates and bring dessert.

"There's one thing I'm not understanding," Rabbie said, leaning both elbows on the table. "Why did she get the idea ye were dead?"

Maddie paused. She'd never needed to think through this part. "Well, I . . ."

"There was a farewell letter in my sporran," Logan said. "To be sent in case I died in battle. I thought I'd lost it, but evidently I'd posted it by mistake."

Rabbie's brow wrinkled. "But that explains why she stopped writing you. Why'd you stop writing her?"

Callum put in, "It isna obvious? He believed she'd lost interest. So many of our sweethearts did."

"He should have had more faith in me." Maddie reached over and squeezed Logan's hand. "You dear, silly man."

He gave her a stern look: *Now you're pushing it too far.*

A prickle of awareness went through her. She didn't doubt that the moment they were alone, he was going to push back.

Chapter Nine

Suddenly, dinner couldn't last long enough.

It was with a heavy sense of foreboding that Maddie bid her aunt and Logan's men good night. As she and Logan mounted the stairs together, she felt the unspoken tension between them reaching new levels.

"I had Becky make up a proper room for you," she told him, pausing at the door of her bedchamber. "It's just down the corridor."

He shook his head. "We're going to share a room, lass."

He opened the door and walked through, making himself at home.

She said, "Where I'm from, most married couples don't share a bedchamber."

"Well, you're in the Highlands now." He flung his boot to the corner. It landed with a thud. "And here, we do. If you think I suffered through that bloody poem of yours just to leave you at the threshold, you're gravely mistaken."

He pulled his other boot loose and set to work on his clothing next.

Maddie couldn't help but stare. She wondered if he had any idea how attractive he was right now, just going about the everyday business of preparing for bed. His every motion fascinated her.

He pulled his shirt over his head and cast it aside. The muscles of his shoulders and back were perfectly defined by the firelight.

He moved to the washstand and poured water in the basin, then went about soaping his face and swabbing his neck and torso with a damp cloth.

He would smell of that soap if he joined her in bed and pulled her close. Soap and clean male skin.

She shook herself.

"You really need your men to believe in this, don't you? Our marriage."

He rinsed his face, then pushed damp hands through his hair. "They've had a rough time of it, marching from one hellish place to another, then coming home to find they've no home left. I dinna want them to worry they'll be forced to move on from here."

As always, Maddie found his devotion to his men

distressingly sympathetic, but she could not let it distract her from the topic at hand.

"You," she said, "are a complete hypocrite."

He answered her while brushing his teeth. His speech was muffled. "How do you reckon that?"

"You would hold me over the flame for telling a lie when I was sixteen. Yet you have also deceived those around you, and for the same length of time."

After rinsing his mouth, he turned to face her. "I did not lie. I merely . . ."

"Failed to contradict mistaken assumptions. For years. It is the same thing, Logan. Deceit by omission, if not an outright falsehood. You let those men believe we've had a relationship, and now you are every bit as invested in maintaining that lie as I am. Do you know what I think? I think you're all bluster. I could refuse to cooperate, turn you out of the castle, and you'd never take those letters to the scandal sheets."

His voice darkened. "It would be a mistake to underestimate me."

"Oh, I don't underestimate you. I can see just how deeply you're invested in your pride. How much the worship of those men means to you."

"It's not their *worship*. It's their trust. And yes, it means everything to me. I promised them that if they stood by me on the battlefield, they'd return to a life here in the Highlands. I am unashamed to lie, cheat, steal, or blackmail, if that's what it takes to keep that promise."

He advanced on her, and Maddie fell back a step, then two, in retreat. Until her legs collided with the edge of the bed. He had her cornered.

"And speaking of traits we have in common," he said, sliding one finger along her collarbone. "I've learned a thing or two about you. I noticed how you flirted with me downstairs."

"Flirted? Don't be absurd."

"You stare at me. You're fascinated."

"It's just the kilt."

"It might be partly the kilt. It's mostly the swagger."

"The swagger?" She tried to laugh. But he was right, he did have swagger. An abundance of sheer male arrogance and the strength to carry it. And it was, to Maddie's eyes, fascinating.

"You were undressing me with your eyes."

"What?" The word came out as a strange little squeak. She cleared her throat and tried again. "Even if I were—and I wasn't—it would be purely out of artistic interest."

"Artistic interest, my arse."

"Sorry to disappoint you, but I have not, as of yet, developed an artistic interest in your arse."

He leaned close to speak in her ear. Heat built between their bodies. "You," he whispered, "are every bit as desperate to consummate this marriage as I am."

"That's preposterous."

"Lass, I dinna think it is."

She put her hand to his chest—partly out of a need to hold him off, and partly out of desire to touch his bare skin. He was so warm, and more solid than she could have imagined. His chest hair tickled against her palm.

Oh, Maddie. You are in so much trouble.

She had to regain control of this conversation, and fast.

"You speak about needing a home, not wanting to move on . . . but it's not only your men you're concerned for. No one's that selfless. You must want this land for yourself, too."

He fell back a step, breaking their contact. "I never had a home to begin with. Didna have one to lose, so I'll never know what I've been missing. I'm the lucky one that way."

Oh, no. Not the tragic orphan story again.

Her heart gave a foolish twinge.

She gathered up some nightclothes and ducked behind the screen, desperate to hide from him and his disadvantaged past, and from her own silly feelings.

A great many people grew up orphaned, she reminded herself as she shimmied out of her frock and donned her nightrail. That didn't excuse him. Maddie had lost her own mother at a young age.

But then again, she'd always had a home. She'd certainly never been forced to sleep with the cows and live on a few crusts a day.

There it went again, that *pang* of emotion.

Maddie resolved to simply ignore it. Logan MacKenzie was blackmailing her into marriage. He'd given her a secondhand engagement brooch. She had no logical reason to feel sympathy for him.

She must have too much feeling pent up in her, that was all. Too much tenderness and affection, with no means to dispel it. Not even any proper pets. Only dead beetles and frigid lobsters.

She took her time washing and brushing her hair and buttoning up her shift all the way to her neck, hoping he might fall asleep before she even finished preparing for bed. At the very least, any ardor he might have been feeling should have cooled.

When she finally emerged from behind the screen, she felt certain she would have no difficulty resisting him.

She was dead wrong. This was even worse than she'd feared.

Pang, went her heart.

Pang, pang, pang.

He was lying in bed, a loose shirt hanging open at the neck to reveal a wedge of his chest. His brow was lightly furrowed in concentration, and those spectacles were perched on the strong bridge of his nose. One muscled arm was flexed and propped behind his head. And in the other hand, he held . . .

Devil take him. Heaven help her.

A book.

Not just any book, but a thick one bound in dark green leather. And he was *reading* the thing.

Those twinges of emotion had grown so strong that they had her nearly doubled over. Little fireworks of longing were bursting in her chest.

Not only in her chest but lower, too. Some cord running from her heart to her womb hummed like a plucked harp string.

He looked up from the book and caught her staring. "Is there something the matter?"

"Yes, there's something the matter. Logan, this is bad."

"What's bad?"

"Here I am, struggling to banish any foolish imagined affections for you so that we can consummate this marriage of convenience in a proper businesslike fashion, as we agreed. And then you go and read a book?"

While he was at it, why didn't he just bring her a basket of kittens, a bottle of champagne, and pose naked with a rose caught between his teeth?

He pulled a face. "I'm trying to get some rest, that's all. I only read when I want to fall asleep."

He turned a page with one hand, hooking it with his thumb and dragging it from right to left while keeping his other arm tucked securely under his head.

The deft, practiced nature of it stirred her suspicion. She eyed the well-creased spine of the volume. The book's pages showed the wear of being thumbed from right to left, again and again, all the way to the end.

He only read to fall asleep, he claimed? Oh, yes. And falcons only took wing out of boredom.

A terrible sense of affinity swamped her. For all her life, making the acquaintance of another book lover had felt like . . . well, rather like meeting with someone from her own country when traveling overseas. Or how she imagined that would feel if she ever traveled overseas.

The love of books was an instant connection, and a true boon for a girl who tended toward shyness, because it was a source of endless conversation. A hundred questions sprang up in her mind, jostling with each other to reach the front of the queue. Did he prefer essays, dramas, novels, poems? How many books had he read, and in which languages? Which ones had he read again and again?

Which ones had felt as though they'd been written just for him?

He turned another page, less than a minute after turning the last.

"You," she accused, "are a reader. Be honest."

It made perfect sense, too. After all, who else would read and reread the rambling, silly letters of a sixteen-year-old ninny?

A devoted reader, that's who. One stuck with nothing else for reading material.

"Fine," he said. "So I read. It's difficult to attend university without some practice in the habit."

"You went to university, too?"

"Only for a few months."

She lifted the coverlet and climbed into her side of the bed. "When you spoke about not having a home, I assumed you had grown up without the advantages of education."

"I was born with no advantages at all."

"Then how did you attend university?"

"When I was ten or so, the local vicar brought me into his household. He fed and clothed me, and gave me the same education as his own sons."

"That was generous and kind of him."

His lips gave a wry quirk. "Generous, perhaps. But kindness had nothing to do with it. He had a plan in mind. He called me 'son' just long and convincingly enough that when every family was compelled to send a son to war, he could send me. So that his own sons—the *real* sons—would be safe."

"Oh." She winced. "Well, that's not so kind. It's rather terrible, actually. I'm sorry."

His gaze darted to his arm.

It was only then that Maddie realized she'd reached out to touch it.

"I'm sorry," she repeated, withdrawing the touch.

He shrugged. The sort of gruff, diffident shrug

boys and men made when they want to say, *I don't care at all about it.*

The sort of shrug that had fooled no woman, ever.

"I got a bed, my meals, and an education from it. Considering what my life would have been otherwise, I canna complain." He closed the book and set his spectacles aside.

No, he wouldn't complain. But he was hurt, and it showed. He'd been given all the material benefits of a family, but none of the affection.

None of the love.

Oh, Lord. Now he was not only an impoverished orphan but an impoverished, *unloved* orphan with a passion for books. Her every feminine impulse jumped to attention. She was vibrating with the worst possible desires. The instinct to soothe, to comfort, to nurture, to hold.

"That pitying look you're giving me," he said. "I dinna think I like it."

"I don't like it, either."

"Then stop making it."

"I can't." She fluttered her hands. "Quickly, say something unfeeling. Mock my letters. Threaten my beetles. Just do something, anything reprehensible."

Tension mounted as he stared at her.

"As you like."

In an instant, he had her flipped on her back. His fingers went to the buttons of her nightrail.

And Maddie had absolutely no will to resist.

He gave her a wolfish look. "I trust this will do."

She heard herself say, "Yes."

Logan made short work of those tiny buttons guarding the front of her shift. He worked with brusque, ruthless motions. There was nothing of seduction in his intent.

This was her penalty for kindness. She had to learn that her sweet-tempered curiosity came with a cost. He would teach her to lay soft touches to his arm. To look straight into his soul with those searching dark eyes and have the temerity to care.

She'd asked for this.

He had undressed a fair number of women. But when he slipped loose the buttons of her chemise, he was trembling to see whatever lay beneath. He wasn't choosy about breasts. Large ones, pert ones. Dark nipples or fair. Alabaster or freckled. So far as he was concerned, the most comely pair of breasts in the world was always the pair he was currently tasting.

But nothing had prepared him for this.

When he pushed the panels of linen to either side, he couldn't believe the sight that awaited him. He'd been expecting an expanse of creamy, delicate skin.

Instead, he found a pale expanse of . . . more linen.

"I canna believe this. You're wearing two shifts."

She nodded. "I put the inner one on backward. Just as an extra layer of defense."

That would explain why he couldn't find another row of buttons.

"You didna trust me?"

"I didn't trust myself," she said. "It seems I was right not to. Look at me."

Logan didn't know whether to be offended by this strategy or impressed at her cleverness. She'd created her own virgin armor.

And he was tempted to play ravishing pirate. Seize the fabric in his hands and rend it down the middle, spilling her bosom free for his plundering.

But why go to that trouble when the linen in question was this fine, this supple and frail? He ran one hand upward, claiming the rounded swell of one breast.

She sucked in her breath. Her flesh quivered beneath his touch. He waited to see if she'd ask him to stop.

She didn't.

"I told you it will be good between us," he murmured.

"I seem to recall that promise. Was it verra good you said? Or verra *verra* good?"

He palmed her breast fully now, kneading and squeezing. With his thumb, he found her nipple and teased it to a tight, straining peak. Back. And forth.

"Verra . . . verra . . . *verra* good."

His own blood pounded in his veins, all of it

making a mad rush in one direction—down. Beneath the bed linens, his cock began to throb and harden.

He moved his attention to her other breast, spreading his fingers wide to stretch the fabric to its sheerest. God, she was lovely. Perfect pink-tinged flesh capped with a small, reddish nipple that looked as though it would taste of berry wine.

Her breath caught. "Could you . . ."

Logan froze at once. When she said nothing further, he lifted his head and met her gaze.

Damn. Why had he given her the chance? Now, even if she hadn't been planning it, she was going to ask him to stop. And then he would have to stop, because he wasn't the sort of man who'd continue.

The business of war and killing stripped a man of his humanity. Over his decade in the army, he'd seen soldiers—even ones that wore the same uniform—commit the vilest of acts against women. Sometimes he'd been in a position to stop it; other times, not. But misusing women was the one line Logan had never crossed.

He didn't view it as a point of pride. He didn't deserve any medals for it. But it let him know he'd held on to a scrap of his soul.

He wouldn't surrender that now. Not even for the chance to hold her tonight.

Don't, lass. Don't ask me to stop.

She said, "Could you at least kiss me when you do that?"

Relief and desire crashed through him.

"Aye. That I can do."

He bent his head and drew that berry-wine nipple into his mouth, suckling her straight through that damned extra chemise.

Judging by her sharp gasp, that wasn't the kiss she'd been expecting. But she didn't complain.

Logan was in paradise. She was sweet. So sweet that his brain went light as air, and he couldn't hold back a low moan.

He licked over her nipple, then moved in widening circles, painting the sheer linen to her breast. He paused to admire the transparent effect, then rolled atop her so that he could better start in on the other side.

What with the two shifts cocooning her body, he couldn't settle between her legs. Instead he braced his knees on either side of her thighs.

And his cock wedged right where it wanted to be.

When their bodies met, she gave a startled gasp. And then he moved against her, and her gasp became a low, sweet sigh.

Yes.

"That's it." He rocked his hips against hers. "Do you feel it? It's only the beginning, *mo chridhe*."

She shut her eyes. Her dark lashes fluttered against her cheeks. "You truly must kiss me when you do *that*."

Logan obliged her, this time pressing his lips to hers.

As he sank into the lush heat of her kiss, a wildness gathered and growled within him.

He wanted her. All of her. Under him. Surrounding him. Taking him into her softness and heat.

And he couldn't get enough of her sweet taste. As if possessed, he pushed her arms against the mattress and kissed her neck, her brow, her lips, her lovely breasts.

Then he moved lower.

He rose up on his knees and began to kiss a trail down her linen-sheathed body. From the hollow between her breasts . . .

To her shy, adorable navel . . .

And further.

From far away, he heard himself murmuring in Gaelic. Words began tumbling from his lips, unbidden. Words he'd never spoken to any other woman in his life.

"Maddie a ghràdh. Mo chridhe. Mo bean."

Maddie, darling. My heart. My wife.

Her fancies had started to addle his brain, too. What was she doing to him?

He spread the linen tight over her hips, revealing the dark triangle of shadow guarding her sex.

And then he bent to kiss her there.

She flinched and bucked, bashing him in the head with her knee.

Ouch.

With a low moan of pain, Logan rolled to the side, clutching his head.

He stared up at the bed's wooden canopy, struggling for breath. Had he been wondering what she was doing to him? He knew what she was doing to him.

She was killing him.

That's what she was doing to him.

"What . . ." She clutched the bedsheets to her chest. "What was . . . Why would you do . . . *that*?"

Why indeed.

"Because humans have more imagination than lobsters, *mo chridhe*. There's more than one way to share pleasure."

She was quiet for a long moment. "How many ways?"

He rolled onto his side to face her, skimming a single finger from her breastbone to her belly. "Here's an idea. I'll demonstrate them, and you keep count."

This time her silence seemed endless.

"Perhaps another time, thank you." She turned onto her side. Away from him.

And that was it, then. Wanting pulsed through his body, coiling and sparking with electric intensity. He didn't dare put his trust in pillows or decency to contain it.

It would be another cold, restless night on the floor.

Chapter Ten

Maddie found it impossible to sleep.

Last night, the whisky and her over-whelmed emotions had left her too exhausted for anything else. Tonight, her body sizzled with unspent energy and frustrated desire.

Whenever she closed her eyes, she thought of his mouth on her.

There.

For that one, heated moment, it had felt good. More than good. A jolt of bliss had streaked through her. She still felt it lingering in the soles of her feet and at the juncture of her thighs.

Would he want a woman to put her mouth on him?

There?

Humans have more imagination than lobsters, he'd said. And yet Maddie—who was human the last time she checked—could not quite bend her imagination that far.

Of course, she might have had a better idea if she'd ever seen *all* of him in the flesh.

She turned onto her side and wriggled closer to the edge of the bed overlooking his pallet on the floor. The bed frame creaked. She froze for a moment. And when she heard nothing but his even breathing, she crept closer still, until she could peek down at him.

The dim glow of the banked fire revealed his figure slowly.

He lay on his side, shirtless, only partially covered by his thin, unbelted plaid. His back was to her. In the firelight, he looked cast in bronze. Except that bronze didn't move, and his back seemed to be . . . convulsing?

At first she thought it merely a trick of the light. Then she had the sudden, mortifying thought that he was awake and laughing at her. But after blinking a few times, she understood what was happening.

He was shivering.

"Logan," she whispered.

No answer.

She quietly lowered her feet to the floor and crept down to sit beside him.

"Logan?"

She laid a light touch to his shoulder. He wasn't feverish. On the contrary, his skin was ice-cold. His entire body was racked with tremors, and he seemed to be murmuring something in his sleep.

She leaned closer to listen. Whatever he was saying, it seemed to be in Gaelic. The same word, again and again.

Nah-tray-me?

Judging by the violent way he was shivering, if she had to venture a guess, she would suppose *nah-tray-me* meant "cold" or "ice" or perhaps "look, a hallucinatory penguin."

Oh, Logan.

Since her attempts to wake him hadn't worked, Maddie turned her attention to warming him instead. She pulled the heavy quilt from her bed. Then she lay down behind him, drawing the quilt over them both.

Propping her head on one hand, she drew soothing caresses over the lines of his shoulders, neck, and back. She made gentle shushing noises. He didn't wake, but gradually his shivers began to subside. The tension in his muscles uncoiled, and his body relaxed against hers. Skin to skin. The masculine, soapy scent of him filled her senses.

Her heart swelled. Tenderness unfurled in her chest like a wisp of smoke, spreading and permeating her entire body.

I dinna do cuddling, he'd said.

She nuzzled the velvety cropped hairs at the nape of his neck, smiling secretly to herself. Perhaps *he* didn't do cuddling, but she did. She was excellent at it, apparently.

Madeline Eloise Gracechurch: Stealth Cuddler.

What Logan didn't know wouldn't hurt him.

But if she wasn't careful, it just might tear her heart in two.

At the first sign of daylight, she rose and slipped into the adjoining chamber, where she dressed herself in a simple muslin frock. She inched her way down the spiraling steps and arrived in the high hall, which Logan's men had turned into their temporary camp.

There she stood, blinking, waiting for her eyes to adjust, and willing her heart to stop pounding in her ears.

Come along, then. Where are you?

Her gaze went to the corner, where the men's belongings had been heaped.

There.

Maddie hugged the perimeter of the room, treading on the balls of her slipper-clad feet until she reached the heap of baggage.

Whether they were in a sporran, a saddlebag, or a knapsack . . . Those incriminating letters had to be here somewhere, and she was going to find them.

She plucked a canvas haversack from the corner and opened it, gingerly poking through the contents. When she found nothing remarkable inside, she moved on to investigate the next. And then to a third.

The contents were humble, and much the same in each. A spare shirt or two, a pair of woolen fingerless gloves, a boar-bristle scrubbing brush, a pair of dice. Nothing much of note.

Until her finger found the sharp end of a needle.

To her credit, Maddie managed not to cry out. But the bag slipped from her grasp, hitting the stone floor with a light thud.

She went absolutely still and turned a wary glance over the hall of snoring Scotsmen. None of them seemed to have heard. The men remained unmoving lumps of plaid huddled under their tartans.

Apparently, the men wore their plaids as kilts by day and then used the same for bedding by night.

She wrinkled her nose. When did they *wash* the things?

When did they wash them*selves*?

"Good morning."

Startled for the second time in as many minutes, Maddie jumped and wheeled.

Apparently if you were Logan MacKenzie, you washed yourself now.

He stood in the doorway to a side chamber, bared

to the waist and dripping. He propped one shoulder against the doorway and clutched his kilt before him with his free hand. His pose was a classic contrapposto. He looked like a renaissance David, sculpted not from cool, stoic marble but from impatient flesh.

A thin trail of dark hair drew her gaze lower.

"You're awake early," she said.

"Not really. I rose shortly after you did." He looked her up and down. One eyebrow rose in interrogation. "Are you looking for something, *mo chridhe*?"

"Oh. Yes. I was looking for something." She twisted the corner of her apron and said the only thing she could. "I was looking for you."

"Me."

She nodded.

His mouth quirked with pure male arrogance. "Well, then. I'm at your service. What did you want with me?"

What indeed. Maddie swallowed hard. She wanted so many things, and most of them were ridiculous. She wanted to reach up and push an errant lock of hair from his brow. To put a shirt on him before he took a chill.

If he could read her mind, he would have a good laugh.

Somehow she had to find a way to calm all these fussy, caretaking impulses. Or channel them into some other activity.

Drat. Why were there never any underfed, shivering puppies about when a girl needed them most?

"I . . . merely wanted to bid you a good journey. I assumed you'd be going to Ross-shire today."

"I'm not going to Ross-shire today."

"But you promised Grant."

"I promise Grant the same thing at least six times a day. We were there months ago, and he doesna recall it. As far as he knows, we're always going to Ross-shire tomorrow."

"Oh. Well, then. If you're not busy doing anything else this morning," she said, "perhaps we could . . . That is, I hoped the two of us might . . ."

He stared at her, expecting her to complete that sentence, and Maddie had no idea what to say. *Braid each other's hair? Play hide-and-seek? Search the loch for sea monsters?* What activity could the two of them possibly share? Other than the bed-related activities that were obviously on his mind—and entirely out of the question.

As she stood there dithering, his eyes narrowed with suspicion. He looked toward the corner where she'd dropped the opened knapsack.

She hopped to the side, blocking his view and giving the knapsack a discreet nudge backward with her foot.

"I thought we could visit the tenants," she said. "Together."

"Tenants?"

"There are a small group of crofters up in the valley. You're the new laird of the castle, so to speak. They will want to make your acquaintance."

To her relief, the suspicion fled his eyes. He rubbed the back of his neck. "I'd like to make their acquaintance, too. That's a fine idea."

He found a fresh shirt in his bag and pulled it over his head, punching his arms through the sleeves. As he did, she made note of the bag—a black-painted canvas knapsack.

The letters had to be in there. Now that she knew, Maddie could be patient. He couldn't hover over the thing every moment of the day.

"Then it's settled," she said. "We'll walk up along the creek together. I can take them a basket of . . . something."

Maddie started to warm to the idea. Perhaps visiting the crofters was the outlet she needed. She could play with the children. There might be a new baby she could hold.

Perhaps they would even have puppies.

As soon as they came within view of the *baile,* a trio of terriers came running to greet them.

The dogs yipped at Madeline's skirts as they approached a cluster of some dozen thatched-roof stone cottages set along the river's edge. High on the ridge, boys watching the sheep turned and looked down to watch them instead.

From one of the distant blackhouses rose the high, thin wail of an infant.

As they neared the *baile,* Logan drew Maddie to his side. "Listen to me. The people here will likely be frightened when they see us."

"Frightened of you?"

"No, of you."

"Me?" she asked. "But I'm just an Englishwoman, and not a very big one at that."

"That's precisely why they'll be terrified," he said. "Have you never heard of the Countess of Sutherland?"

"Of course I've heard of her. One can't fail to hear of her. She's a fixture in London society. An accomplished painter, too. Quite elegant."

"Oh, yes. So accomplished and elegant that she's become the most ruthless landowner in all the Highlands."

"I don't believe that."

He sighed with impatience. The lass was so bloody sheltered. Everything had been handed to her on a gilt-edged tray. She had no idea how the common folk of the Highlands lived. A futile sense of anger swelled in his chest.

"The countess inherited half of Sutherland when

her parents died. In the past few years, her agents have evicted village after village, forcing Scotsmen off the land by the hundreds and thousands. Stealing their farmlands to make way for sheep, burning their cottages to the ground, and offering them little in the way of compensation. Often with the assistance of the British Army."

He looked down at his redcoat with regret. He would have done better to wear a traditional great kilt today.

"Believe me, *mo chridhe*. The Highlands is the one place on earth where no one will underestimate the ability of a quiet-looking, gently bred Englishwoman to destroy lives."

"That's terrible."

That was vastly understating matters. "Try criminal. Shameless. Unconscionable. Any of those words would better serve."

She regarded the cluster of blackhouses. "So you're worried they'll think we're here to evict them?"

"I wouldna doubt it," he said. "Showing your face for the first time, with an officer of the Royal Highlanders at your side . . . ? They'll likely fear they're about to lose everything."

"Oh, goodness."

They were close enough now that Logan could glimpse faces in the windows of the cottages, peering out at them.

"Dinna worry," he said. "I'll assure them they've nothing to fear."

"If you say so."

A little smile curved her lips. Logan was irritated that she didn't seem to understand what he was telling her.

"At least you've brought gifts. What's in the basket?"

She rummaged through the contents. "A few sweetmeats and lozenges. Packets of raisins. But mostly it's Aunt Thea's surplus cosmetics and remedies. She sends away for every product advertised in every ladies' magazine. I like to see them put to some use."

He blinked at her. "These are your gifts?"

"Your men have depleted our stores of food, and I didn't have time to prepare anything else."

"What are they supposed to do with"—he held up a brown bottle and peered at the label—"Dr. Jacobs' Miracle Elixir?" He plucked a small jar out next. "Excelsior Blemish Cream?"

"Women are women, Logan. Every girl needs a bit of luxury and a chance to feel pretty now and then."

He passed a hand over his face. This was going to be a disaster.

"Miss Gracechurch! Miss Gracechurch!"

No sooner had Logan finished his stern warnings than the youngest occupants of the blackhouses began pouring out from their homes and rushing to meet Maddie in the lane. Soon she had children gathered around her, tugging at her skirts.

"What was that you said, Logan? That they'd be frightened of me?"

She reached into her basket and pulled out a handful of sweetmeats, distributing them into the waiting hands of the children.

"You might have mentioned that they'd know you already," he said.

"And spoil your informative lecture on the evils of the Clearances? That would have been a pity."

He shook his head. The canny minx.

"Hullo, Aileen." She crouched at the side of a gap-toothed girl who could not have been more than four or five years old. "How is your scar then, dear?"

She lifted the edge of the girl's sleeve and examined a thin red mark on her upper arm.

"Very cleanly healed. Good girl. You'll have a biscuit for that." She reached into her basket for the treat. "There, darling."

Once Aileen had run off, Logan remarked, "That was an inoculation scar."

Maddie nodded. "I've been visiting regularly ever since I took possession of the castle. When I learned none of the children had been inoculated, I made certain to order the cowpox matter from Dr. Jenner. We performed the inoculations a month or so ago."

Damn, she just kept on surprising him. First with her beauty. Then with the illustrations. He'd been forced to accept that there was more to her character than he'd gleaned from her letters, but none of it fell too far outside the borders of his carefully mapped mental territory labeled "Madeline." She was privileged, sheltered, intelligent, curious, and far too crafty.

But this . . .

This was different.

As he watched her with the tenants' children, his conception of her pushed against its established boundaries. He was forced to add new descriptors to his list. Ones like "generous" and "responsible" and "protective." She was conquering new places in his understanding, brazenly invading territory he'd rather die than surrender.

This was all wrong. He'd come here to marry her and claim what he was owed.

He didn't want to *like* her—not any more than she wanted to like him.

"Not all of us English landowners aspire to the Countess of Sutherland's example," she said. "My father always adhered to strong principles of land stewardship, and inoculation is something I care about. My mother survived smallpox as a young girl. Though she recovered from the pox, her heart was weakened. I believe it was why she died young."

Logan knew, of course, that she'd lost her mother. Her father's happy remarriage had been detailed in many a letter. However, she'd never written much about the woman herself, and it hadn't occurred to him to ask.

"I was hoping this year to start a school," she said, deftly changing the subject. "Perhaps once your men finish their own cottages, they can work on building a schoolhouse."

"First they need to work on finding wives and making the children to fill it."

"That can likely be arranged. Several of the men hereabouts went to war and didn't return. More than one young woman found herself at loose ends."

Just looking around them, Logan glimpsed a few potential candidates—a cluster of lasses stood together in a doorway, whispering and giggling amongst themselves. They were quickly joined by others. Soon it seemed the entire population of the small village had come out to greet them, crowding around.

"You weren't exaggerating," he said. "They do appreciate your aunt's castoffs."

She looked up from her basket. "They're not usually *this* eager. That must be for you. When I . . ."

Her voice trailed off. When Logan turned to look at her, he could see she'd grown still. He recognized that pale, disconnected expression on her face. It was the same look she'd worn at their wedding.

She'd called it shyness, but to Logan, it looked rather like shock. He'd seen it in soldiers, particularly the ones who'd survived the ugliest of battles. Their eyes stared for miles, and their minds seemed to be somewhere far away.

"Maddie?"

She shook herself.

"This is Captain MacKenzie," she told the women, pushing the basket into Logan's hand and backing away. "He's going to distribute the gifts today."

"Wait," he said. "You mean to just leave me here with all this . . ." He fished a small tin out of the basket. " . . . rose-hip beautification balm?"

"I've just remembered a woman down the lane who's entered her confinement. I meant to look in on her."

"It can wait until you've finished here."

She shook her head, and then she was gone.

Chapter Eleven

Maddie hastened away, ducking behind a long, narrow stone cottage with a sloping thatched roof.

Once alone, she wrapped her arms around her middle, hugging herself tight. Her teeth chattered, and her skin prickled all over.

She felt a touch guilty for leaving Logan on his own, and under false pretenses. There wasn't any woman who'd entered her confinement in this humble village. Not that Maddie knew of, at any rate. But she found a ewe nursing a pair of lambs in the stone enclosure behind the cottage, and she decided that made her honest enough.

When the crowd had closed around her, the cold had closed in, too. She'd known she had to get away, and the truth never made a useful excuse.

Over the course of her life, she'd learned this lesson over and over again. If she begged to be released from a social obligation on the grounds that she was simply too shy, her family and friends never took her at her word. They insisted she only needed to give it a chance. They wheedled and nudged, telling her of all the fun she would have. This time, they promised, it would be different.

It was never different.

Maddie had long ago accepted the truth. The same occasions that brought joy and merriment to others were torture for her. And no one would ever understand.

Once she'd recovered her composure, she walked back to the cottage's corner and peeked around it to observe.

The women were still crowded around Logan and his basket of beauty supplies. They tapped the bottles he offered and peered into jars of cream, talking and giggling amongst themselves. He uncorked a bottle of *eau de toilette* and held it out for a young woman with coppery hair to sample the aroma.

After taking a cautious sniff, the young woman laughed and smiled. A wash of pink touched her freckled cheeks. Maddie suspected it had nothing to do with the bottled scent and everything to do with its handsome purveyor.

Goodness, he looked fine today. The morning sunlight brought out the ginger highlights in his hair and turned his skin a warm bronze. The air about him was one of command and ease. He was in his element. He'd likely been raised in a *baile* much like this. He knew just how to greet each of the cottagers who came forward, from the oldest grandmother to a curious youth who came down from the grazing slopes.

When she could see that Logan's basket was emptied and the women had begun returning to their cottages with their new treasures, Maddie emerged from her hiding place. They bid their farewells to the dogs and children and began the walk back.

Logan didn't seem happy with her. "That was quite a trick you played, abandoning me to play tinker with the lasses."

"I don't think it was my gifts that those lasses were interested in. I think they were more curious about you."

"I would have done better to walk out to the fields and have a talk with the men."

"I suppose that would have been more lairdly, you mean."

He made a dismissive noise. "It's not being lairdly. It's doing my duty. Getting to know the neighbors. Letting them know they needn't worry about their future." He slid her an assessing look. "Speaking of worries, what happened back there?"

"I don't know what you mean."

"I think you do. When the women surrounded you, it was like you went away somewhere else. Or pulled inside yourself somehow. You weren't there. I noticed the same during our wedding."

She bit her lip. "Do you think the women noticed?"

"I canna say. But I noticed."

She looked into the distance. "I've told you. I'm shy."

"That seemed like something more than shyness to me."

She shook her head. She was used to her family and friends not understanding. But it was a new low when even her imaginary sweetheart refused to accept the truth.

"I'm timid in groups, that's all. I always have been. And I hate that it sometimes makes people feel I'm not interested, but I don't know what else I can do."

"Dinna worry. You'll have a chance to make a good impression on Beltane."

"Beltane?"

"The first of May. It's a traditional Highland celebration, reaching back to the pagan times."

"I've heard of it," she said. "But I'm not sure why I'd be making an impression on that day."

"I've invited them to the castle and asked the lasses to spread the word. We'll extend the invitation to anyone living in the area."

"You're having a party, then?"

"It would be more accurate to say that *you* are having a party. The lady of the castle is the hostess, is she not?"

Maddie's steps grew agitated, and she nearly stumbled over a rock. "The first of May is barely a fortnight from now. That isn't enough time to pre-pare the castle. Or, for that matter, to prepare myself. I've never hosted anything."

"These people need a connection to the traditional ways," he said. "A celebration to look forward to. And they need to know that the land is in good hands. It's important that they see us working together."

"I just wish you'd asked me first."

"I might have asked. But I was decided on invit-ing them no matter your answer."

"Well. How very commanding of you."

"I'm not accustomed to making decisions by com-mittee, *mo chridhe*. For mild-mannered discussion, you should have posted your letters to some cleric from Hertfordshire. If you didna want a Highland officer, you shouldna have wished for one."

Shouldna, couldna, wouldna.

"Silly me. I dreamed big."

He gave her a sly grin. "And you got it."

The lewd implication in his statement made her blush.

"Can we please discuss the fact that we are egre-giously mismatched?" she asked. "Two days in, and our marriage is already a disaster. I keep thinking there must be some other solution. If you will not accept a lease . . . perhaps I could sell some of the land to you."

He snorted. "Sell it to me for what? Do I look like a wealthy man?"

"You're an officer. Or you were. Your commission must have been worth a significant amount."

"I attained that rank through a field promotion. My captaincy wasn't worth the same as a gentleman's. It gives me and the lads enough to start on, but that's all."

"Oh. Well, that's too bad."

"If I had the gold to purchase land outright, I would have done that on my own. It would have been a great deal easier."

Maddie didn't know how to take that statement. Was she supposed to believe he'd been driven to this dishonorable act—forcing her into marriage—out of honorable motives? Or was she supposed to feel like she was his second choice?

She fingered the brooch affixed to her tartan sash.

Well, there was her answer.

She *was* his second choice.

"Say I'd never written a single letter," she said, her voice softening. "Say your men didn't need any help. What would you have wanted for yourself, Logan? A home, a wife, a family? A trade, or a farm . . . ? What did you dream about?"

"I dreamed of nothing."

"You can't say nothing. Surely you must have—"

"No." His tone was curt. "Lass, I never dream at all."

Damn.

Logan hadn't intended to say that. It wasn't something he talked about often. In point of fact, it probably wasn't something he'd spoken of to another soul, ever. He knew it marked him as strange.

But he'd spoken of it now, for some daft reason.

She stopped in the middle of the path and turned to him, searching him with those clever, dark eyes that had the power to see not only what was there but also what wasn't.

"I don't believe you," she said. "Everyone has dreams."

"Not me." He shrugged. "When I close my eyes at night, there's naught but darkness behind them. Just emptiness until I wake."

It was Logan's greatest fear—the thought that had likely preserved him through many a battle and campaign—that when it came for him, death would be nothing but an endless night. He'd be a shivering boy again, caught alone in the empty darkness.

Forever.

"But last night, you—"

"Last night I what?"

She pressed her lips together. "Nothing. It's just so strange. I've never known someone who didn't dream at all."

"Never developed the talent, I suppose. I was an orphan with nothing. What use would dreaming be? I wouldna have known what to dream about, even if I'd tried."

"Surely it's not too late to learn." She reached out to brush a bit of fluff from his sleeve. As if she wanted to touch him but had thought better of it. "You don't have to be trapped in a marriage to me. Not if you don't want it."

He pulled her to him, roughly. Letting her feel his body pressed against hers. "I dinna think you can doubt what I want."

"Yes, but there's wanting, and then there's *wanting*. The desire of your body might not be the desire of your soul."

He made a dismissive noise. What soul?

"This life you're so determined to create for your friends and the tenants—a cottage, crops in the ground, cows at pasture . . ." She touched the front of his shirt, somewhere close to his pounding heart. "A bonny Scots lass to welcome you home from the fields every evening, keep you warm at night, give you bairns . . . Maybe you want that for them so badly because it's what you really want, too."

He pushed the idea away. "You're the one with an excess of imagination. And I must say, it hasna made your life much better, has it?"

"Perhaps not."

"It doesna matter what I want. Much less what I dream about. My soul has no say in the matter. None of this has anything to do with me. I came here to marry you because it's what the men need. I'm taking one for the clan."

She flinched at his words.

He knew at once he'd hurt her.

And it didn't feel nearly as satisfying as he'd hoped it would. It made him feel rather small, actually. Like a boy caught winging rocks at songbirds.

She exhaled slowly, then nodded. "Thank you for that. After watching you with the tenants, I was in far too much danger of liking you."

As she strode away from him, the feisty swing in her gait beckoned him to follow.

"You did want a new reason to despise me, after all. I'm just trying to oblige."

"You're doing a fine job of it, too."

"So you're upset with me."

"Yes."

"Insulted. Angry. Irritated."

"All three."

"Excellent."

He caught her arm and pulled her to face him, letting his gaze wander over the flushed skin at her throat and the rise and fall of her corseted breasts. An attractive spark of defiance lit her dark, secret eyes.

"Then our next stop is the bedroom, *mo chridhe*. You should be ready to make this marriage real."

Chapter Twelve

Oh, no.

Maddie immediately rued her foolish words.

"Don't be absurd," she said.

"I willna be absurd. I mean to be incendiary."

Maddie wished she could think of a tart, sophisticated reply to set him in his place and get herself out of this. But the brisk wind whipping at her skirts seemed to have stolen her wits, as well.

So in lieu of a sophisticated reply, she made a juvenile one.

She stammered nonsense for a moment, then panicked and fled.

The winding path back to the castle was suddenly much too long. Maddie needed to be home at once. Home in her bed, inside a cozy tent of pillows and blankets.

With Logan safely on the other side of the bolted door.

Lifting her hem, she left the footpath and began a route straight overland, walking as fast as the muddy ground would allow her.

"Don't walk that way," he called after her.

She ignored him.

I will walk where and how I please, thank you. I'm not one of your foot soldiers. You do not command me.

"Ack."

Maddie nearly tripped over her own hem. She looked down. In her haste to prove her independence, she'd independently taken a grave misstep. The entirety of her half boot had disappeared into black, fibrous mud.

When she tried to pull it loose, her other leg immediately sank, too—all the way up to her knee. What was this muck? It acted like quicksand, drawing her further and further down.

"Logan?" she called. "Logan, please come at once. I can't move my feet."

He stood a few feet to the side and surveyed her situation. "You've stepped in a bog. Happens all the time."

"So it's happened to you?"

"Och, no. I'm not that stupid."

Of course not, Maddie thought bitterly. Of course this would only happen to her.

"But I have unmired many a cow and sheep," he continued.

"Wonderful. If you'd just be so kind as to unmire me. Quickly?"

A hint of amusement gleamed in his eyes. That look told her something terrible.

He was going to help her, but he was going to enjoy every minute of this first.

Maddie twisted and pried at her leg, to no avail. It was well and truly stuck, and her heart was rabbiting about her chest.

He clucked his tongue. "The first rule of bogs: dinna panic."

"What's the second rule of bogs? I think we should just skip to that."

"No thrashing about," he said. "You'll fatigue yourself. Just be calm and wait for your body to reach its equilibrium."

Easy for him to say.

She tried to reach for something, anything, to grab onto. Her hands caught only air and loose grass. The bog tightened its grip, swallowing her hips.

"Logan," she cried. "Logan, it's getting worse."

"That's because you're struggling."

"Of course I'm struggling! I am being swallowed alive. And you're just standing there."

He crouched to her eye level. "You'll be fine. Most bogs are no more than waist deep."

"*Most* bogs," she repeated. "So some bogs are deeper."

"Almost no one dies of miring."

"*Almost* no one? If you're trying to reassure me, you're going about it all wrong."

"Relax," he said. "The ones who do perish, they die of the exposure or thirst. Not because they're sucked under."

"So you're saying . . ."

"You'll be fine. We'll build a little roof over your head and bring you bannocks twice a day. You can live here quite happily for years."

Maddie clenched her jaw to keep from smiling or laughing. Every time she made up her mind to despise him, he showed a flare of that disarming humor. She refused to reward him for it.

"Not to worry," he said. "It takes hours for the weight of the peat to cut off circulation to your limbs."

She groaned in despair as she sank further still. The peat and mud sucked at her legs, pulling her waist-deep in muck.

She was truly beginning to panic. Landing knee-deep in a bog was a funny situation, even she would admit—for a minute. Maybe two. But immobilized in freezing, waist-deep mud with the distinct possibility of never working herself free?

This was not her idea of a pleasant afternoon. Especially when it seemed likely to become her final afternoon.

Logan, by contrast, seemed to be having the time of his life. He sat down on a bit of rock nearby. "Say, remember that time when you got mired in the bog?" He chuckled to himself. "What a memory. We were there all day. Made a picnic of it. We sang songs for an hour or two. Counted to five thousand, just for larks. Then you insisted I go for sandwiches, and . . ."

She cast him a beseeching look.

He looked at the mud. "If I pull you free, will you promise to bed me for my pains?"

"Here's what I'll promise, Logan MacKenzie. If you don't get me free, I will come back from the grave and haunt you. Relentlessly."

"For a timid English bluestocking, you can be quite fierce when you choose to be. I rather like it."

She hugged herself to keep her hands out of the creeping mud. "Logan, please. I beg you, stop teasing and get me out of this. I'm cold. And I'm frightened."

"Look at me."

She looked at him.

His gaze held hers, blue and unwavering. All teasing went out of his voice. "I'm not leaving you. Ten years in the British Army, and I've never left a man behind. I'm not leaving you. I'll have you out of this. Understand?"

She nodded. She was beginning to comprehend

why his soldiers would follow him anywhere, and why the tenants trusted him on sight. When Logan MacKenzie took a soul under his protection, he would die before he let them suffer harm.

Maddie's wasn't a soul under his protection, not truly. He meant to use her for her lands, plain and simple. But at least she had the comfort of this knowledge: He couldn't leave her here.

So long as their marriage remained unconsummated, she was of no use to him dead.

"First, draw a good breath," he told her. "In and then out. Slowly."

"I don't want to waste time with breathing. Can't you just pull me out of this?"

"Breathe," he repeated.

It would seem he wouldn't help her until she obeyed him. She closed her eyes, drew a breath, then released it.

"That's it, again. More slowly this time. And again, until you've calmed."

Those half dozen slow, forced breaths were the most torturous moments of her life. But at the end of them, she did feel somewhat improved. Her rioting heartbeat had calmed to a slightly less deafening clamor.

"When you're ready," he said, "you can begin to move back and forth."

"How?"

"Just rock to and fro. As if you're dancing."

"Oh, Lord. That's it. I'll die here. I don't know how to dance."

He chuckled. "Lass, the bog doesna know that."

She did as he directed, swaying back and forth. She felt like a clock's pendulum moving in treacle. At first, she could only move an inch or two to either side, but after a few minutes' effort, she could manage a reasonable sway.

"That's it. Can you feel water circulating about your legs?"

She nodded.

"Then you're doing it right. Keep it up. Perhaps even a bit faster. It would be best to have your legs free before . . ."

"Before what?" Maddie asked.

Heavy raindrops splattered her face and shoulders.

"Before that."

Wonderful. Now she would be wet and chilled from both sides.

She rocked with renewed vigor and was rewarded with a bit more breathing room. "What do I do now?"

"Lean back a touch," he directed. "As though you're going to float atop the bog."

"But—"

"Just do it."

He lay on his stomach behind her, reaching forward with both hands. As she reclined, he caught her under the arms.

"I have you," he whispered in her ear. "And I'm not letting go."

She swallowed hard. "What next?"

"Whichever of your legs feels the loosest, keep wriggling it side to side. And pull it up."

"I'm confused. Am I supposed to move it side to side, or up?"

"Both."

Dear Lord. What was next? Do this all while juggling torches and smoking a pipe? She wasn't certain she had the coordination for this. London ballrooms, Highland bogs . . . was there no place in the world that was safe for an awkward English spinster?

She worked on her right leg first, shaking it beneath the surface of the mud as she slowly drew it upward. The incremental progress was agonizing, but at last her knee emerged from the muck.

"Good," he said. "Now the other. This time, you wriggle. I'll pull."

"I'm trying."

And she *was* trying, but it wasn't enough. The mire was quickly closing on her again, drawing on her leg. She was suddenly, sharply aware of how fortunate she was to have Logan nearby. If Maddie had been on her own, she never could have worked herself free.

Even with him here, it didn't seem a certainty.

"One last time," he said. "Move your leg back and forth, with as much vigor as you can manage. I'm going to pull on the count of three."

She nodded.

"One . . . two . . ."

She gritted her teeth.

"Three."

His arm muscles flexed. As he pulled, she felt a terrible wrench in her hip joint. Maddie knew she would pay for that later. She'd be sore for days.

But a full year of soreness would still be better than one more minute spent stuck in that bog.

At last, she was free.

Breathless and panting, she crawled a few feet up the slope and flopped onto a bit of damp turf. She was caked with mud below the waist and soaked with rain everywhere else.

Logan seemed winded, too. He collapsed beside her.

"Life is so strange," she said, swiping a strand of hair from her rain-spattered face. "When I invented a Scottish sweetheart, it was with the aim of *avoiding* humiliation. Look at me now. How do I get myself into these things?"

"By wishing for them, *mo chridhe*." He rolled to face her, propping himself on his elbow. "It's everything you asked for. A remote castle in the Highlands and an officer in a kilt. Be glad you didna manage to kill me off, or you'd still be stuck in that bog alone."

There he went again, accusing her of murderous intent. He couldn't seem to let go of that idea. And every time he brought it up, he spoke with an edge of resentment in his voice.

"Logan, I'm sorry if I hurt you."

He made a dismissive noise. "You didna hurt me."

Right. How could a little Englishwoman possibly hurt a hulking Scottish warrior? Naturally, he would never admit to *that*.

"For what it's worth," she said, "my true fantasy was not a Highland castle and a man in a kilt. I just wanted to be understood, accepted. Loved." Her gaze fell to her damp tartan sash and that heart-shaped lie pinning it together. "Don't worry. I've learned my lesson."

"I canna say much about love and acceptance, but I do understand you. I understand you just fine."

"You really don't."

"Oh, I do." His eyes roamed her face. "You're deceitful, fanciful, clever, unbiddable, generous, talented with a drawing pencil . . ." He smeared his muddy thumb down the slope of her nose. " . . . and dirty. Verra, verra dirty."

"I'm no dirtier than you."

She pressed her hand flat to his face. It left behind a starburst of five muddy fingerprints . . . and one unamused Scot. Added to his intense blue eyes and unshaven jaw, the markings gave him the look of an ancient Highland warrior, painted for battle.

Ready to strike.

His big, muddy hand went to her waist, tangling in the damp gray wool of her frock.

"If it's dirty you want . . . ?" He tugged her close, startling a gasp from her. "It's dirty you'll get."

His mouth fell on hers, hot and masterful. His hands were everywhere, smearing even the cleaner parts of her frock with mud. All Maddie could do was cling to his coat while the forbidden sensations swamped her.

His tongue swept into her mouth. Seeking, demanding. She could taste the frustration in his kiss. Whether it was left over from last night, this morning, or the entirety of the past decade, she couldn't guess. Whatever the cause, he obviously meant to avenge it with this sensual onslaught.

And Maddie could not bring herself to object.

She loved the rough, possessive way he was touching her. His hands roamed her breasts, her hips, her backside. Her nipples came to tight points, as if they recalled last night's attentions and were ready to beg for more. When his thumb found one of the aching peaks and teased it, she moaned with helpless pleasure and relief.

She let her head fall back, and he lavished soft

kisses on the vulnerable skin covering her pulse. His gentleness and thoroughness made her feel cherished. Precious.

Wanted.

She'd never dreamed she could feel this desired by anyone. It was almost . . .

Oh, how ironic. It was almost a dream come true.

No, she told herself. *Don't be a ninny*. She couldn't let herself think that way.

She'd been struggling to keep her foolish heart out of this, keeping him at arm's length with conditions and rules. It was too dangerous to do otherwise. All too easily, she could create a story in her mind. Spin a tale of devotion that would be just another lie—one she told herself. She didn't want to imagine that Logan could care for her.

He *didn't* care for her.

But he *wanted* her.

This heat between them was real. This grappling kiss was the truth. And the hot ridge of his arousal pressed against her thigh was far too big to be any trick of her imagination.

He lifted his head and looked down at her. "*Maddie*."

When he whispered her name, the cold was forgotten. So was the mud, his teasing, the pain in her leg. The rain kept falling, pushing her further into the shelter of his embrace. Melting her will to resist.

She touched a hand to his cheek. Gone was the fierce Highland warrior. The rain plastered his hair to his brow and dotted his face, giving him a wet-puppy look: lost and in need of love. Every bit as confused as she felt inside.

"Oh, Logan."

And now, despite all her best attempts to avoid it, here it came.

Her heart started telling her a dangerous, dangerous tale. The story of a decent, loyal man who'd treasured her letters, dreamed of her nightly, survived battles and marched across continents to come home—not to a castle or a glen but to her. And even now, when he held her in his arms, he lacked the words to explain all the emotion in his heart.

It was nothing but a silly fiction.

It had to be.

But she couldn't block it out any longer. She put her arms around his neck and wove her fingers into his hair, pulling him close.

Chapter Thirteen

*L*ogan should have pulled away. They needed to seek shelter.

But he couldn't bring himself to let her go.

The rain had plastered her frock to her skin, leaving little to his imagination. He saw all of her, in perfect contour—her pale skin, her puckered nipples, the blue tint to her quivering lips. She was vulnerable and trembling.

She needed warmth.

And he needed this.

To hold her. Guard her. Feel her pounding heart pressed close to his and know she was alive.

Because, though he would die before he'd admit it, he'd been frightened for a moment there, when she'd been caught in the mire.

He'd drawn her close to reassure himself. He'd kissed her because she'd seemed to want him to.

But now his shy, timid bride was kissing *him*, and he'd lost control of everything.

Her fingers sifted through his damp hair. Her sweet, tentative tongue stroked his. The longing pierced him to the core. He felt faint with it.

He tightened his grip in the back of her dress, pulling her body flush against his. She sighed into the kiss, wriggling closer still. Her belly brushed over the ridge of his cock. A tremor moved through his thigh muscle.

God, he wanted her.

This was madness. They were both caked with peat and mud below the waist. There was no way he could take her virtue here, on the ground in the rain and cold.

But he couldn't bear the growing tension anymore. His cock throbbed in vain, trapped beneath the wet woolen folds of his plaid. He was desperate for some kind of contact. Resistance. Touch. Heat.

He had to take control.

In a swift motion, he rolled her onto her back, wedging himself between her thighs. When his cock finally found the friction it craved, he groaned with pleasure.

She cried out in pain.

Logan pulled onto his elbows immediately.

He searched her startled expression. "What's the matter? You're hurt."

"It's just my leg. I . . . I wrenched it coming out of the mire."

Jesus. She'd been wounded all this time? And here he'd been mauling her on the hillside as if she were a lamb and he were the last Highland wolf.

"Dinna be worried. I'll have you back to the castle at once."

He loosened the extra folds of tartan draped over his shoulder. Tucking her close to his chest, he wrapped the plaid around Maddie's body to warm her.

Then he hefted her into his arms.

"I hope you know, you're ruining your chances in the bedroom," she said. "It's impossible to despise you when you keep kissing me like that and sweeping me off my feet every day."

He set his jaw grimly. "You can learn to hate me again tomorrow. You're not walking anywhere today."

When they arrived back at the castle, wet and muddy and chilled through, Logan began barking orders before he'd even set Maddie down.

He directed Becky to bring blankets.

Cook was ordered to start heating water for a bath.

And he insisted that Munro, his field surgeon, have a look at Maddie's leg.

"It's nothing," she assured the surgeon once she'd been wrapped in an old quilt and deposited on the chaise longue in her bedchamber. "I've only wrenched it. I was stupid enough to step in a bog."

Munro wiped the mud from her limb and gingerly turned her foot this way and that, testing. "The swelling is mild. It doesna look serious."

"That's what I tried to tell Logan. But he doesn't listen to me."

"If you wanted to walk on it now, I wouldna stop you."

She nodded. "I'm sure you sent soldiers back into the fray with far worse."

"But you are no soldier." His graying eyebrows rose. "If your injury is delicate yet, I could tell the captain you need some rest. And that he needs to keep the honeymoon waiting for a few days."

Yes.

This was just the stroke of luck she needed. She'd take any excuse to hold Logan at bay for a few more days.

"Now that you mention it, my knee is quite tender. I do think the rest would do me good."

Maddie smiled to herself as the surgeon packed up his examination bag. Logan was not going to be happy with her, but he was the one who'd insisted on a doctor's opinion. He couldn't ignore medical advice.

As the surgeon unrolled the cuff of his sleeve, she glimpsed a gnarled, misshapen scar on his right forearm.

She winced. "What happened there?"

"Oh, that? A bayonet. It's not as bad as it looks. It would have healed better, but you know what they say. The cobbler's children run barefooted, and the field surgeon goes without proper stitching."

"I suppose from time to time even the doctor needs healing."

He nodded. "And from time to time, even the commander needs to be told what to do. Sometimes the captain could do with a bit of being ordered around." He gave her a sly wink. "You dinna need to be timid with him, lass."

Maddie smiled. "Thank you for the advice."

Once Munro left her, Becky came in with two ewers of steaming water, which she added to a deep tub for Maddie's bath.

Ah, a bath.

Here was one of Logan's commands she had no desire to countermand. After the mud and the chilly rain today, a hot bath was just what she needed.

She used old towels and rags to scrub as much of the peat from her body as possible so as not to muddy the bathwater. For once, she made use of one of Aunt Thea's purchases, adding a healthy dollop of a lavender-scented liniment to the bath. Then she twisted her hair into a giant knot atop her head and lowered her body into the steaming tub.

An involuntary moan eased from her throat as the hot water enveloped her to her neck.

So lovely. It was almost as soothing as a warm hug.

The tension in her muscles began to unknot.

All her relaxation was ruined, however, when Logan flung open the door with a crash.

Maddie gasped and flinched, sinking lower in the bath and using her arms to cover her most secret bits. "Did you never hear of knocking?"

"Not in my own house, no."

She cast a longing glance at the towel at the end of her bed. Too far away for her to reach for it without exposing herself.

"According to Munro," he said testily, "I'm not to touch you. For days."

"Oh?" She tilted her head at an innocent angle. "What a pity."

"Stop playing as though you didna ask him to say it."

"You are the one who insisted he examine me. You can't ignore his advice." She ran the sponge down her arm, squeezing lather from it as she went. "Since we are forbidden from any strenuous activity, I think it would be best if you used the bedchamber Becky made up for you."

"That will not be necessary. I'll be damned if I'll sleep down the corridor." He exhaled gruffly. "I'm leaving."

"Leaving?"

"Dinna sound so hopeful. It's only temporary. I need to order timbers for the new cottages, so I'm traveling to Fort William. The journey should take me two or three days. When I return, I expect you'll be in perfect health."

He gave her a pointed look, and his meaning was perfectly understood. Despite the warmth of the bathwater, gooseflesh rippled down her arms.

When he returned, his patience would be at an end. Maddie would have no further tactics for delay.

At the end of three days, she would either be free of him . . .

Or she would be his wife.

Chapter Fourteen

*M*addie didn't suppose Logan had been foolish enough to leave them behind, but if those letters *were* anywhere in this castle, she was determined to find them before he returned.

She was coming to care for him too much, too foolishly. She couldn't repeat the same mistake she'd made when she was sixteen. Pitching those letters into the fire was her only hope if she didn't want to spend the rest of her life caught in a lie of her own making.

Unfortunately, after many dusty hours of searching, she hadn't found so much as a clue. Over the past two days, she'd opened every drawer in every piece of furniture—checked behind and beneath them, too. Now she'd turned her gaze to the walls themselves.

This afternoon, she stood back and surveyed the Long Gallery, a room on the castle's top floor that stretched the full length of the tower. The oak paneling featured a molded ledge where the wall met the ceiling. From where Maddie stood, it didn't look deep enough to hide a packet of letters . . . but there was no way to be certain other than to check.

She pulled a straight-backed chair to the edge of the room and climbed atop it, standing on tiptoe to reach her fingers into the cobwebby, linty crevice.

Nothing . . .

Nothing . . .

She stretched in an effort to reach the corner.

Noth—

"What's all this, then?"

Maddie nearly fell off the chair. After regaining her hold on the paneling and securing her footing, she turned to face the intruder. "Oh. Good afternoon, Grant."

"How do you know my name?" He searched the gallery, wary. "What's this place?"

His hand went to his hip, as though he were reaching for the weapon he expected to be there. Maddie was suddenly aware of how large he loomed, and how small she was in comparison.

And how alone they were right now.

Her heart began to beat a little faster. If she didn't manage to calm him, this situation could grow dangerous indeed.

Maddie stayed very still and held up both empty—if dusty—hands. She repeated the words she'd heard Logan and his comrades say so many times. "The war's over, Grant. You're back home in Scotland. This is Lannair Castle, and you've been staying here for almost a week. Callum, Rabbie, Munro, Fyfe . . . they're working just outside, collecting stone."

His brow creased. "Who are you?"

"I'm Madeline. Captain MacKenzie's sweetheart who wrote him all those letters. We're married now." She motioned toward her plaid sash and the luckenbooth.

"Are ye?"

She nodded.

The man's face relaxed. "He's a lucky bastard, then."

"Thank you. And you're my favorite person."

He grinned. "Then I'm a lucky bastard, too."

Maddie couldn't help but smile. This man must have been quite the charmer once, when he'd been healthy of body and mind.

His gaze shifted about the room uneasily. "Do you know where my wee ones are? Have we been to Ross-shire? I'm keen to see the bairns."

She shook her head. "I'm sorry. I don't know."

"I'll ask the captain if we can go tomorrow."

Her heart broke for the poor man. Again and again, he woke from that fog obscuring his mind, looking for his children. And every time, Logan put him off.

Well, Maddie couldn't take him to Ross-shire. But perhaps she could help him in some other way.

She climbed down from the stepstool and clapped the dust from her hands. The letters search would have to wait for another time. Logan had probably taken them with him in that black knapsack. She hadn't been able to find it, either.

She crossed the room and took Grant by the arm. "Do your children like shortbread?"

"O'course they do. Never seen the bairn what doesna like shortbread."

"Let's go down to the kitchen. I think Cook has prepared some fresh this morning, and I could do with a cup of tea. And while we eat, I'd love for you to tell me all about them."

It was hours past nightfall when Logan finally reached the glen. He hadn't intended to travel by night, but the moon was near full, and the prospect of camping on the damp heath didn't particularly appeal.

Not when there was a warm bed waiting for him at Lannair Castle.

He'd given her time. She'd had her opportunity to rest. He wasn't sleeping on the damned floor tonight.

A bleary-eyed footman let him in the side stairway. Logan felt as weary as the manservant looked, but instead of going straight up to bed, he stopped on the first landing and peeked into the High Hall. There he did a silent count of the men as they slept. It was an old habit from his days of watching over cattle and sheep as a youth, and one he'd never abandoned as a commander of troops. He'd never lost a lamb or calf, and he'd never left a soldier behind, either.

One, two, three, four. . .

He counted twice and still came up one short.

Grant was missing.

Christ.

His weary heart kicked into a faster rhythm, and he crossed the length of the hall. When he found out who'd shirked his duty tonight, that someone's bollocks were getting a sharp twist.

But truly, Logan had no one to blame but himself. He never should have left them on their own. After tonight, he ought to start posting a man as sentry. This was a bloody castle, after all. A military fortress. Perhaps he ought to be running it that way.

As he searched the nearest rooms, he sent up a

silent prayer. Grant couldn't have wandered far, could he? Hopefully he hadn't wandered out into the night. If he lost his way on the moors and his mental slate wiped clean . . .

A soft noise reached his ears.

A voice, murmuring.

No, *voices*.

He followed the low, soft rumble of indistinct conversation down the corridor to where it ended with a flight of steep stairs. The voices were coming from the kitchen.

As he crept down the stairs, the murmuring grew more distinct, and the knot of worry in his chest began to loosen. He recognized Grant's voice.

"Squeal louder, lass. Squeal louder."

And then a ripple of soft feminine laughter.

When he turned the corner, he saw them there. Grant and Maddie. Seated together at the table, huddled around two mugs and a single lamp.

Logan braced himself against the archway as the emotions pummeled him. He was relieved and incensed at the same time. He'd been worried that Grant could have harmed himself. Now he knew it was even worse—he could have harmed Madeline.

"Good evening," he said.

Her head whipped up. "Logan. You're home."

God. The words set his world spinning. She almost sounded happy to see him. And those words.

Logan. You're home.

He'd never expected to hear those words. Not in all his life.

And damn, she looked lovely. She was wearing only a dressing gown wrapped tight over her nightrail. Her hair was a loose plait draped over one shoulder. Soft, dark tendrils worked loose, framing her face with curls.

But something else drew his gaze and held it.

Her braid was tied not with a scrap of plain muslin but with a bit of plaid.

His plaid.

It was all too much. His sense of relief at finding them both safe. The softness in her eyes, the welcome in her voice. That swatch of his tartan in her hair. He'd traveled long and hard to be here tonight, and it all just made him feel he might collapse.

And what was he going to do? Take her in his arms and tell her he'd missed her every moment he'd been gone? Tell her how jealous he was that Grant could make her laugh with that stupid joke, when Logan hadn't managed it once?

Of course not. Because those things would be reasonable, and he couldn't hold on to a shred of sense around her. Because when someone so blithely offered him the one thing he'd been denied all his life and had sworn to never crave, his first impulse had to be distrust. And anger.

Stupid, unreasoned anger.

"What's going on here?" he demanded.

"We're just talking," Maddie said. "Are you hungry? I could get you some—"

"No."

"She's making me a sketch of the bairns." Grant lifted the paper and showed it to him proudly. "Look at that. It's just like 'em the day I kissed 'em good-bye. I suppose they've got bigger now."

Logan took the paper and examined it. He didn't have his spectacles on, but even without them he could see the skill in her drawing. Two fair-haired children, one boy and one girl, holding hands beneath a rowan tree.

"Say, can we go to Ross-shire tomorrow?" Grant asked. "I'm keen to see them for myself."

"Aye, *mo charaid*. Tomorrow. For tonight, it's time to sleep. Go on, then. The others are just up the stairs."

Grant nudged him with an elbow as he moved past. "Do you know you're married to her?" he asked, tilting his head toward Maddie.

Logan gave her a look. "Yes."

The big man reached out and ruffled Logan's hair. "Lucky bastard."

Once Grant had left, Maddie quietly rinsed the teacups and put them away. She moved the lamp to a hook, wiped the table clean, and hung the towel to dry. All in silence.

She was avoiding him.

Very well, then. Logan would wait. He had all night.

When she finally turned to him, he lifted the sketch of Grant's children. "What is the meaning of this?"

"I beg your pardon." She frowned. "I gave that to Grant. It's his."

"He'll forget in ten minutes. He's not going to miss it."

"Perhaps not, but he's missing *them*. They're his children."

Logan shook the paper as he advanced on her. "This is not the way to help. What good does it do? It's only going to upset him, wondering where they are."

"Perhaps talking about the memories will help his mind to heal."

"It's been over a year. He's not going to heal. He needs consistency. A safe, familiar place where he won't be agitated all the time."

Maddie circled to his side of the table and leaned her weight on the edge. She crossed her arms over the front of her dressing gown and regarded him with that solemn, searching expression. Looking for his empty spaces.

"So this is why it's so important to you," she said, "for the two of us to keep up appearances. To be properly married. It isn't only about the land. If

Grant believes *you've* had your happy homecoming with the sweetheart who sent you letters, you can keep him believing that his own happiness is just around the corner. That you'll take him to Ross-shire to see his nan and the wee ones. Always tomorrow. Never today."

Logan didn't try to dispute it. He wasn't ashamed. "I just want him to be at peace. As much as he can be."

"But you can't lie to him forever, Logan. What happens when he starts to get older? When he looks around to see that everyone's hair is gray, and his hands are spotted with age, and his friends have all married and had children—even grandchildren—of their own?"

Logan sighed heavily and pushed both hands through his hair. "We have years before that happens."

"But it will happen. You're telling yourself you can keep him safe. You can't." She took the sketch from his hand and set it aside. "I know what it is to live in a world built from lies, Logan. It's anything but comforting. It means living in constant fear. At any moment, the slightest thing could bring it all crashing down. It's not good for Grant, and it's not good for you, either."

"It's not your place to make that decision."

"It is my place. This is still my castle. And I've come to think of Grant as my friend. You can try to tell me what to wear and where to go and what to serve for dinner. But you can't forbid me from caring for him."

The mere mention of caring gave Logan's heart a kick and sent it spinning to some uncharted place.

"I can, and I will."

She huffed out her breath in silent disagreement.

He leaned in, bracing his hands on the table. "You shouldna be alone with him. He's a big man, with unpredictable moods and an addled memory. There's no telling what could happen. When I came around that corner and saw the two of you . . ."

She tipped her head to one side and looked up at him through that fringe of dark lashes. "You were worried for me. I know. It's sweet."

He clenched his jaw. "It isna *sweet*. I saw a dangerous situation. I reacted."

She dropped her eyes and touched the lapel of his coat. "I was worried about you, too. We expected you home yesterday, Logan. It's why I'm down here with Grant at all tonight. Passing the time."

Holy God.

Her fingertips touched a button on his coat. "It would be natural to be frightened."

"I wasna frightened. I'm angry."

"I can see that." Her eyes lifted to his. "But I don't understand why."

Logan didn't understand it, either. Any more

than he understood how much he'd thought of her in the past three days. He was losing control, and he hated losing control.

And since he didn't seem to have any hope of regaining it, he'd decided he'd settle for making her lose control, too.

He leaned forward, capturing that lush, pink mouth in a possessive kiss. She didn't need any coaxing to kiss him back. Her lips parted beneath his, and when he slid his tongue deep, her tongue moved forward to welcome his.

Yes.

God, he wanted her.

He put his arms around her and gathered her to him, running his hands over the quilted velvet of her dressing gown and tugging at the knotted belt.

"What are you doing?"

He didn't answer. He just kept on doing, expecting his intent would become perfectly clear.

He pulled the belt loose and let the length of braided fabric drop to the floor. Then he slid his hands inside her dressing gown to meet the cool, crisp linen of her shift—and the soft, pink heat of her body beneath it.

He smiled against her mouth. She was only wearing one shift tonight.

With a low, weary groan, he dipped his head and began to draw a line of kisses down her neck. He skimmed one hand down the firm slope of her thigh, gathering the muslin and giving it an upward tug.

"Logan," she gasped.

If she meant him to stop, she was going about it all wrong. He loved hearing his name from her lips. It made his blood pound. His cock came to attention, hardening beneath the heavy weight of his kilt.

"You said you'd give me time," she said. "Time to find another solution. I can't let this happen."

"It's already happening." He reached beneath her shift, stroking the tantalizing curve of her calf and teasing the hollow of her knee. "You want this, *mo chridhe*. I know you do. Oh, you can try to deny it with words. But if I were to touch you, right now, is that the same tale your body would tell? Or would I find you hot and wet and trembling beneath my fingertips?"

He skimmed his touch higher, climbing the silky expanse of her thigh. She sighed, and her flesh quivered beneath his fingertips. So soft. So sweetly warm.

"Tell me you didn't miss me," he whispered. "Tell me you don't want my touch."

"Logan, I can't . . ."

When her voice trailed off, he kissed her, deciding to end the sentence right there.

No, you can't, lass. You can't tell me that because it isn't true. You want me every bit as much as I want you.

He had to believe that, or he'd go mad.

He ran a caress up her thigh and settled his touch at the heart of her. His fingertips slid easily up and down her crease. She was ready for him, just as he'd known she would be.

She gasped and clutched his arms with both hands. "Logan . . ."

"Just this, *mo chridhe*. Just touching."

In acquiescence, she let her head fall forward to rest on his shoulder. Her breathing had grown rough, needy.

He parted her folds with a gentle touch, slipping a finger into her heat. God, she was tight. So tight, and so wet. She gave delicious little gasps of pleasure as he slowly worked his finger in and out, delving deeper by incremental degrees. When he slid fully inside and the heel of his hand made contact with her mound, her hips bucked. He kept still, giving her a moment to adjust to the sensation, grinding his palm against her most sensitive place.

And then he went still, waiting.

Come along, then. You're a clever lass. You know what your body wants.

Soon enough, she began to roll her hips. Riding his finger. Rubbing her mound against the heel of his hand. Chasing the sensation, just as he'd known she would.

Her shameless pursuit of pleasure made him

wild. His cock pushed against the rough weave of his plaid. Every whisper of friction sent a thrill to the base of his spine. He'd never craved release so desperately in all his life. Not even as a randy youth.

Small puffs of her breath caressed his neck. She lifted her head and looked up at him with those dark, sleepy, enticing-as-anything eyes. Her shy, pink tongue darted out to moisten her lips.

He couldn't keep silent any longer. Words started to tumble from his lips. Tender words, crude words. Words he would disclaim when he recalled them in the morning. All in Gaelic, thankfully.

She would have laughed to hear him confessing how often he'd thought of her in his absence. She would have doubted when he said no other woman had made him this achingly hard. And if she ever heard him comparing her dewy lips to the first blush of heather on a Highland summer morn, it would ruin everything.

But he couldn't help himself.

She made his blood catch fire.

"Maddie a ghràdh. Mo chridhe. Mo bean."

She lifted her arms and laced her fingers at the back of his neck. And then she drew him forward, drowning him in her kiss.

Her hips rolled, and he moved with her, adding a second finger as he plunged into her eager body again and again. Her tongue tangled with his, searching and desperate. Her fingernails bit into his neck.

Logan thought he might spend right then and there.

No sooner had he thought it than she shifted her weight, leaning back on the table. Her thigh came in contact with the aching curve of his cock. And even with the layers of velvet, linen, and wool between them—that, plus the pulsing heat enveloping his fingers, was enough to send him right to the edge.

He fought the urge to grind against her until he reached climax. He hadn't come into the folds of his kilt since he was a lad of fifteen, and he wasn't about to do it now. To lose control that way . . . it would be too much like surrender.

He was in command here.

"Come, *mo chridhe,*" he whispered. "I need to feel you come for me."

Her body went rigid, save for a delicious tremor in her thigh that let him know her peak was near. He kept his rhythm steady, ignoring the soreness in his wrist and the ache of unspent need in his groin.

She bit her lip, and her eyes squeezed shut.

"That's it. Let it happen."

And then he felt it. Her body seizing around his fingers, shuddering with the bliss of orgasm. The cries of pleasure she made were timid and subdued, but no less arousing for it.

When she slumped against him, limp with pleasure and damp with sweat, he told himself the balance of power had been restored.

He slipped his fingers free of her body and pulled her shift back down over her knees.

"The other day," he said, caressing her back, "you told me Becky had made up a bedchamber for me."

She nodded drowsily against his chest.

"I'll sleep there tonight."

"No, no." She lifted her head. "Logan, you needn't be alone."

"You just told me you still wanted time."

"That's not what I mean." Her hand pressed against his chest. "There's more than one way to share pleasure, and there's more than one way to share a heart."

"I've told you—"

"And you lied. You loved someone once. Enough to want to marry her. Enough to carry a memento of her with you for years, through battle and worse." She pounded his chest with the flat side of her fist. "I know there's something in there, you stubborn creature. That beneath that hard exterior, you're nothing but squish. You're not fooling me."

He made his voice cold. "You're fooling yourself."

"Perhaps." She shrugged and looked away. "I suppose it wouldn't be the first time."

The truth of it was, he was a coward. Too afraid to

admit that whatever remained of his dark, shriveled heart *was* growing involved.

Maddie had a great deal about him wrong, but maybe she was right about a few things. Perhaps Logan wasn't quite as empty inside as he'd wanted to believe. And that thought scared him. He didn't want to need her, not that way. If he needed her, that gave her power over him, and he'd danced long enough at the end of her string.

All those letters, all those years.

All that wanting and yearning she'd rekindled in him . . .

Only to be left for dead.

The senseless anger swirled in him. The urge to hold her, punish her, pleasure her, possess her. Tonight, he would be a greater danger to her than Grant could ever pose.

He gathered what willpower remained to him and stepped back. "Good night, *mo chridhe*. Take yourself up to bed. And when you get there, bar the door."

Chapter Fifteen

Over breakfast the next morning, Rabbie cocked an eyebrow at him. "Still no progress on the bedding front?"

Logan stared straight forward. He refused to acknowledge the question.

"That's a no, I take it."

"Are you certain you're applying yourself?" Callum asked.

Logan gave him a sharp look.

"You've got to be the Rob Roy of her imaginings. Are you calling her a 'bonny lass'? The English-women's hearts go all a-flutter at that."

"What do you know about the hearts of English-women?"

"He's got the right of it," Rabbie put in. "'Bonny lass' is good. 'Wee bonny lass'—well, that's even better."

"'Yer wee bonny lassie,'" said Callum, taking the improvement one step further. "Throw in lots of 'och' and 'aye' and 'dinna fash yerself,' too."

Rabbie shook his head. "You're all missing the obvious answer."

"What's that?" Munro asked.

Logan was glad Munro had asked, because he sure as hell wasn't going to. But truth be told, he was coming to the end of his patience. If he didn't have her soon, he was going to go mad with wanting. At this point, he was willing to listen to any idea, no matter how ridiculous—even if it came from Rabbie.

Rabbie hunched over to whisper. "She's got to see him with his kit off. Shirt, plaid, all of it."

A coarse whoop rose up from the men.

Logan rolled his eyes and stabbed his meat with his knife.

"No, I mean it," Rabbie said, standing up. "Here's how it goes. You rise early one morning, Captain. Choose a misty one, when the gloom's settled like a blanket over the valley."

He waved his flattened hand before them like an artist painting a landscape. "You strip down to your skin, and then you have a dip in the loch. Wait until she comes looking for you. Because she will. They always do. But pretend not to notice when she does. And then— just when she's close enough to see and she's been watching for a while, you rise up out of the water. Like a dolphin. Or a mermaid. Shooting up through the mist and pushing your hair back with both hands"—Rabbie thrust both hands through his hair to demonstrate—"with all the little beads of water trickling down over the ridges of your shoulders and chest." He danced his fingers down his belly. "Like so."

Munro snorted. "So he's supposed to go down to the loch at half-crack o' the morning, paddle about in the frigid water for an hour or two, and then emerge? I'm finding it difficult to believe she'd see anything impressive."

Everyone laughed. Even Grant.

"You lot can laugh," Rabbie said, "but mark my word, Captain. Get your kit off. The next time you have her in your arms, she won't be able to resist."

"I've been married," said the habitually silent Fyfe. "I'll tell you what she wants. She wants your secrets. She wants your soul. You've got to crack yourself open and find that broken, shameful piece of your heart that you'd hide from the world and God Himself if you could manage it. And then serve it up to her on a platter. They won't settle for anything less."

The mood around the group grew solemn.

"Well, I like my idea better," said Rabbie, winking at Logan. "Try it first."

"I might," Logan muttered.

Even if he was willing to crack himself open, he would find little there to offer her.

"You're all making this too complicated," Munro said.

"She's a lass. Bring her flowers. Take her dancing. Give her an excuse to put on a pretty frock. That's all it takes."

"But Madeline's different. She doesna like those things," Logan said.

"Trust me. They all like those things."

Logan rubbed the back of his neck and exhaled. Perhaps Munro was right. In the village, Maddie had said the same.

Women are women, Logan. Every girl needs a bit of luxury and a chance to feel pretty now and then.

Wasn't that what her letters had been about? She didn't think she could ever be a success at a party or an assembly. And her dream had been a man who would want her anyway.

He didn't want to be her dream man. But maybe he could play the role for one night.

Perhaps all Madeline Gracechurch had ever needed was a bit of everyday courting. The same sort of attention any girl her age would receive. And she deserved that much and far more.

Logan knew exactly what he had to do.

"Bloody hell," he said. "I'm going to have to attend the Beetle Ball."

"You want to attend Lord Varleigh's ball?" She replaced a pen in its inkwell and turned to face him. "Logan, we can't."

"Why not?"

"It's impossible. For a dozen reasons."

She folded her arms over her ink-stained work smock. She tucked her bottom lip under her teeth. And that single fingertip went to her collarbone again, tracing back and forth. Driving him wild with wanting.

He crossed his arms and jammed his own hands in his oxters. It was the only way he knew how to keep from reaching for her. "Tell me the reasons. One at a time."

"Firstly, we already declined the invitation. I told Lord Varleigh we weren't attending."

"Easily mended. You write a message telling him we've changed our minds. I'll dispatch one of the men to deliver it this afternoon. Next reason."

"I . . . I have nothing to wear." She gestured at her frock. "I've been wearing half-mourning for years. All my gowns are gray wool."

"We'll find you a ready-made gown in Inverness tomorrow. Next problem."

"And I suppose you could wear your best uniform. An officer's dress is always acceptable attire. But you've invited everyone here for Beltane, and that's less than a fortnight from now."

"All the more reason to find you a new gown and give the skirts a spin or two. The lady of the castle canna welcome her guests in gray wool."

She sighed. "Lord Varleigh lives in Perthshire. It's too far to travel."

"I've heard they have these new things called inns. Often located near roads. We'll find one nearby to stay the night."

Now Logan was really starting to appreciate this idea. The Beetle Ball itself sounded like many-legged torture, but the prospect of spending a night with Madeline in a tiny room at a coaching inn, with an even tinier bed, away from his men and her aunt—now *that* sounded worth a few hours of anything.

It also sounded like the perfect way to finally make this marriage real.

"But it's a ball." She turned away from him, continuing the work of straightening her desk. "I don't go to balls. I'm miserable at them. I can't dance."

"Neither can I. Not that sort of dancing, at any rate." He came to stand behind her, lightly placing his hands on her waist. "We dinna have to dance, *mo chridhe*. We'll just go and listen to Lord Varleigh talk about his beetles. Most importantly, you'll be there to see your work unveiled."

"I don't really want that kind of attention." She tapped a pencil against the blotter on her desk. "But I confess, I would like a chance to meet a man who'll be there."

Now this made him take notice. "A man?"

"Logan, don't be jealous."

He tightened his grip on her waist. "You like it when I'm jealous."

"Very well, perhaps I do." He could hear a little smile in her voice. "Lord Varleigh told me of a scholar he knows in

Edinburgh. One who'll be attending the ball. Apparently this scholar is planning an encyclopedia. *Insects of the British Isles,* in four volumes. He might be in need of an illustrator. Lord Varleigh promised to make the introduction."

He turned her to face him. "See? So you do want to attend."

She didn't answer, but she didn't need to. Now that Logan had removed the barriers, a pretty flush had started to warm her cheeks. Once he got her into a proper silk gown rather than this scratchy mourning attire, half the battle would be won.

"That's only six reasons so far," he pointed out. "You said there were a dozen. Hurry up, then, so I can remedy the rest."

"On second thought, perhaps there's only one more reason. But it's the biggest reason, and there's no remedy to be found for it."

"Try me."

"I can't leave the lobsters."

Holy God.

She moved toward the tank, peering into it. "Fluffy's become more active over the past day. It's a sign she might be ready to molt. I have to stay close, or I could miss the mating entirely. I've been waiting too long to let that happen. So has Rex, for that matter."

Curse it, couldn't she see that Rex wasn't the only frustrated male in this castle? If the bloody lobster ended up satisfying his natural urges before Logan did, he would be tempted to climb the highest tower of Lannair Castle and fling himself off it.

"Let me worry about the lobsters," he said.

"But—"

"Trust me." He put his hands on her shoulders. "I'm a captain, remember? I know how to set a watch, draw up a plan, command troops. We'll remove Rex to a separate tank for the night. My men will set up shifts for the lobster watch. If there's any sign of Fluffy molting, Rabbie will ride hell-for-leather to Varleigh's estate and let you know. You'll be home with plenty of time to put Rex and Fluffy together and watch the sparks fly."

She glanced at the seawater tank. "I'm not sure how many sparks will be involved."

"Watch the bubbles blub. Watch the antennae wave. Whatever it is that happens when lobsters make love, I swear on my plaid you willna miss it. I make no promises I canna keep."

She looked up at him with those calf's eyes. As usual, he could sense a whole world's worth of thought going on behind them.

Logan couldn't hold back anymore. He touched his thumb to her collarbone, sliding up and down the narrow ridge. Soothing her the way she would soothe herself.

Her skin was so soft. He was dying to touch her everywhere.

"Let me worry about everything." His voice was

suddenly hoarse. "I just want you to enjoy yourself. You deserve this, Maddie."

She drew in a deep breath, then released it. "Fine."

Fine.

That wasn't exactly the overjoyed acceptance he'd been hoping to hear.

But he'd take it.

"Perhaps it's more than fine." She lifted her head and looked into his eyes. "Perhaps it's perfect."

Perfect. Now that was better.

"Maybe this is the compromise we've been searching for."

Logan supposed maybe she'd been searching for one, but he had never been interested in compromise. "I want what I want, lass. That's all."

"I know. I do understand. That's what makes it perfect." She whirled away from him, as if powered by her own little breeze of excitement. "See, you have a dream."

"I told you, *mo chridhe*, I dinna—"

"You don't dream. Fine. Call it a goal, then. You want to give your men a *baile* here, in this glen. I have a dream, too."

"A dream with bugs."

"Exactly. A dream of all the insects in the British Isles. If Mr. Dorning hired me on for his encyclopedia, I would have a small, but steady, income to support myself. And then I would be established, with excellent prospects for more work thereafter. I wouldn't even need to live here."

Logan shook his head. "We've already discussed all this. A lease willna be acceptable, and I canna buy the land."

"Perhaps we can work out another sort of bargain. A trade."

"A trade? What kind of trade?"

"Your goal for mine."

He could only stare at her. She wasn't making sense.

"I could never think of attending a ball on my own," she said. "I'm shy, I'm awkward. I want to flee and hide. But maybe I won't be that way if you're near." A little smile played about her lips. "It's as if you make me so irritated, I forget to worry about myself. If you escort me to Lord Varleigh's ball, perhaps you can help me make a good impression on Mr. Dorning. And if he gives me the encyclopedia post . . ." She turned to face him. " . . . I'd give you this castle, and gladly."

What?

Logan couldn't believe that offer. He certainly didn't trust it.

"I didna ask for that," he said, "and I dinna want it. No one's ever given me anything. I've worked for everything I've ever had."

"I know. And you're going to work for this. Perhaps it doesn't seem equal if you look at it in terms of money or land. But to me, it will be an even trade. Your dream for mine."

He didn't know what to say. "You're certain?"

"I'm certain. Well, and there's one other thing." She bit her lip. "I'd need those letters back, too."

"Right," he said. "The letters. Of course."

That might be a wrinkle in this plan of hers, but Logan decided he would swim that loch when he came to it. He'd just make certain she signed her side of the papers before he handed his over to her.

She laced her arms around his neck, lightly swaying to and fro in a flirtatious manner. "And perhaps, if we're not playing this will-we-or-won't-we-consummate game any longer, we can enjoy a few lesser carnal pleasures."

Now she had his attention.

"You did say men are more creative than lobsters."

"Aye, lass. That we are."

"And you also said that I'm curious. Maybe you were right about that, too. Especially after last night."

Her hands flattened against his chest, soft and warm. Exploring. Enticing.

This plan of hers . . . well, it sounded nigh on perfect. Too perfect, he worried. Or at least it might have been if there hadn't still been one significant hurdle to clear.

He had just promised to take a lady to a ball—one hosted by a bloody earl, at which beetles would be the main topic of conversation—and make her a success.

And he didn't have the damnedest idea how.

Perhaps he could find something in a book.

Chapter Sixteen

When Maddie prepared for bed behind her screen that night, she emerged to find the most terrible sight yet.

"Oh, really, Logan. That just isn't fair."

He looked up from his reclined pose in her bedroom chaise longue, his face partly hidden behind a book bound in dark green leather. "What?"

"You're reading *Pride and Prejudice*?"

He shrugged. "I found it on your bookshelf."

Seeing him read any book was bad enough. But her *favorite* book? This was sheer torture.

"Just promise me something, please," she said.

"What's that?"

"Promise me that I'm not going to come out from around this screen one night and find you holding a baby." That seemed the only possibility more devastating to her self-control.

He chuckled. "It doesna seem likely."

"Good."

"While we're on the topic of books . . ." Logan rose from the chair and tossed the book to the side. "I have a question for you. If these are the kinds of stories you prefer, why did you invent a Scottish officer for your imaginary suitor? You could have created a Mr. Darcy type."

"Because Scotland is far away, and I needed you to be someone who'd never come around."

He gave her a half smile. "How did that work out?"

"Not quite as I'd planned. More's the pity." At the dressing table, she finished plaiting her hair and tied the ends with a bit of plaid. "Any further questions?"

"Aye. I have one."

She turned around and found him staring at her with unabashed desire.

"Why did you never send me a drawing of yourself?"

She paused, surprised. "I don't know. I suppose the idea never occurred to me. But are you saying the idea occurred to you?"

"Of course it did. I'm a man, amn't I?"

Yes. He most definitely was a man. And his manliness was on full display as he undid the cuffs of his shirt, exposing his bronzed, muscled forearms.

"Every time they delivered one of your letters," he said, "I'd have this swell of anticipation. Maybe . . . just maybe . . . this time there'd be a sketch of a woman in there." He pulled his shirt over his head and hung it over the back of the chair. "No such luck. All I got was moths and snails."

Maddie barely heard the last part of his speech. Aside from the usual stupor that accompanied the sight of him shirtless, her mind had seized on a word toward the beginning of his statement. The one that had sounded like . . . anticipation.

"You . . ." The word died on her tongue. She cleared her throat and tried again. "You looked forward to my letters?"

He answered her from the washing stand. "War is a brutal occupation, *mo chridhe*. It is also deadly boring and verra uncomfortable. Socks are cause for celebration. A toothbrush?" He held up the one currently in his hand. "Worth its weight in gold. Letters are manna from heaven."

After he rinsed his face, he crossed to the edge of the bed and slid one finger along her collarbone. "The slightest glimpse of this softness would have seemed a miracle."

He undid the top button of her shift, pushing the fabric to the side to reveal a small swatch of her skin. "Only one shift tonight?"

She nodded. "I trust you now."

With a heavy sigh, he leaned against the bedpost, his eyes never leaving her body. "Then sketch a picture for me. No pencil. No paper. Just you, right here, right now."

Maddie's pulse stuttered. His suggestion should have been unthinkable. But her body had ideas of its own.

She said, "Tell me how."

"Start by taking down your hair."

She reached for the scrap of fabric tying the end of her plaited hair. She pulled the knot loose and began to tease the strands of the braid apart, shaking her head gently to distribute them.

In this moment, she would do almost anything he asked. But she wasn't doing any of it *for* him. Oh, no. This was all for herself. She loved the way he was looking at her right now. She never wanted it to end.

"Now this."

He pushed the sleeve of her shift down her shoulder. She tensed.

"I just want to look, *mo chridhe.*" His voice was hoarse. "Let me have this much."

He pushed the panel down to reveal her breast. With just the pad of his fingertip, he circled her pink areola. Her nipple tightened to an aching peak.

Maddie glanced up at him. The expression on his face was pure, unfiltered yearning. She never would have believed she could inspire that look in anyone, much less a man who'd been privy to her worst sins. He swallowed, and the hard bob of his Adam's apple was the most sensual, arousing thing she'd ever seen.

Her whole life had been an exercise in avoiding attention. Observing, rather than being observed. She'd mastered the art of hiding in plain view. And for the first time, she never wanted this attention to end.

She slipped her arm from the loosened sleeve entirely. Then she undid a few more buttons of the shift, pulled her other arm free, and let the cloud of white linen settle about her waist.

Her heart pounded in her throat.

"Lie back on the bed."

She followed his instruction, reclining against the bed. In an impulse of sheer wantonness, she pushed the wadded shift over her hips and peeled it down her legs. Leaving herself completely bare, from head to toe.

Her choice of position was instantly more fraught than she had anticipated. Should she lie on her back, or on her side? Bent legs or straight? And for heaven's sake, what should she do with her arms? Stretch them overhead? At her sides? One of each?

Her sincerest impulse was to flail them about in indecision, but that wasn't the erotic picture she hoped to present.

In the end, she lay on her side, crosswise on the bed. Legs together, bent gently at the knees. With one arm, she propped up her head. The other hand lay draped— casually, she hoped—on her thigh.

He stared at her.

He stared at her so long without speaking that she began to grow concerned.

"Maybe this was a bad id—"

He shushed her. "Sketches don't talk."

She touched the backs of her fingers to her elongated neck, drawing them slowly downward. She waited for him to complain that sketches didn't move, either.

He didn't complain.

Unless a strangled groan counted as a complaint, and she didn't think it did.

She let her fingertips drift lower, down into the hollow between her breasts. He muttered something Gaelic that she assumed to be the best kind of blasphemy.

With his eyes never leaving her body, he undid a fastening of some kind on the inside of his kilt. The heavy plaid fell to the floor, leaving him every bit as naked as she was.

Every bit as naked, perhaps, but considerably more tanned, muscled, and covered with hair.

More solid, too.

One particular bit of him was very, very hard.

Maddie worried it would be impolite or lewd to stare, but she couldn't tear her gaze away. She was fascinated. Not only as an artist but as a woman as well.

Good heavens. His male organ jutted out from its nest of dark hair, a thick, dusky curve of flesh that appeared, at first glance, quite alarming in size. As she stared at him, her mind was doing estimations, drawing diagrams.

How could . . . ? Why did . . . ?

Her brain could scarcely complete a question. She needed more observation.

Which meant she needed to give him something to watch, too.

With her fingertips, she traced the globe of her breast. Slowly circling her fingers round and round.

He gave a low groan. With one hand, he gripped the bedpost.

He wrapped his other hand around his staff.

The jolt of arousal was immediate. Electric. The moment his hand closed around his rigid staff, her own breeding parts went soft and quivering.

Perhaps she ought to have felt embarrassed—and to be truthful, she did, a bit. But she couldn't look away. The visible proof of his arousal, the strength of his grip, the tension in the sinews of his neck as he stroked up and down . . .

She'd caused that. All of it.

The surge of power was intoxicating.

Most thrilling of all was the way he looked at her, or rather looked through her. *Inside* her. Somewhere behind those eyes, he was making love to her in bold, passionate strokes.

And something told her it wasn't the first time he'd been lost in that particular fantasy.

The idea was wildly arousing.

She let her fingertip circle one nipple, then the other. Then she drew that single fingertip down her belly. To her own most sensitive place.

He nodded. His eyes, heavy with desire, lifted to hers. "Go on."

Maddie could scarcely believe she was doing this, but her arousal was so powerful that it pushed out any sense of shame. At his urging, she touched herself there. Just the way she knew it would please her most if she were alone.

But she wasn't alone. Logan was watching her, and that meant every sensation was heightened. There was danger here between them, but also trust. The most frightening sense of safety she'd ever known.

He stroked himself faster, bracing his head against his propped arm. His breathing was rough.

Her pleasure spiraled toward a steep, fast-approaching peak.

She wanted to hold back, the better to watch him and absorb every detail of the sight. But all too soon, the pleasure broke over her. She curled in on herself, closing her eyes and letting the waves of bliss rock her again and again.

She was dimly aware of his low groan. When the haze of her own climax lifted, she looked up to find him wiping himself clean with his discarded shirt.

Her breath heaved in her chest.

Good heavens. What did they say to each other after that?

Nothing, apparently.

Without a word, Logan lay down on the bed alongside her. Not touching. Just beside her. No pillows or tension between them—only warmth.

His breathing calmed, and a delicious languor spread through her body. Neither of them seemed willing to ruin the pleasant truce by speaking.

So they were quiet.

And then they were asleep.

Logan's sleep was much as it always was.

Dark. Cold. Empty.

Seemingly endless.

Then, out of nowhere, a face appeared to him in the darkness. A pale, pretty face with dark eyes.

She called to him in a sweet, husky voice. "Logan."

Well, Logan thought. If he was going to develop the talent for dreaming, these were the kinds of dreams he could enjoy.

He reached for her, wanting to draw her close.

And then the face began to recede. Back into the darkness.

No.

No, come back.

"Logan."

This time, there was fear in her voice.

He had to get to her. Hold her. Keep her from slipping away.

But he reached for her in vain. Looking down, he saw to his horror that his feet had sunk into the ground. His arms weren't his own anymore. They were freakishly thin. Child-sized. He couldn't stretch them far enough, no matter how he tried.

And he did try.

Again and again and again.

"Logan."

He sat bolt upright in the bed, shaking and breathing hard. The bed linens were bathed in perspiration.

Maddie sat up next to him. Her hand went to his shoulder. "Logan, are you well? You were having a dream."

He shook his head. "It's not possible. I never . . ."

"You do. You do dream, you **stubborn** man. I've seen this more than once. You **dream, and** you talk. Sometimes I'm able to settle you **in your** sleep, but this time was different. I'm sorry **to wake** you, but I couldn't bear to watch you suffer **that way.**"

Logan's breath heaved in his chest.

He didn't know how to receive this news. Apparently he'd been embarrassing himself nightly in front of her . . . and she'd been soothing him when he'd been insensible to it?

He pushed both hands through his hair, frustrated in more ways than one.

"You're fine now," she crooned, sweeping her fingers down his spine. "We can go back to sleep."

He shrugged off her touch. "It's nearly morning. We might as well rise and be dressed if we're going to be in Inverness when the shops open for the day."

"Very well, then."

Logan tried to ignore the crestfallen look on her face. He knew he was hurting her by brushing away her sweet gestures. But he would hurt her more deeply later if he allowed them.

Dreams had no place in his plans. This had been a ruthless scheme from the outset, and it needed to remain that way. If he meant to secure this land for his men, he had to conquer Madeline, one way or another. Either she would surrender this property, or she would surrender her virtue. Emotions could only complicate matters.

He could not encourage her to care for him.

If only because it would grow too tempting to care for her in return.

Chapter Seventeen

Aunt Thea leaned close to him. "I'm going to guess you don't have a great deal of experience shopping for ladies' formal attire?"

Logan scratched his neck. "What gave it away?"

They sat on two narrow chairs in the midst of an Inverness dressmaker's shop, waiting on Maddie to make her choice of a gown. The sheer quantity of lace and plumes in the establishment had him feeling itchy.

"Not much experience attending balls, either?" she asked.

"None."

"You must be so anxious. I couldn't eat for weeks before my first presentation."

If he hadn't been anxious already, he was growing anxious now.

Thank you, Aunt Thea. Much obliged.

"While we're waiting, I'll give you a bit of advice." She pushed to her feet and prodded him in the elbow. "Come along. Stand up. A man should never be sitting while a lady stands."

Logan reluctantly stood. He didn't especially want etiquette lessons at the moment, but he didn't know what else to do with himself in this place, either. At least she offered a way to pass the time. It was better than fidgeting. If he tapped the heel of his boot any more times, he would wear a hole in the carpet.

"Now," she began, "when you first make a new acquaintance, the person of lower social rank is presented to the higher."

"No need to memorize any of the social ranks," he said. "I'm going to be on the same end of that exchange every time."

He couldn't imagine there would be anyone of lower rank present at an earl's residence. Even within a humble Highland *baile*, Logan had always been the lowest of the lowly, one step above the animals. Sometimes he'd been fed *after* the dogs.

"Regardless, you will then bow. No need to bow deeply from the waist. That's for toadying footmen. But something more than a nod is in order with the aristocracy. Think of a hinge in between your shoulder blades and lean forward from there. That should do."

Logan obeyed as best he could, feeling rather like a marionette.

"Now kiss my hand."

He brought her hand to his lips and kissed the backs of her fingers.

"That part isn't strictly necessary." Her eyes twinkled. "It was mostly for me."

He couldn't help but smile a little. He didn't know where Madeline had inherited her shy nature, but it certainly hadn't been from her aunt's side.

"Now for the dancing," she said.

"We won't be dancing."

"Most of the steps aren't difficult. Wait for a country dance and watch the gentleman next to you. Or, if you're feeling adventurous, you could try the waltz."

Logan shook his head. "Maddie told me she won't want to dance at all."

"Perhaps she won't. But I do. It's been ages since I danced the gavotte with the Comte de Montclair. Humor me?"

He cast a wistful look at the heavy drapes that guarded the dressing room, willing them to open and give him an excuse to refuse.

No luck.

So he allowed Aunt Thea to position his arms just so and teach him to step this way, then that. One-two-three, one-two-three. He wouldn't remember any of it later, but if it made an old woman happy, he supposed he couldn't object.

"Not bad," she said. "Not bad at all."

Logan bowed and kissed her fingers again.

She kept his hand and squeezed it. "I never had children, you see. That's why my Madling is so precious to me. I've thought of her as my own. Mothered her the best I could. You do realize what that means, Logan?"

He shifted his weight from one foot to the other. "Is this the moment where you warn me that if I hurt her, you'll slip poison in my tea?"

"No, no. What I have to say is much worse. If you're Maddie's husband, that means I'm going to mother you." She gave him a quick, tight hug before releasing him. "And you'll just have to endure it."

Logan was stunned.

He'd never been mothered by anyone. He wasn't certain he'd recognize the feeling, much less know how to return the sentiment. But he understood loyalty. The familiar protective impulses rose as he helped her take her seat. In that moment, she'd been added to a short roster of people he would give his life and soul to protect.

It wasn't a decision, just a fact. He would guard this daft old woman's happiness with his life. No matter how she tried to kill him with tonics and salves.

And just when he'd begun to recover his wits, Madeline pushed aside the dressing room curtains.

And he was stunned again.

Madeline stood before him in a gown of rich, emerald-green silk. The low-cut bodice did miraculous things for her bosom, and the vibrant color made a striking contrast with her pale skin and dark hair. And her lips . . . something about the green brought out their richness. They looked like two lush slices of a ripened plum.

His mouth watered.

She turned and twisted in front of the mirror, trying to get a look. "It needs some alterations, but I think it will do." She turned to Logan. "Don't you?"

He nodded dumbly.

"Very well, then."

She disappeared once again, drawing the curtains closed.

He was still nodding dumbly.

What had just happened? She'd parted those curtains for all of ten seconds, perhaps, and he felt like a prophet who'd glimpsed divine revelation. Now his world was on end.

Aunt Thea tugged on her gloves. "Well, that's done. While Madling finishes with her fitting, you stay here. I'm going to duck down the street and have a peek in the apothecary."

Logan nodded. Again.

"Are you feeling quite well?" Aunt Thea asked. "You haven't spoken a word since Madling emerged. And your face is all flushed."

"Is it?" Logan rubbed his face. "Perhaps I need one of your tonics or possets."

"I don't think so." She arched one slender, silver brow. "I've seen this affliction before. It's a heart malady. And there isn't any cure."

"No, wait. It isn't like that. Aunt Thea—"

Once the older woman left, Logan leaned forward in his chair and let his head drop into his hands.

Brilliant. Just when he'd started to worry about breaking Maddie's heart, he now had to worry about her aunt's, as well.

"Where's Aunt Thea?" Maddie asked.

He looked up to see she'd emerged again, this time in her usual gray frock. Rationally, he should not have found her even lovelier than he had a few minutes ago—but he did. It was the familiarity that stirred him. He knew this frock. He knew *her*.

"She said she wanted to stop in at the apothecary's."

"Oh, dear." She pulled a face. "Well, I happen to need new gloves. I don't suppose you can tolerate a quick stop by the draper's? I think it's just down the street."

Together they left the shop and made their way toward the other side of the lane. It was midday, and a market day, and the street had grown considerably busier while they'd been in the dressmaker's shop.

A trio of laughing boys racing down the lane divided them. Logan was forced to release his grip on Maddie's hand. When he reached the pavement on the other side of the road, he turned to look for her.

She wasn't at his side.

"Maddie?"

Madeline had come to a dead halt in the center of the road. She stood pale and trembling. People and horses moved about her like trout swimming around a rock in the stream.

Jesus Christ. If she didn't move, she was likely to be hit by a cart.

Logan pushed his way to her side.

"Maddie. What is it? Are you going to swoon? What's wrong?"

She didn't answer. Only stood there, her eyes unfocused and her whole body quivering.

He was tempted to pluck her off her feet and carry her in his arms, but he worried that would create even more of a scene. He didn't want to draw more attention.

Placing his arm around her shoulders, he guided her to the side of the main thoroughfare, scouting their surroundings for a safe place where she could sit and recover her breath. There was a tea shop nearby, but it was crowded with patrons at this hour.

Out of desperation and a lack of alternatives, Logan steered her toward the kirk.

Of all places, a kirk. He hadn't been inside a proper house of worship in years.

But the space was dark and quiet and empty, and that was what Maddie needed right now.

He walked her down the center aisle and helped

her find a seat on a narrow wooden bench. Then he put his arms about her, attempting to soothe the tremors racking her slender frame. He thought of the way she'd touched him that morning, when he'd woken shaking and covered in sweat. Tracing his fingers down the linked pearls of her spine, he tried to imitate her soothing caress.

He held her like that for several minutes, until she felt ready to speak.

"I can't do this." She choked on a sob. "I'm sorry. I know we had an agreement, but I can't even walk down a street without panicking. I don't know how I thought I could go to a ball."

"Easy, *mo chridhe*. I have you now. It's over."

"It isn't over. It's never over." She pulled a handkerchief from her pocket. "I hoped at last I could move past this, but I've been this way almost all my life. At least, ever since . . ."

"Ever since what, *mo chridhe*? What happened? You can tell me."

"You'll think me so stupid and foolish. I *was* stupid and foolish."

"I'd never think you stupid. Foolish, possibly. Tell me the story, and I'll let you know."

She plucked at the lacy edge of her handkerchief. "When I was seven years old, it was Christmastime and my mother was dying. I knew it, even though no one would tell me so. I could see it in the way she'd grown so pale and thin, and I could smell it on her breath. It was the strangest odor, like mineral spirits and rose petals. There weren't any callers, other than doctors. My lessons were suspended. I had to be very quiet at all times, so as not to disturb her rest. So I learned at quite a young age how to be invisible. Any game I played, any joy I found—it had to be undetectable. I spent a great deal of time out of doors. Taking interest in other small, quiet things.

"One day, one of the local farmer's girls told me there was to be a Christmas pantomime in the village square. I was curious to see it, but I didn't dare tell anyone. I crept out and walked all the way into the village myself to see it. I pushed my way to the front of the crowd. It was wondrous. The costumes, the joking. There was a man who juggled flaming batons. I laughed until my sides hurt. For a few minutes, I forgot all about the sadness at home. And then . . ."

When she paused, Logan reached over and took her hand.

"I don't know precisely what happened," she went on. "A horse startled, perhaps?" Her brow wrinkled with concentration. "Maybe a dog got loose. I can't recall. The whole crowd went into a panic, and I was caught in the middle with no one to protect me. If I hadn't managed to wedge myself under the scaffolding, I surely would have been trampled. I still don't remember how I got home. I only remember that it was dark, and so cold. I stuffed my frock in the coal bin to hide the rips and stains, then spent the night trembling in my bed. I thought surely they'd find me out in the morning. They would have heard the news from the village, or they would have noticed the frock. But when my father woke me, it was to say my mother had slipped away in the night. So no one discovered my misbehavior. And I never told them."

"No one?"

"How could I? Confess that while my mother lay on her deathbed, I'd stolen away to laugh at a pantomime? I was so ashamed."

He shook his head. "You were a girl. You wanted a respite from grieving and sadness. That's nothing to be ashamed about."

"It was difficult to believe that as a child, though. For the longest time, I felt my timidness was a deserved punishment. You see, I've tended to freeze in crowded places ever since. Markets, busy streets, theaters . . ."

"Ballrooms," he finished for her.

"Ballrooms." She lifted her shoulders, then let them drop. "Whenever there are too many people around, I become that seven-year-old girl again. Alone and frozen with fear."

Logan wasn't sure what to say. He stroked the back of her hand with his thumb. "It's understandable."

"Is it? Because I don't understand it, really. Is it

truly the crowd that frightens me? Maybe I'm still punishing myself for an old mistake. Or perhaps it's superstition. I'm afraid that if I enjoy myself, something terrible will happen."

She swallowed. "In any event, there was no way I could face a London season, and no way I could explain the reasons to my father. So I lied. And years later, here we are."

"Here we are."

"See?" She forced a smile. "I told you the truth was stupid. Just another foolish story of Maddie Gracechurch making one mistake and then letting it ruin the next ten years of her life. It's a pattern, apparently."

He regarded her, thoughtful. "That pattern isna what I see when I look at you."

"It isn't?"

"No."

In the dim, misty interior of the kirk, her eyes were pools of dark liquid. "Then what *do* you see?"

He waited a moment before responding. "I see a bug."

She laughed in surprise. Just as he'd hoped she would.

"No, truly," he said. "One of those insects that starts out as a grub and then makes itself a case. What's it called?"

"A cocoon?"

"Right. It makes itself a cocoon and goes into

hiding. And when it finally emerges, it's something entirely different. Something beautiful."

"Well, sometimes it's beautiful. A great many insects make themselves cocoons. It's not all pretty moths and damselflies, you know. If you're right, and I've been hiding in a cocoon, I could emerge to find that I'm an earwig or a termite."

Logan doubted it. He knew what he'd seen when those velvet drapes had been pushed aside in the dressmaker's shop, and it hadn't resembled an earwig. But she needed to discover that for herself.

He said, "There's only one way to find out."

"You're saying I should screw up my courage and go to the ball."

He nodded. "You have more courage than you give yourself credit for. You're brave enough to take me on, and that's not nothing."

"I suppose that's true. You are rather formidable."

"There are trained soldiers who fled at the sight of me. You've always held your ground."

"It must seem unspeakably ridiculous, having to coax me to go to a party when you've led troops into battle. How did you manage it without being frightened?"

"Battle, do you mean?"

She nodded.

"I didn't. I was always frightened. Terrified, every time."

"Oh."

"But it helped to know I wasna alone. That there was always someone at my back who wouldna desert me." He pulled her arm through his, tucking it close. "We'll be in it together. I'll be there for you. I sure as hell wouldna be at the Beetle Ball for anyone else."

"Thank you," she whispered.

As if it were impulse, she kissed his cheek.

And then, as if it were destiny, he bent and kissed her lips.

The embrace was brief and chaste. But sweet. So sweet. And somehow more affecting than any kiss he'd known before. With Madeline, or with anyone.

This day grew more and more perilous. He'd woken from his sleep to find Maddie too close to caring for him. Then her aunt had made it clear there was a second set of hopes he stood at risk of destroying.

Now the worst, most unthinkable revelation of all.

What could be worse than knowing there were two hearts in danger of breaking?

Suspecting there might be three.

Chapter Eighteen

Aside from a small delay due to muddy roads, the journey went much as planned. They reached the coaching inn with plenty of time to dress for the evening.

One of the inn's serving girls helped Maddie with her gown and hair. The young woman was remarkably talented with curling tongs, Maddie thought, surveying the girl's work in the looking glass as she considered whether perhaps she ought to hire a proper ladies' maid.

But even if her hair looked tolerable, there was still . . . the rest of her. Her cheeks were pale. Her stomach was a writhing mass of nerves. She hadn't been able to eat a thing all day.

And Logan wasn't helping in the least. While she

dithered over her choice of earbobs, he walked the room.

Back and then forth.

And back and then forth.

Worse, he seemed to pick up speed with every pass. Until he was striding with agitation in every step.

She watched him in the mirror. "You're making me nervous. I do wish you'd stop flouncing."

That suggestion drew him to a halt. He turned to her. "I'm not flouncing."

"It looked like flouncing to me."

"Men canna flounce."

"They can if they're wearing a skirt."

"A kilt isna a skirt. 'Tis an entirely different thing." He turned on his heel and resumed his agitated strides.

"Flounce," she said lightly, looking pointedly at the bouncing hem of his plaid. And again with each of his heavy strides. "Flounce, flounce, flounce."

She couldn't help but tease him. Needling him took away some of her own anxiety.

"It isna flouncing," he said. "It's *pacing*."

"If you say so, Captain MacFlouncy."

"Or prowling."

"*Prowling*." She arched one eyebrow. "Like a kitten?"

He gave an exasperated sigh. "Call me a kitten once more, and I'll . . ."

"You'll what?"

"I'll pounce on you and lick you like a dish of cream."

Maddie smiled to herself. That didn't sound like such a terrible punishment.

"You've been sitting at that dressing table for the past two hours," he said. "I know you're anxious. But if you want to meet this Mr. Dorning, we must be on our way."

"I know, I . . ." She lifted her head and met her own gaze in the mirror. "I'm just nervous."

"This is hardly an appearance at St. James's. They're only a group of naturists."

"Naturalists. If they were naturists, that would make getting dressed much easier." She reached for a small jar on the dressing table. "I'm trying to decide whether to brave this rouge Aunt Thea gave me."

She picked up the small pot of cosmetic and squinted into it. Then dabbed the contents gingerly with the tip of her little finger.

Logan crossed to her, took the rouge from her hand, carried it to the room's single narrow window, and pitched it out into the twilight.

After a count of three, she heard it land with a faint thud.

"Just as well. I'll be more comfortable if I don't attract notice." Maddie rose to her feet with a sigh and gathered her gloves. "We can leave now."

Now he blocked her path, forbidding her to take a single step. "Hold just a moment."

Goodness. His sudden nearness was so affecting. He looked so fine in his dark green-and-blue tartan, and his freshened officer's coat fit him snug as sealskin. Every button and bit of gold braid gleamed. He'd even acquired a white cravat and tied it with reasonable skill.

And he'd shaved. Recently enough that even his formidable stubble hadn't yet managed to reappear. His jaw was smooth, save for a small red nick where he'd cut himself with the razor.

She was seized by the desire to touch his cheek.

Press her lips to that small, endearing wound.

And she wanted so much more.

Her hands fluttered with nerves, as if she and he had been strangers and this had been their first meeting.

Despite it, she tried to sound nonchalant. "I can't imagine what's come over you. First you're rushing me to leave, and now you're telling me to wait? I thought women are the sex with changeable moods."

"We need to talk about that comment you just made. Something about how you won't attract notice?"

"Yes. Well, what of it?"

He put his hands on the dressing table, one on either side of her hips. His blue eyes pinned her, as surely as if she'd been a butterfly pinned to a board.

"Like hell you won't attract notice," he said. "You have *my* notice."

Maddie squirmed, trying to escape. "Really, we'll be late. We should be leaving."

He didn't budge. "Not just yet."

"But I thought you were in a hurry."

"I have time for this."

The words were a low growl that sank to her belly and simmered there. He leaned close enough that she could breathe in the scent of his clean hair and skin, along with the faint aromas of soap and starched linen. She'd never drawn a more arousing breath.

"You may say you dinna want to attract notice. Well, I notice all of you." He tipped his head, letting his gaze saunter down her body. "In fact, I'm starting to fancy myself a sort of naturalist. One with verra particular interests. I'm becoming quite the expert in Madeline Eloise Gracechurch."

"Logan . . ."

"And lass, you canna stop me."

Logan took his time, drinking her in.

Holy God, she looked lovely tonight. The green of her gown brought out the rosiness of her cheeks and lips. The silk clung to her figure, and that little lacy ruffle decorating her bosom drove him mad with desire. He tilted his head, staring into the soft darkness of her cleavage.

He needed to touch her. Taste her. Possess her in some small way.

"What do you mean to do?" she asked.

"I mean to put some color on your cheeks."

"How?"

"I'm going to kiss you."

"Don't you dare. The maid spent an hour with the curling tongs."

"I willna muss your curls." A sly smile tugged at his mouth. "Not the ones on your head, at any rate."

"Now you're not making any sen—"

He dropped to his knees before her, tossing up her petticoats with both hands.

She squeaked in response. *"Logan."*

"Just a kiss, *mo chridhe*. Just a kiss. Let me give you this much."

This wasn't only about giving. He was taking, too.

He ran one hand up her stocking-covered leg, skimming over her garter to caress her silken thigh. Then he swept his touch higher, settling in the dark triangle where her thighs converged.

"Logan, please. I don't want . . ." Her words trailed off in a breathy sigh.

He smiled a little, rubbing up and down with the

pad of his thumb. "Oh, you want. You most definitely want. I can feel it." He gave her inner thigh a lick. "I can taste it."

She might have been shocked by his crude language, but her body didn't object. He slid a finger along her crease and found her to be wet. So wet and ready for him.

"It took too long to dress," she whispered. "I don't want to be mussed."

"Then lean against the dressing table." He settled her backside against the edge. "Hold your skirt like so." He lifted the silk hem and folded it upward, placing it in her hands. "And now be verra, verra still."

Before she could muster another objection, Logan sank back to his knees and laid his mouth to her core.

She gasped.

He moaned.

Holy God. She tasted of ambrosia. Like peaches and blossoms and honey and musk. And just a touch of salt, to make the unbearable sweetness even sweeter still.

He went slowly, running his tongue up and down the full length of her slit. Teasing, tasting. Enjoying the hitch of her quickening breath. Feeling the little tremors in her thighs. Savoring the perfect softness of her most intimate places.

And then, when she began to arch against his

mouth, he slid upward and touched his tongue to the place he knew she needed it most.

She cried out a little. Her hips bucked.

He reached under her petticoats, cupping the twin globes of her arse in his hands to hold her still.

So . . . very . . . still . . .

As he worried that sensitive bud with the gentlest flicks of his tongue.

Soon her hips were rolling in an instinctive rhythm. Moving with him, against him. If he withdrew his tongue, she chased it.

Yes.

Arousal surged through him. Beneath his plaid, his cock was hard as a staghorn dagger handle. A thought whispered through his lust-frenzied mind.

He could have her.

He could make her his. Right here, right now. Forever.

If he rose to his feet this moment, lifted her sweet little arse onto the table, and positioned his cock at her entrance . . . would she tell him no?

He didn't think she would.

But damn if he wasn't enjoying this too much. The seduction. The chase. Learning the sweet taste of her, and finding every slight caress that made her sigh and moan.

Still, he needed to be inside her in some way. He released her backside with one hand and ran his fingers up the slope of her thigh. Never ceasing his attentions at the crest of her sex, he slid the tip of one finger inside her.

"Yes?" he whispered, pressing his brow to her belly.

There was no hesitation in her reply. Only trust. "Yes."

He advanced his finger, thrusting in and out, pushing deeper by slow degrees. She was so damned tight. He felt a primal thrill at the way her inner muscles gripped his finger so fiercely. This was something she'd only shared with him.

And she loved it.

"Logan. Oh, Logan, that's so . . ." A moan caught her words and stole them away. "So lovely."

"You're lovely." He kissed her just where he knew she needed it. "Beautiful." Made a tender pass of his tongue. "Perfect."

Then he settled into a rhythm. Sliding his finger in and out. Teasing her with the tip of his tongue. Her breathing and motions grew frantic, but he kept up his slow, steady pace. She released her hem with one hand, tangling her fingers in his hair.

"Don't stop," she pleaded.

Logan had no intention of stopping. He would stay like this—kissing her, stroking her, worshipping her—just as long as she needed him to.

That's it, mo chridhe. Mo chridhe. Come for me.

Her fingers tightened in his hair. With a sharp cry, she convulsed around his finger. He felt the pleasure shudder through her whole body.

Then she slumped back against the dressing table, panting and spent.

Logan needed a moment to gather himself, too.

"See? You had no need of any rouge." He settled her skirts about her. "Now there's plenty of color on your cheeks. On your throat and bosom, as well. Everyone at the ball will see it. And because I've no intention of leaving your side, they'll know just who put it there."

She reached to straighten his cravat. Evidently he'd become a bit mussed.

He liked having her fuss over him.

Her eyes tipped up at him from beneath those dark lashes. And she said, as though it were the sweetest of endearments, "You are terrible."

"If it's an apology you're wanting, lass?" He dropped a kiss on her brow. "You'll be waiting a while."

She'd be waiting for the rest of her life.

Because Logan had already made up his mind.

There wasn't going to be any compromise. No bargain, no trade.

Madeline would have her dreams, *and* she would be his wife. Tonight, if there was any justice. And once he held her in his arms, he was never going to let her go.

Chapter Nineteen

When Maddie and Aunt Thea had purchased this coach in York, the carriage vendor had informed them that it seated four persons comfortably, six in a pinch.

Maddie supposed it might fit that many persons—but only if none of those persons was a six-foot-tall Scotsman in full Highland dress.

As it was, the two of them made a tight squeeze.

He'd insisted on sitting across from her on the rear-facing seat so as not to crush her gown. Well, so as not to crush it *further.*

For what must have been the twentieth time in as many minutes, he ducked his head to peer out the carriage window. He'd only spared her the briefest glances, spending most of his time looking out at the road and countryside.

"We shouldna be more than a mile away now."

"Indeed," she said.

Stupid reply. All they'd exchanged since the inn were inanities. She didn't seem able to string more than two syllables together, ever since . . .

Ever since.

Mercy. After the wicked things he'd done to her . . .

Never mind speaking. She scarcely knew how to *look* at him now. Whenever she recalled the sensation of his tongue on her flesh—which was approximately seven times a minute—she burned all over. Her legs went quivery beneath her petticoats. Perspiration gathered between her breasts.

The carriage jounced in a rut. His knee knocked against her thigh.

Logan's eyes snapped to hers. "Are you well?"

"Indeed."

She knew at once that his thoughts had been taking him to the exact same place—underneath the tent of her splayed petticoats. For the first time since they'd left the inn, his eyes stopped roaming the hills and crags of the countryside and roamed her body's curves instead. Slowly, with a raw, possessive hunger.

A low, simmering heat sparked and built inside her, feeding off that desire in his eyes the same way a flame fed off coal.

He'd once called her uncommonly pretty in conversation, and at the time she had been tempted to argue back. But tonight, for the first time in her life, she felt irresistible. Ravishing.

Truly *beautiful*. In his eyes, if no one else's.

Oh, this was so dangerous.

The carriage rolled to a stop.

"We're here," he announced, still staring into her eyes.

"Indeed," she answered.

Her ever-helpful nerves quickly pushed aside any other inconvenient emotions. By the time Logan alighted and extended his hand to help her down, sheer, dumb terror had replaced any lingering thrills.

He put his other hand under her elbow, being careful to support her weight as her slippers found the gravel drive.

At last she was able to look up at the scene before them.

So this was Varleigh Manor.

Good heavens.

The castle was an imposing spectacle of squared turrets, trimmed with an iced-gingerbread border. The entire surface had been veneered with rose-tinted harling, with small stones crushed in the plaster so that the façade glittered in the dwindling twilight.

Lights gleamed in every window, large or small. And all around them, exquisite gardens perfumed the night. She hadn't properly seen them yet, but the scent engulfed her senses and made her dizzy.

Maddie could do nothing but gape. She'd been expecting an impressive home. Perhaps even elegance. But this?

This was opulence, writ large.

Add in the crush of coaches surrounding them, the white-tie gentlemen and ladies bedecked in jewels and plumes . . .

"Oh, no," she whimpered. She clutched Logan's arm. "No, no, no. We can't go in there. Just look at it. Just look at everyone."

Just look at me.

The hastily altered silk gown that had looked quite passable in a dimly lit coaching inn now felt hopelessly dowdy and out of fashion. She ought to have worn her mother's pearls. She ought to have bought new gloves.

"I was expecting a small, quiet gathering of science-minded aristocrats. Not this."

"We're here now, lass. There's no going back."

Perhaps there was no going back, but Maddie's feet were not eager to move forward, either.

She stayed close to him as they walked toward the entrance and queued up for their announcement in the ballroom.

"First rule of balls," he whispered, tucking her arm tight in his. "Dinna panic."

"What's the second rule? I think we should just move on to that."

"Remember when we went to the Beetle Ball and had a smashing good time?" he murmured.

"I do, as a matter of fact. You were quite well behaved and charming. In fact, I seem to recall that you even danced with the dowager countess herself."

He shrugged. "I am surprisingly good with older women."

"So I've heard."

"But I only danced with her to be polite. The true enjoyment came later. When I cornered you in an alcove and pleasured you until you screamed."

Maddie clapped a gloved hand over her startled laughter. At least her cheeks would be pink without any rouge.

It was their turn to be announced. The major-domo looked at them, waiting for Logan to provide the names.

Logan cast an uncertain glance in Maddie's direction and tugged at his cravat.

In that moment, Maddie realized something. She'd been unbearably self-centered. As out of place as she felt in this setting, Logan must have been feeling a hundred times more uncomfortable. True, she'd never attended a proper ball, but she'd been trained in how to behave at them. She'd been raised within this class of society.

Logan was an officer, but he had not been born a gentleman. For an orphaned country lad who'd grown up sleeping with cattle in the byre, this scene must be completely foreign. He might as well have been launched to the moon.

A soft tendril of emotion uncurled in her heart.

Stop that, she told herself. *He's not here for love of you. He's here for the castle. The land. His men.*

They had an agreement. After tonight, he would have his lands, and Maddie would have her life back. No more hiding. No more lies.

She leaned toward the manservant and gave their names. "Mrs. Madeline Gracechurch and Captain Logan MacKenzie, of Invernesshire."

As they were announced, they moved into the ballroom.

Maddie spoke through a smile. "This is my debut. That's the first time I've heard my name announced like that."

"I hope you enjoyed it. It's also the last time you'll hear your name like that."

A strange thing for him to say, but Maddie supposed he had the right of it. It seemed unlikely she would ever attend another ball.

She murmured, "Now we go in and make a slow circle of the room."

"Right," he said. "See, I told you they'd all stare."

"Of course they're staring. They're staring at

you." And Madeline was so glad of it. She'd been worried about being noticed, but she might as well have been invisible next to Logan. "You really don't know, do you?"

"Know what?"

"How wildly magnificent you look tonight."

He made a dismissive noise. "It's the kilt."

"It's partly the kilt. It's mostly the swagger."

This was, after all, a gathering of naturalists—and Logan was a rare specimen. She wondered if there was any sight so handsome as a Highlander in full military dress. Everyone in the room was plainly fascinated.

"I dinna see Varleigh," he muttered.

"I imagine he's probably preparing for his lecture."

Logan nodded. "Did you want to dance?"

"No," she quickly replied.

"Thank God. I'll stay close to you then so no one else asks."

She didn't know which was more endearing—his faith that someone else would bother asking her to dance, or the deliciously possessive sentry post he adopted at her side. They accepted glasses of punch from a passing servant. Made a show of inspecting a carved marble bust. Watched the dancers as they moved through a quadrille. Through it all, he never strayed more than two feet from her elbow.

She knew this was partly to protect her and partly to protect himself, but to the casual onlooker he must have appeared completely besotted with her. Maddie had no complaint. She'd always imagined what it would be like to have a strong, handsome Highland officer slavishly hanging on her every word and action. Now she knew.

It was every bit as wonderful as she'd dreamed.

Soon, the music stopped, and the guests began filtering toward a gallery.

"Here." Maddie fished a small object from her reticule and pressed it into Logan's palm.

"What's this?" he asked.

"A cheroot."

"I dinna smoke cheroots."

"Well, you could smoke one tonight. If you wanted."

He frowned at her, plainly confused.

"It's your ticket out of doors if you want an escape. The naturalist lecture will be starting soon. I know you're not interested in hearing about nineteen new species of Amazonian beetles, and I think I can bear sitting in the back of a lecture on my own. If you'd rather take a turn outside, I'll understand."

He looked at her for a moment. Then he crushed the cheroot into the nearest potted plant. "I'm staying with you."

In that moment, Maddie wasn't sure she cared

to hear about nineteen new species of Amazonian beetles, either. Perhaps she'd rather find the nearest alcove and make that memory Logan had teased her with. But considering how much trouble he'd gone to, she had to hold up her end of the bargain.

That was the point of the evening, she reminded herself. Trading her dream for his. Logan surely hadn't forgotten it, and she shouldn't, either.

They found seats toward the rear of the room.

Logan suffered through the lecture admirably, boring as it must have been for him. Even Maddie's attention wavered. She was anxious that at any moment Lord Varleigh would call on her to stand and be recognized. The firm press of Logan's thigh against hers was reassuring. And deliciously distracting.

Her worries, however, proved to be in vain. A smattering of applause let her know that the lecture was over.

Maddie was still in her seat.

"He didna mention you," Logan muttered. "Why not?"

"I don't know," she whispered. "Maybe he means to acknowledge me later."

"But it's over. Everyone's wandering away." Before she could stop him, Logan shot to his feet and called, "Lord Varleigh."

The people stopped wandering away.

"Yes, Captain MacKenzie? Did you have a question?"

"Just a compliment to offer, my lord." Logan cleared his throat. "I wanted to congratulate you on the superb quality of these illustrations."

Lord Varleigh looked him directly in the eye. "Thank you."

Maddie felt Logan's immediate flare of anger. He might have dressed in fine clothing and put on suave manners tonight, but he was still a warrior beneath it all, and now his battle instincts had charged to the fore.

Someone was going to get hurt.

"The bastard."

She tugged on his sleeve, urging him to sit. "It doesn't matter."

"Of course it matters. That's your work on the walls, and he's stolen all the glory."

"He deserves to have the attention tonight. He's the one who traveled to the Amazon."

"He got on a damned boat. That's all. And once there, I've no doubt he paid a crew of native Amazonians to do all the work. He's probably stolen from them, too. But you, Maddie . . . You took his ugly, dried-up husks of things and brought them life." He touched her cheek. Only briefly, as though he didn't trust himself to be gentle just now. "That's the most remarkable thing about you, *mo chridhe*. The way you have of bringing things to life."

A lump formed in her throat.

Desperate, she pulled him away from the lecture group and into a side room. A small library of some sort.

Lord Varleigh joined them. "Is there some sort of problem, Captain MacKenzie?"

"You know damned well there is."

"Logan, please," Maddie murmured.

In concession, Logan moderated his tone from a quiet roar to a steely growl. "You invited her here to be recognized. You offered to introduce her to Mr. Dorning. Now what kind of explanation can you offer to Miss Gracechurch for your behavior?"

Lord Varleigh straightened his waistcoat. "I should still be glad to introduce Miss Gracechurch to my colleagues. That is, provided she assures me that she will remain Miss Gracechurch."

"What?"

"I need to know," Varleigh said, "that there is no chance that she will shortly become Mrs. MacKenzie."

Logan muttered an oath.

"But why should that matter, my lord?" Maddie asked.

"Miss Gracechurch, I cannot, in good conscience, recommend you for a lengthy project if you are to be wed. A wife has obligations to her husband and family, and those duties will supersede your artistic employment."

"But that is absurd," she said. "Surely many of your colleagues are married gentlemen, with duties to their families and wives. No one questions their scholarly dedication."

"Perhaps," Lord Varleigh said, sliding a condescending glance in Logan's direction, "if were you married to a gentleman of some social or scholarly standing, that would be a different matter."

Now it was Maddie's turn to experience a flare of anger. Never in her life had she struck another person, but she wanted to punch Lord Varleigh in his aristocratic nose.

"Did you just insult Captain MacKenzie?" she said. "I will have you know, he is a highly intelligent man. He reads. Every evening. He even attended university."

"Mo chridhe." Logan gently pulled her back. He addressed Lord Varleigh. "Miss Gracechurch will be with you in a moment, my lord."

After the man quit the room, a silence fell.

Logan began pacing back and forth in the small room. "I told you he wanted you. He probably planned this whole ball as a means of impressing you—perhaps he even meant to propose to you. Now he's taking his petty revenge because he's angry that you're here with me."

"Now that's absurd."

"Is it?"

"I can't believe that any man would care enough to go to all that trouble. Not for me."

He stopped pacing and approached her. He put his hands on her shoulders and forced her to meet his intense blue gaze. "I am wearing a cravat and cuff links at the godforsaken Beetle Ball. Does this not count as going to trouble for you?"

"But . . . that's not for me. Not really."

"Maddie, *mo chridhe*." His grip on her arms softened to a caress, and his gaze dropped to her mouth. "Like hell it isn't."

Her heart swelled in her chest. If he kissed her right now . . .

If he could *love* her . . .

Perhaps nothing else would matter.

Losing work was a disappointment. Maddie wanted that encyclopedia post. Even more than that, she wanted to be recognized for her illustrations. Lord Varleigh's snub had settled in the pit of her stomach like a bitter, queasy lump.

But the prospect of losing Logan tore at her heart.

In a strange, illogical way, he'd been a fixture in her life since she was sixteen years old. And despite all her best attempts not to, she'd come to care for him—the *real*, imperfect Logan. The man who set her body aflame with incendiary kisses and infuriated her with his arrogant presumptions and pushed her to emerge from her icy, frozen cocoon.

She'd fallen in love with him.

"I suppose it doesna matter," he said. "All you have to do is go tell him we're not marrying."

Maddie swallowed hard. "I'm not certain I can do that."

She wasn't certain she *wanted* to do that.

He glanced over her shoulder at the ballroom. "I think they're going into supper. It isna so crowded anymore."

"It's not the crowds. Logan, please. Let's just go home."

"Then we'll just go out there and find this Mr. Dorning ourselves," he said. "To the devil with Varleigh. You needn't be afraid of him. I'll tell everyone the truth."

"Just take me home," she said. "It doesn't matter anymore."

"No. I'm not going to let you hide behind me again."

"What if I'm not hiding behind you?" She put her hand in his. "What if I'm choosing you instead?"

He stared down at her. "Maddie, I—"

Tap-tap.

Tap-tap-tap.

They turned, seeking the origin of the frantic tapping noise. A familiar face was pressed to the library windowpane.

"Rabbie?" she said in disbelief.

He nodded and mouthed a word: *Open.*

And then another: *Hurry.*

Logan cursed and hurried to the window, pushing it open and extending a hand to help Rabbie through.

Once inside, Rabbie straightened and plucked bits of greenery from his sleeves. "There you two are."

"What the devil are you doing?"

"They wouldna let me in the front. I've been peeking in every window, looking for you. Narrowly escaped a thrashing from a pair of footmen."

"What's happened?" Logan demanded. "Is it Grant?"

"No, no. Grant's fine. It's the lobster."

Maddie gasped. "She's molting?"

Rabbie pulled a face. "Och, no. Well, I canna be certain. Not exactly."

Logan knew that look on his soldier's face. It didn't bode well.

"Tell us at once," he said. "The full truth."

"The lobster's gone missing. She escaped."

Chapter Twenty

They left the ball at once.

Logan offered to go ahead home on his own. "You needn't leave with me," he told her. "You should stay and meet Mr. Dorning. Rabbie can see you back to Lannair afterward."

Maddie wouldn't hear of it. "I can't do this without you. And if Fluffy's missing, I have to help search. She's more than just an assignment. You know that. She's a pet."

Logan led the way outside, ordering their carriage with a brisk command. Since Rabbie's horse was spent, he would have to ride with them. In the coach, the journey would take . . . Logan did a few mental calculations . . . four hours to return to Lannair. If they were lucky.

Which meant Logan had four hours to pass before he could be of any practical use in easing the worried look on Madeline's face.

And he was going to spend every minute of them scolding Rabbie.

While the coach was brought around, Logan grabbed him by the coat front. "You had *one* task."

Rabbie swallowed hard. "I know."

"Watch the lobster." Logan gave Rabbie a little shake. "That was the only duty I gave you. How could you manage to muck that up?"

"Well, you see. I was watching her in the studio. But 'tis a mite uncanny up there, ye ken?"

Yes, Logan knew. The place made his skin crawl too, but that was no excuse.

"So I put her in a bucket and brought 'er downstairs while the lads and I played cards. Someone must have kicked it over. Next I looked, she was gone."

The sheer idiocy of the entire scenario left Logan speechless. Their coach was brought around, and he helped Maddie in first before joining her.

"Not to worry," Rabbie said, climbing in. "By the time we get back, the other lads will have already found her. How far can a lobster travel under her own power, anyway?"

"I dinna know," Logan gritted out. "That is a question a *dutiful* soldier would never need to ask."

As they started home, Maddie was quiet. And pale and distressed.

Logan wanted to punch a hole through the carriage top. It was a hard top, which meant he would have bloodied his knuckles in the effort—but he was certain his rage would have made it happen.

He turned to her. "How long can a lobster live without being in water?"

"A few days if she's inside the castle, where it's cool and damp. But if she found her way outside to the loch?" She shook her head. "The freshwater would kill her."

"We'll find her. Dinna worry. We'll search all night if need be."

She rested her head against the side of the coach and said quietly, "It doesn't matter anymore."

"Like the devil it doesna matter."

"This is all my fault. It was wrong of me to trap her in that tank. No wonder she leapt at her first chance to escape. If she wanted to mate with Rex, she would have done it by now. Perhaps he's all wrong for her. Perhaps he's a brutish lout of a lobster with poor hygiene, and she wants nothing to do with him."

"What about your life-cycle drawings?"

She only shrugged. "Apparently I'm a woman with no future prospects in illustration."

Right.

Logan kept his calm for the remainder of the journey. Barely.

When they arrived back at Lannair Castle, the men had not yet found the lobster on their own. Damn.

Logan gathered the men in the kitchen. He sketched out a plan on the slate the cook used for the day's menus.

"Here's the layout of the ground floor," he said. "Entrances and exits are here and here. The first thing we do is set up a perimeter. Make certain no lobsters go in, no lobsters go out. Munro, you're on the front entrance. Grant stays with you. The rest of us will search."

"Try this." Rabbie whistled a trilling, birdlike song and cupped his hands around his mouth. "Here, Fluffy, Fluffy, Fluffy! Here, girl!"

Logan blinked at him. "I'm highly doubtful that method is going to work."

Rabbie shrugged. "We'll see then, won't we?"

Logan drew a cross through the castle schematic, dividing it into quadrants. He assigned three of the four to Rabbie, Callum, and Fyfe.

"I'll take this one," he said, marking the spot with the chalk. "Take a torch. Search every possible nook and crack in the exposed rock. Before it's cooked, a lobster's blue, not red, so she'll be difficult to spy at night. Take care where you step. If you find her, bring her here to the kitchen straightaway. We'll rendezvous in two hours, regardless. And whatever you do, keep her away from freshwater. Any questions?"

Fyfe raised his hand. "Does the one what finds her get to eat her?"

"*No.*" Logan put his hands on the kitchen table and addressed the gathered men. "This lobster is of great importance to Madeline. Which means it's of great importance to me."

The words were the truth. He wasn't sure when it had happened, but he cared now. About Madeline and about her illustrations. This was more than a lobster. It was her *dream*. No one was going to take that from her—not Varleigh, not Rabbie, and not Logan.

"I need you to move swiftly and surely, lads. In all our years together on campaign, we never once left a soldier behind to die. We're not leaving this lobster, either."

Just before leaving the room, he pulled Maddie aside. "Dinna worry. You have my word. We'll find her in no time at all."

Hours passed.

Nothing.

While the men continued their search, Maddie went upstairs to change out of her gown. She would be of more help in practical clothing.

As she went, she scanned every niche and pocket in the stone. It seemed highly unlikely that a lobster would have managed to climb stairs, but she kept her eyes open anyway.

She went into her bedchamber and set about undoing the closures of her green silk, when her eye fell on something that caught and held her attention.

Not Fluffy.

Logan's black canvas knapsack.

He'd worn a small dress sporran to the ball tonight. But there on a hook hung his military-issue satchel for coins, spectacles, gloves . . . and, presumably, several years' worth of Maddie's embarrassing letters.

She abandoned her plan to undress and hurried to seize it in her hands. Those letters had to be in here. They just had to be. She'd searched everywhere else.

Her fingers trembled as she loosened the buckle holding the strap.

And then she paused.

What would she do with them if they were inside? She'd been planning to destroy them at first opportunity, but now she wondered. Would she truly be able to throw them in the fire?

Maddie didn't know. So much had changed.

She took a deep breath, opened the knapsack, and peeked inside.

Nothing.

Well, not nothing. There were the usual odds and ends inside, but no packet of letters. Drat.

"What are you looking for?"

Logan's voice.

She wheeled to face him. "Oh. Nothing. Well, I'm looking for Fluffy, of course. The knapsack was lying open, and I thought she might have crawled inside. It's . . . a little known fact that lobsters love the smell of canvas."

In a lifetime of telling stupid lies, Maddie knew she had just told her stupidest.

But Logan looked too fatigued to question her, or perhaps simply too weary to care. His eyes were red with exhaustion, and his jaw had grown over with stubble again.

Her heart softened. He'd been working so hard for her.

"No luck on your end, either?" she asked.

He shook his head. "But we're not giving up. Not if it takes all night and into morning."

"You should rest. It's just a lobster."

"She's not just a lobster. She's your dream, and that was our bargain. Your dream for mine."

"It's over, Logan. It's over. You saw the way Lord Varleigh treated me tonight. Even if he had introduced me to Mr. Dorning, it would have been for nothing. I'm a woman. That's already a strike against me in most people's eyes. And if I'm newly married? They'd never hire me for a long project. They'd assume I'll get pregnant at any moment and abandon the work."

"Why are you speaking as though we're married?"

"Because maybe we should be." She forced herself to meet his gaze.

"You don't want that."

"Don't I?"

"No. You don't."

"What makes you so sure?"

"Aside from the fact that you've been telling me so, in no uncertain terms, ever since I arrived?" Heavy footsteps carried him closer. "The letters, *mo chridhe*. You'd spun a tale of a Scottish officer and a home in the Highlands. But that was just a story. Your true dream was in the margins. All those moths and flowers and snails. I'm not letting you give that up just because Lord Varleigh is a bastard and one lobster crawled away. It means something to you."

Perhaps it did. But it meant *everything* to her that he understood.

"Maybe we could mean something to each other."

"Maddie . . ."

She reached to touch him, grasping the lapels of his coat to draw him close. Her heart was pounding in her chest, but she told herself to be brave.

He was ragged and weary, but she was weary, too. Exhausted from holding back this tide of affection and tenderness inside her. She couldn't control her emotions for another moment.

She wanted to hold him. She wanted him to hold her.

"Don't you see?" She slid her hands inside his coat, skimming over the rippled surface of his abdomen and reaching to encircle him in her arms. "If we could have a marriage that was real . . . one that *meant* something . . . Lord Varleigh and Fluffy and the encyclopedia wouldn't matter. Nothing else would matter."

"Don't." His voice was hoarse. "Don't talk like this. We still have a great deal of castle to search."

"Let the men search. Stay here with me."

She sensed his will to resist weakening. His breathing grew ragged. She found the spot where his open collar gaped. She kissed the dark notch at the base of his throat.

"Stay with me, Logan." Stretching onto her toes, she kissed his jaw, then his cheek. "Make love to me."

She kissed him.

And any feeble, insincere protests Logan might have made were lost, washed away in the sweetness.

"Stay with me." She pulled him toward the bed, and he followed. "It's time to make this real."

Together they fell onto the mattress. At last, she was under him. Soft and warm and welcoming. Spreading her thighs to make a cradle for his hips and tugging at the hem of his shirt.

Belowstairs, he could still hear the men thundering from one room to the next, shouting directions to each other in their lobster search.

"You're . . ." When her hand slipped inside his shirt, he moaned against her mouth, "You're certain you want this now?"

"Yes. Now. Always." Her whispered words warmed his skin and inflamed his desire. "Make me feel like you did earlier, on the dressing table. Let me do the same for you." She pushed up the fabric of his shirt and ran her hands over his bared chest. "Logan, I want you."

Holy God. The words were like sparks dropped into whisky. In an instant, he was afire for her. Primed to explode.

She was a grown woman, he reminded himself. She understood what this meant, and she was making her own choice.

All he had to do was seize his prize.

She held him tighter, running her fingers through the hair at the nape of his neck. The edge of pleasure was keen. He clutched her to him, sinking into the kiss.

"Just do it," she urged, reaching between them to

pull up her skirts. "Hurry. Make me yours before I can . . ."

Her voice trailed off.

But she didn't need to complete that statement. He knew what she'd almost said.

Make me yours before I can change my mind.

A whisper of guilt moved through him. He ignored it. Running headlong toward the fear, just as he'd always told his men to do in battle.

For a glorious moment, he believed he could conquer it.

And then . . .

In an instant, it simply became too much. There was no thought in his decision. No desire or conscious intent. Just the instinct: Pull away.

The flash of hurt in her eyes was immediate. And eviscerating.

He felt like he'd glimpsed paradise by peering between the bars just as the gates were closed on him forever.

"Before you can change your mind," he finished for her. "That's what you almost said, isn't it? You want me to take you here and now, before you come to your senses." He rolled onto one elbow, breathing hard. "I dinna like the sound of that."

She flung her arms overhead and sighed. The gesture did incredible things for her breasts. "Now you're suddenly full of scruples?"

"I don't know. Maybe I am."

"Logan. This is what you wanted. What you demanded and threatened to ruin me to get."

"You're only upset right now because of what happened back there. I know you're disappointed, *mo chridhe*."

She reached for him. "Then make it better. It would be no sacrifice to give up my work if this were a real marriage in every sense. One with love. A family. We could have that together, Logan."

Jesus. So now he had to promise he could be worth giving up everything for? He couldn't do that. He didn't know how to replace her career, a family, a community of colleagues and friends. It was impossible.

He wouldn't be enough. She'd grow to resent him.

And then she'd leave.

"We don't have to lie to anyone. We could make this all the truth. Tonight. Don't you care for me at all?"

Of course he cared for her, and more than a bit. The truth was, he cared for her too much. He just couldn't take her dreams away. Not like this.

"We'll find another way," he said.

It was the wrong thing to say.

"We've been through this, Logan. Or did you forget? You have rejected every one of my ideas. Including this one, mortifyingly enough." She rose to a sitting position and buried her face in her hands. "I feel like such a fool."

"I just can't give you what you're asking," he said. "I've told you that from the start. Love and romance . . . it's just not in me."

"I refuse to believe that. I know that's not true." Her dark eyes flashed with anger. "You're the most caring, loyal man I've ever known. I see it in the way you treat your men, the tenants. Even my aunt. I'm the only one who can't seem to inspire your devotion."

"That's not fair. And you know it's untrue. I would protect you with my life."

"But I'll never have your heart. Will I?"

He didn't know how to answer her.

She rose from the bed and went to the dressing table. "I'm done with this. I'm done dreaming of you." She yanked at the tartan sash draped across her torso, pulling open the luckenbooth brooch and holding it in her outstretched palm. "I want the truth. Who was she, this A.D.?"

"I've told you. It's not important."

"It's important to me! I've been wearing this day in, day out. A heart-shaped lie on my chest for everyone to see. I accepted it as my due. A mark of shame that I'd brought on myself by deceiving everyone. But now I want to know the truth. Did you love her?"

"Maddie . . ."

"It's a simple question, Logan. No explanations necessary. Just one word will suffice. Yes or no. Did you love her?"

"Yes," he answered.

"A great deal?"

"As much as I knew how. It wasn't enough."

"So she left you."

He nodded.

"Clever woman."

Logan winced. "Perhaps she was. I was holding her back."

And he would be holding back Maddie, too. She had far more than sketches to offer the world. She had a gentle heart and abundant love. The wish to raise a family. All of these were things he couldn't bring himself to accept.

She would be wasted on him.

"So even though she left you, and even after all this time," she said, "you've never been able to forget her."

He shook his head in honest answer. "No."

She tossed the luckenbooth toward him, and it landed on the rumpled quilt. "Take it back. I don't want to wear it anymore. I'm leaving."

"Wait." He pushed to his feet. "It's scarcely a week until Beltane. Whatever arrangement we work out between us, I need you to be there that night."

"You just *rejected* me. What makes you think I

have any interest in striking some kind of agreement with you?"

"Do I need to remind you about the letters?"

"Those stupid letters." She choked on a wild laugh. "They don't even matter anymore. Go ahead, send them to the scandal sheets. What do I have left to lose? I've no employment prospects to protect. No romantic prospects, either. I'm accustomed to public humiliation. Loneliness, too. I can't be any more isolated than I have been living here."

She flung open her closet and reached for an empty valise on the top shelf. It tumbled down on her, glancing off her head as it fell to the floor.

Ouch. Logan winced in sympathy.

"Just what this moment needed," she said numbly. "One more humiliation."

She opened the valise and placed it on the bed, then began pulling handfuls of linen and stockings from the closet and shoving them inside.

Logan grabbed the valise by one handle. "You canna leave. Not yet."

She took the other handle and tugged back. "I can. And I will. You can't stop me."

"What will you live on?"

"Anger, for the present. It feels as though I have enough to fuel me for some time."

Her eyes were as determined and brave as he'd ever seen them. This was just the fire he'd been wanting to see from her. The strength he knew she'd possessed all along.

And of course, it *would* come just as she'd resolved to leave him.

He pushed a hand through his hair. "Forget about me."

"Oh, believe me. I intend to."

"None of this has been for me. My men need a home, and you know that. I know you care about them, too. Think of Callum, Rabbie, Munro, Fyfe. Think of Grant."

"I will miss them all. Especially Grant." She paused, a clutch of striped woolen stockings in one hand. She pressed the stockings to her heart. "Grant is my favorite person. Do you know why? He made me feel beautiful on my wedding day. No matter how many times we're introduced, he's always impressed. He makes me laugh." She stuffed the stockings into her valise. "He thinks you're a lucky bastard to have me. What a poor, addled fool."

"Grant might be addled, but he's no kind of fool. And neither is he the only one who found you beautiful on our wedding day." He took her in his arms. "I canna let you leave."

"Why should I stay?"

"Because I . . ."

Logan knew what she wanted to hear. But somehow he just couldn't force the words. He didn't believe in those words. Not coming from anyone else, and not from his own lips, either. Sooner or later, they were always a lie.

She gave him a sad smile. "That's what I thought."

"Maddie."

A shrill, high-pitched scream propelled them two steps apart.

His protective instincts kicked into a gallop. But before he could gather his wits to investigate, Rabbie's head appeared in the doorway.

"Found her!" the breathless, red-faced soldier reported. "Or rather, she found Fyfe's finger. One lobster, alive and well."

"Excellent. Thank you so much, Rabbie." Maddie gave him a smile that faded just as soon as he'd left the room. To Logan, she added, "Just in time. Now she can leave with me."

"You'll finish your drawings elsewhere?"

"No. I'm going to do Fluffy the favor I should have done myself. I'm going to set her free."

Chapter Twenty-one

"Madling?" Aunt Thea poked her turbaned head through the door. "Becky told me you're packing your trunks. Is everything all right?"

"Aunt Thea, do sit down. We need to talk."

She steeled her nerves. It was time. Long past time.

This bog of lies had sucked her in further and further over the years. She had landed in it up to her neck, and this time she wasn't going to have any assistance from Logan.

It was up to Maddie to get herself free.

First rule of bogs: Dinna panic.

"What is it, Madling?" Aunt Thea asked.

Breathe, she told herself.

"I . . . I'm going to have a great deal to say. May I ask you to bear with me until I've said all of it?"

"Of course."

"When I was sixteen years old and came home from Brighton, I told you I'd met a Scottish officer by the seaside." Maddie swallowed hard. "I lied."

There it was. The grand confession, in two syllables. Why they'd been so impossible to say aloud for so long, she could not fathom.

But now that she'd said them once, it seemed no trouble to say them again.

"I lied," she repeated. "I never met any gentleman. I spent the entire holiday alone. When I came home, everyone was expecting me to go to Town for my season. I felt panicked at the thought of society, so I invented this wild falsehood about a Captain MacKenzie. And then I just kept telling it. For years."

"But . . . unless I'm going demented in my old age, there is a man in this castle. One whose name is Captain MacKenzie. He looks quite real to me."

"He is real. But I'd never met him before." Maddie put her head down on her crossed arms. "I'm so sorry. I've been ashamed, and afraid of you learning the truth. I wanted to tell you years ago, but you were so fond of the idea of him . . . and I'm so fond of you."

"Oh, my Madling." Aunt Thea rubbed her back in soothing circles. The way she'd done when Maddie was a young girl. "I know."

"You know that I'm sorry? You can forgive me?"

"Not only that. I know everything. The lies, the letters. That your Captain MacKenzie was merely whimsy and imagination. I've always known."

Stunned, Maddie lifted her head. "*What*?"

"Please do not take offense at this, dear—but it wasn't a terribly plausible tale. In fact, it was rather preposterous, and you're not especially talented at deceit. Without me vouching for you, I don't think the story would have lasted a month with your father."

"I don't understand what you're telling me. Do you mean that you never believed me? All this time, you've known that my Captain MacKenzie was a complete fabrication, and you never said a word?"

"Well, we agreed that you seemed to need time."

"We? Who is 'we' in that sentence?"

"Lynforth and I, of course."

"My godfather knew I invented a suitor, too?" Maddie buried her face in her hands. "Oh, Lord. This is so embarrassing."

Embarrassing, but also oddly freeing. If this was true, at least she did not need to feel she'd inherited this castle under false pretenses.

"Naturally he did. And he understood. Because, my darling Madling, the two of us were close."

"Close."

"Lovers for twenty years, on and off. And he knew I'd once lied to avoid marrying, too."

Maddie thought her brain would twist from all these revelations. "You weren't debauched by the Comte de Montclair and ruined for all other men?"

"Oh, I went to *bed* with him. It wasn't terrible, but it wasn't magical, either. And no, that night did not ruin me for other men. To the contrary, it made me realize that I was far too young to shackle myself to one man for the rest of my life simply because my parents deemed him suitable, only to learn on the wedding night that he might or might not possess an erotic obsession with feathers."

"Feathers?"

"We needn't dwell on that. My point is, the importance of compatibility in the bedchamber cannot be overstated. Anyhow, I loudly proclaimed my ruination as an excuse to avoid marriage. I was able to take lovers when and how I pleased, but for his last two decades or so, I was rather devoted to Lynforth. His passing was quite the blow. It's why I so gladly came north with you. I was in mourning, too."

"Yes, but your mourning was real." Maddie edged closer. "Oh, Aunt Thea. I'm so sorry."

Her aunt dabbed at her eyes. "We knew it was coming. But one is never truly prepared. Nevertheless, life changes. We discover new passions. While you've spent your time drawing beetles, I've penned a torrid novel in my tower upstairs."

"You, a novelist? But that's . . . Well, that's perfect."

When she thought about it, Aunt Thea had been writing melodrama for years, with Maddie in the starring role.

"It's more of a memoir, really. Or as the French call it, a *roman à clef.* Nearly everything in the events is true to life, but the names have been changed to protect the wicked."

Maddie shook her head. "Why didn't you tell me? Why have we been lying to each *other* all this time?"

She clasped Maddie's hands in her own. "I didn't know we were, dear. For years, I rather thought it was all mutually understood. Sometimes a woman doesn't quite fit in with her expected role. We do what we can to make our own way, carve out a space for ourselves. I thought you were happy here in Scotland, and I encouraged your father to leave you be. But then that enormous, glorious man appeared . . ."

Maddie laughed wryly. "Did he ever."

"And then I didn't know what to think. Perhaps you'd been telling the truth all along. I devised a test or two for him. The poem, the dancing lesson. I tried to make myself available should you need to confide in me. But mostly, I decided . . . you are a woman now. A strong, intelligent woman whom I admire. It wasn't my place to interfere."

Maddie picked at the crocheted edge of her handkerchief. "He's a complete stranger. Can you believe it? My letters were delivered to him somehow, and he knew everything about me. About our family. But I'd never met him before he arrived in the parlor. And now . . ."

"And now you love him. Don't you?"

"I'm afraid I might." Her eyes stung at the corners, and she blinked hard. "But he doesn't love me. Or perhaps he could, but he won't let himself. I don't know what to do. We quarreled terribly after the ball last night. I gave him back the engagement brooch."

"A mere lovers' quarrel, perhaps."

"Is it? I don't know if we're lovers at all. I want to be loved so desperately, I'm afraid I'm just imagining he could love me in return. I'll end up stuck in another lie of my own creation."

Aunt Thea smiled. "After what I put him through in preparation for that ball, he must genuinely care for you. At least a little."

"He's a loyal man. But I . . . I think I've wounded him somehow. Deeply. Perhaps my lies didn't hurt you or the family, but they hurt Logan. I don't understand how or why the silly letters of a sixteen-year-old could have such an effect. But I wish I knew how to make it right."

Even offering her love hadn't been enough. What more could she give him than that?

She stared at the table. "I just feel so twisted up inside, and hopeless."

"I have just the remedy for that condition."

Maddie cringed. There was nothing to ruin a heartfelt moment like one of her aunt's remedies. "Oh, Aunt Thea. In the interests of honesty, I must say . . . I don't know if I can choke down one more of—"

"Don't be silly. It's just this."

Her aunt leaned forward and caught her in a warm, tight hug. It was a hug that smelled like a cosmetics counter, but so welcome nonetheless. They held each other, rocking back and forth.

By the time they pulled apart, Maddie had tears in her eyes.

Aunt Thea cupped her cheeks. "You *are* loved, my precious Madling. You always have been. Once you know and believe that in your heart, everything else will be clear."

Logan kept his distance from Maddie for the next several days. It wasn't easy staying away, but he didn't see that there was anything to be gained from approaching her. She was already on the brink of leaving, and he didn't have anything new to say.

He could only hope that time—or perhaps the lingering threat of those letters—changed her mind.

That seemed even less likely when on the afternoon of Beltane, he found her in the dining hall amid dozens of crates and boxes.

The table was covered with china, silver, glassware, linens, pewter candlesticks. And humbler items, too: pots and kettles, fireplace pokers, candles and small jars of spice.

He asked, "Are you having a tea party?"

"No," Maddie said. "This isn't a tea party. I'm building the men's trousseaux."

"Trousseaux?"

Her brow wrinkled. "*Can* men have trousseaux? I don't rightly know. It doesn't matter. When they move into the new cottages, they will need to set up house. They'll be in need of these items."

"Isn't the castle in need of these items?"

"Not anymore." She packed a pewter jug in straw. "I'm going home to my family. Someone ought to make use of these things."

Logan set his jaw. It rankled him, the calm, matter-of-fact way she spoke of leaving. Not only leaving the castle but leaving him as well.

He followed her as she moved to the other end of the table, counting out equal piles of spoons.

"Do I get a parting gift, too?" he said, no doubt sounding more petulant and transparent than he would have liked. "Perhaps a side table and a pair of candlesticks?"

"Actually, I have something else in mind for you."

"Oh really? What's that?"

Her dark eyes met his. "I want you to have this."

"What, a spoon?"

"No, this." She tilted her head to glance at the vaulted ceiling. "The land. This castle. All of it."

Logan stared at her. What was she saying? "Maddie, you can't mean to—"

"It's already done." She reached toward the center of the table and plucked an envelope from atop a pile of folded tablecloths. "I drew up the papers by copying the documents that transferred the property to me. Becky and Callum signed as witnesses. The news will have spread through the castle by now. By this evening, everyone will know." She handed the envelope to him. "Lannair is yours."

He took the envelope in his hand. He couldn't do anything but stare at it.

"But that bargain you suggested . . . I didna hold up my end."

"The truth is, Logan, it just doesn't belong to me. It never did. I didn't work for it. I have no attachment to the land. This place belongs to the Highlands. To the people who've lived here for generations. To those whose ancestors piled the stones of this castle with their bare hands. And I can't imagine a better person to watch over it."

"I want no charity from you or anyone. I've worked for everything I've ever had."

"Oh, I know that. I know well that accepting this will make you uncomfortable, and that's part of my fun. I'm taking great pleasure in watching you squirm. For me, it's a victory of sorts."

And victory looked well on her.

"So when are you leaving?" he asked.

"Tomorrow. I plan to stay for the feast, of course. And for the bonfire tonight. We've all worked hard on the preparations. Even if I'm no longer the lady of the castle, and even if I won't be your bride . . . I want to be there."

"I want you there, too."

I want you here always.

The words hovered on the tip of his tongue, but he didn't speak them. It was too late. Too useless. In giving him this castle, she'd taken away his last bargaining chip. He didn't have any worldly possessions or influence she hadn't already refused.

Another man might have offered her something from within himself. His heart, perhaps. A certain warmth of emotion. Maybe even a dream. But Logan had forgotten how to dream, if he ever had known how.

And when he looked inside himself, he saw nothing but emptiness and cold.

He lifted the envelope. "Thank you for this."

She nodded. "It's been an honor to know you, Logan. I do hope you'll understand if I don't write."

Chapter Twenty-two

*M*addie found unexpected enjoyment in being a hostess. She found it far easier than being a guest. She was so busy keeping the ale flowing and monitoring the progress of dishes in and out of the kitchen that she could keep to the borders of the hall and duck out for a moment whenever the crowd became too much for her.

Most convenient of all, she scarcely had time to think about Logan. She saw him once or twice in passing. He greeted her with a brusque nod, but she didn't pause to chat.

It seemed entirely likely that she might not speak to him again before she left in the morning.

Just as well. There just didn't seem to be anything left to say.

When afternoon was waning, everyone pushed back

from the tables lining the High Hall and walked, full bellies and all, up to the highest peak overlooking the loch.

As the day faded into twilight, a small group of villagers gathered to make a bonfire. Instead of bringing coal from someone's hearth, they fashioned a crude machine of sort with sticks—almost like a drill. After nearly an hour of the biggest and strongest taking turns with it, a curl of smoke rose from the rubbing wood. A woman hurried forward with a handful of dried moss and wood shavings.

With a bit of patient blowing—and perhaps some cursing and prayer—the small glow became a flame. And with many hands bringing more fuel, the flame became a bonfire.

Whisky was passed around, along with wedges of fruited oatcake. Maddie politely declined the former but happily accepted the latter.

"Be sure it's not the marked one," Rabbie said.

"What do you mean?"

"'Tis tradition. One of the cakes is marked with charcoal. Whoever draws that one, we toss them into the bonfire." He winked.

"What a charming tradition." She inspected her oatcake. "No charcoal."

"Ye'll live to see the next Beltane, then."

A bright, merry fiddling struck up, and when she looked, its source was a shock to her.

"I didn't know Grant played the fiddle."

"Oh, aye," Rabbie said. "He had one that he brought with him on campaign. Hauled it over the Pyrenees and back, but it was ruined in a river crossing. The captain just brought him that one from Inverness the other day."

Maddie nibbled at her oatcake and played a game of peek-a-boo with a little fair-haired girl hiding behind her mother's skirt. After a few rounds of dodge-and-hide, she offered the girl the remainder of her oatcake and received a shy, gap-toothed smile in return. Maddie thought it an excellent trade.

Every once in a while, she saw Logan out of the corner of her eye—usually talking with a farmer or one of his men, or passing another round of whisky. They never made eye contact.

Once she thought she felt the heat of his stare. But when she turned to look, he was nowhere to be found. She supposed she was imagining things. It wouldn't be the first time.

Maddie stood close to the bonfire, hugging her shawl tight about her shoulders and watching couples dance to the music Grant supplied. Judging by the way the men and ladies queued up, the reel didn't seem too different from a traditional English country dance.

As the dancers queued up for a new dance, Callum appeared at her side. "Would you like to join in?"

"Oh, no," she said without thinking.

"Ah. I see. Very well, then."

Something in his disappointed demeanor sparked a realization. She'd been so caught in worrying about herself, she'd misunderstood. Callum hadn't been asking whether or not she enjoyed dancing. He'd been asking her *to* dance.

With him.

And she'd refused him with one word and a shudder. *Really, Maddie.*

"Callum, wait!" She reached out to catch him before he could disappear. "I'm so sorry. I didn't realize you were asking me to dance."

"No matter. You dinna need to explain."

"No, I want to explain. The truth is, I'm honored to be invited to dance. It means a great deal to me. More than you could know." She squeezed his arm. "Thank you."

His eyes warmed with a smile, and the knot in her stomach began to loosen up. As difficult as it was going to be to walk away from Logan, leaving Lannair Castle was going to break what remained of her heart. She would miss her new friends here. So very much.

"The problem is," she told him, "I don't know how to dance."

" 'Tis nothing. The steps are not difficult."

"Perhaps not for most, but I've never danced. I'm afraid I'll be terrible at it."

He held up his pinned, shortened sleeve. "I'm at a disadvantage myself. So if you are terrible, at least we'll be equally matched. Shall we have a go at it anyway? 'Tis only for laughs."

Perhaps it was the heat of the bonfire. Or maybe

she just couldn't bear to disappoint the enthusiastic look in Callum's eyes. It was possible a small part of her hoped Logan might see them and be jealous.

But most likely . . . it was just time to stop standing in the cold. Rabbie had said she'd live to see the next Beltane. But she wouldn't be here in the Highlands. She might only have this one chance to dance a Scottish reel, and it would be a pity to waste the night on nerves and fretting.

Perhaps this was a moment to be seized.

A moment to simply *be*.

For whatever reason, Maddie found herself saying yes. To dancing. For the first time in her life.

And it made her immediately wonder why she hadn't done the same years ago.

Which is not to say that it went especially *well*.

The dance itself was rather a disaster—but an amusing one. The particular reel they'd joined involved a great deal of twirling, and once Maddie started spinning, she had a hard time ceasing. Add in the fact that Callum wasn't in the best position to reach out and catch her, they resembled nothing so much as two billiard balls colliding and spinning away from each other, repeatedly.

Before long Maddie was laughing so hard that she could scarcely catch her breath. At the end of the reel, they were supposed to grab hands—but they missed one another entirely.

She lost her balance and careened away, still twirling and laughing.

Until she collided with someone. Someone helpfully big and solid and impossible to knock over.

"Oh, goodness. I'm so sorry, truly. I—" She looked up. Her stomach sank. "Oh. It's you."

Logan.

"Are you enjoying yourself?"

"I am, quite. Thank you for asking."

Suddenly she was every bit as nervous with him as she would have been at sixteen. Who could help it?

Tonight he carried with him a new air of . . . not swagger. Swagger was nothing more than bluster arranged to mask uncertainty. Tonight, he looked confident. Protective. Ready to lead.

Lairdly, in the truest sense of the word.

Dressed in his full great kilt and a crisp ivory shirt, he also looked ready to pose for an illustration in Sir Walter Scott's next novel.

The dance ended, and Callum came to find her. He gave Maddie a grin. "Sorry to have stolen you from her, Captain."

"No need to apologize," Logan replied. "Madeline belongs to herself."

"We were just dancing," she said.

"I saw."

"Not very well."

His mouth quirked. "I saw that, too."

"Yes. Well. I'm sorry to have collided with you. It's just so dark."

She looked around, desperate to avoid the confusing look in his eyes. There were no other lights, anywhere. Not at the castle, not at the *baile* on the riverbank.

The world had collapsed to the orange-red glow of the bonfire and the vast, starry sky above.

"'Tis the tradition," Callum said helpfully. "On Beltane, we douse all the fires in every home. At the end of the night, each family will take coals or a torch and relight their hearth from this bonfire. 'Tis a fresh start."

"A fresh start. What a lovely thought."

It helped her understand why Logan had been so determined to have the land in his ownership before Beltane—he wanted his men and the tenants to know this was a fresh start.

It also made her wonder what she and Logan could be to each other if only they could make a fresh start of their own.

He was a good man. Caring, protective, intelligent, loyal.

And on a shallow level, so attractive.

Maddie was going to forever regret not having made love to him. At least Aunt Thea had been properly ruined by the Comte de Montclair. Feathers and all.

But it was no use pining after what couldn't be.

Logan didn't love her. He *couldn't* love her. Some other woman had gotten to him first and left him ruined for all others.

She hoped this A.D., whoever and wherever she was,

properly appreciated what she'd missed. Maddie hoped the woman rued her mistake daily. Maddie was also not above wishing her to be a frequent sufferer of boils.

"What was that?" Logan asked.

Had she spoken aloud? "Oh. Nothing."

A woman cloaked in a traditional arisaid approached them. She began speaking to Logan in fervent Gaelic, and before Maddie knew what was happening, the woman had placed an infant in her arms.

Wonderful. This was exactly what her heart didn't need right now.

She started hoping that the infant would squall or soil its clout or vomit up soured milk. Something, anything to stop her womb from turning these frantic *use-me* cartwheels.

But the babe refused to be anything less than entirely adorable. He was an angelic little bundle in Maddie's arms, swaddled in a length of cozy flannel.

Meanwhile, the babe's mother thanked Logan—even without knowing the language, Maddie could recognize the look of gratitude, and Callum translated the rest. The young woman had been recently widowed, and she had thought she would be forced to leave Scotland. Apparently Logan had engaged her services to do laundry and cook for the men while they completed their new cottages. She and her son would be able to stay.

Maddie's heart wrenched. She stared down at the little bundle, who cooed and waved his tiny fists.

A bright something winked at her from the child's bunting, and Maddie peered at it.

"He's wearing a luckenbooth." She showed Callum. "But surely he's a bit young to be engaged. And I thought those were for lasses."

"He's not engaged." Callum tickled the little one's cheek. "'Tis the custom. A man gives the luckenbooth to his bride on their betrothal, and then 'tis placed on the bunting of the couple's firstborn child. People believed it wards off evil."

"How interesting. So that means these markings here . . ." Maddie fingered the tiny markings scratched on the heart-shaped brooch. "They're not the child's initials."

"No, no. Those would be his mother and father's."

"I see."

She stared down at the babe in arms, and that heart of gold that flickered in the light of the bonfire.

L.M. and A.D.

The world slowed down. Her heartbeats thumped singly in her ears.

Did you love her?

As much as I knew how. It wasn't enough.

So she left you.

Yes.

A clever woman, then.

Maddie cringed at the memory. Oh, good Lord. If her suspicions were correct . . .

The widowed woman had joined in the dance,

and Logan had moved away. When Maddie looked up, she locked gazes with him over the bonfire. His eyes narrowed, intent and searching. The red firelight played over his furrowed brow.

He seemed to know something had changed.

"Callum," she said, swallowing a lump in her throat, "does the word *nah-tray-me* mean anything to you?"

He tilted his head. "*Na tréig mi*, do you mean? 'Tis not a word, it's a phrase."

"What does it mean?"

"It means, 'dinna leave me.' Why do you ask?"

She tried to hide the sudden catch in her voice. "No reason."

No reason. Except that everything makes sense now, and I realize I've been a complete and utter fool.

"I have to do something. Can you take him?" She turned to place the child in Callum's arms.

"No, no. Hold a moment. Me?" He stepped back, waving his amputated arm. "I canna take him with one arm."

"Of course you can. Mothers do it all the time." She tucked the babe into the crook of his full arm, making sure his hand supported the infant's bottom. "There now. Someday you'll hold your own child the same way."

On impulse, she kissed both Callum and baby on the forehead.

Then she turned back to look for Logan, searching the crowd.

He wasn't there.

Chapter Twenty-three

*L*ogan walked away from the bonfire with long, purposeful strides.

But he apparently didn't walk fast enough.

"Logan, wait."

He didn't slow his pace. He couldn't talk to her. Not right now, after watching her rock that babe in her arms and dance with Callum. After feeling her body against his, even for that short moment.

She'd made her choices, and so had he. He could bear to part ways with her tomorrow. But if she came anywhere near him tonight, he'd be sure to pull her close and do something they'd both regret.

"Go back to the fire," he told her. "It's too dark. No lights at the castle to guide your way. You'll stumble. There might be bogs."

"*Na tréig mi.*"

The words stopped him in his tracks. His heart stopped for a moment, too.

He kept his voice calm. "You're learning Gaelic now?"

"I'm learning *you* now. Finally."

What the devil did that mean?

She caught up with him. From what he could make out under the silver moonlight, she looked angry.

Good. It was safer that way.

"You lied to me, Logan."

"I didna lie to you."

"You let me continue under a false assumption. That luckenbooth. You didn't have it made for another woman. Did you?"

"This again? I've told you, she means nothing to me. Not anymore."

"Now that is a lie." She drew nearer. "The baby I was holding by the fire had a luckenbooth pinned to his bunting. Callum explained everything. The L.M. on that brooch wasn't yours, was it? They were your father's initials. You were named for him. And A.D. . . . Oh, Logan. Your *mother*. What was her name?"

He exhaled slowly. "I dinna rightly know. I wasna old enough to remember."

"I'm so sorry. Why didn't you tell me the truth? I

would have been proud to wear it had I known. Did you just enjoy making me envious?"

Envious. The word made no sense to him.

"Why the devil would you be envious?"

"Because," she cried, throwing up her hands, "I thought some bonny Scottish lass had stolen your heart and broken it. Of course I was eaten alive with envy. I wanted your heart for myself."

"I told you, I can't give you that."

"Yes. You told me. And you lied then, too."

She drew close enough to lay a touch to his arm. Just the lightest brush of her fingertips on his sleeve. It electrified him.

"I know how much you care for those men," she said. "I know how tender you can be, how gentle and protective. I know how you tended to me in Inverness. How you stood up for me at the ball . . ."

He grabbed her by the arms and forced her away. "I know how *you* are. You're overimaginative. You make too much of things. You lie to yourself. I should have thought you'd learned your lesson by now."

He walked away, and once again, she followed.

"Are you ever going to stop punishing me? When I lied and wrote those letters, I was young and stupid and selfish and wrong. I deceived everyone. I unknowingly made you my accomplice. It was wrong of me. I know that, and I'm so sor—" Her voice broke off. "I can't say I'm sorry. I'm *not* sorry."

"Of course you're not sorry. Why should you be sorry? You were given a castle and an independent life."

She hurried in front of him, blocking his path. "I found *you*."

"You left me for dead."

There it was. The seed of all his anger, raw and pulsing like an exposed wound.

"And it wasn't the first time you were left for dead. Was it?"

He didn't answer her. He couldn't.

"*Na tréig mi*," she whispered. "Don't leave me. Do you know you say that in your sleep?"

"I don't—"

"You do. *Na tréig mi, na tréig mi*. Over and over, while shivering." She slapped a hand to her brow. "I don't know how I didn't see it before. It explains everything. Your mother wrapped you in a plaid, pinned the luckenbooth on to keep evil away . . . and then she abandoned you."

"Yes. Yes, all right? That's exactly what she did, and 'twas on a hillside not much different from the one we're standing on now."

"Which means you weren't an infant. You were old enough to remember." She hugged herself. "Oh, Logan. The things I said . . . that she must have been a clever woman if she left you. You must know I didn't mean it that way. I'm so sorry. So sorry for what happened."

"Sorry for what happened? Don't be sorry for what happened. Be sorry for what you did."

"What did I do?"

He moved back, taking time to breathe and walk a slow circle. He was angry now. Not only with her. But partly with her. He'd been angry with Madeline Gracechurch for a long, long time. And since she'd asked, he was going to let her have it.

Here, in the dark.

"Do you want to hear something verra amusing?"

"I don't suppose it's a joke that ends with 'Squeal louder, lass. Squeal louder.'"

"Oh, far better than that. When your first letter reached me, I wasn't a captain. I was a private. Lowest rank in the army. Undisciplined, uninterested. Too poor to afford shoes. Here came this letter to Captain Logan MacKenzie. What a joke. They teased that I must have chatted up a girl before leaving, made myself out to be more than I was." He pushed a hand through his hair. "Before long, they were calling me 'captain' whenever my back was turned. My sergeant had me whipped for putting on airs."

"And you blamed me."

"Of course I blamed you. You were to blame. I'd read your letters. I knew they were nothing but fancies for a spoiled English debutante who didna fancy a turn about Almack's that season. But the letters kept coming. The mockery, too. And after a while, I started to wonder . . . could I not make captain? That would show them all."

"That sounds very like you. Ambitious. Determined."

He snorted. "It was absurd. Do you have any idea what a stupid notion it is for an enlisted private with no money and even fewer connections to set his sights on making captain?"

"But you did it."

"Aye. I did it. It took me four years, but I did it, one promotion and field commission at a time. The address on the envelope became the truth. The men's teasing became respect. And the letters inside, they were changing, too. They were . . . kinder. Thoughtful. Bloody odd, but thoughtful. You sent me news of wee Henry and Emma. Here were children praying for me every night, as though I were part of their family. You canna understand, Maddie. I spent my youth in the byres, or huddled beneath my tattered plaid on the ground. I'd never had that. Never in all my life. I felt like a fool for it. But I started to pray for them, too."

"Logan . . ."

"And then there was you. This strange, sweet woman that wouldna recognize me in the street but told me all her secrets—and made more of me than I could have made of myself. Someone who was dreaming of me, wishing to hold me in her arms.

It felt . . ." His voice caught. "It felt as if I'd tugged on a loose thread of God's tartan, and a world away, someone tugged back. What was lies and foolishness to you was more than that to me. Your letters gave me the dream I didn't know how to imagine for myself. They brought me to life. And then you left me for dead."

Maddie pressed a hand to her mouth. "Logan, I'm so sorry. I cared for you. What you felt . . . I felt it, too. I never would have kept writing for so long otherwise. I knew it was real somehow."

"Dinna say that." He seized her by the arms and gave her a little shake. "Dinna tell me I was real to you and then you walked away to never think of me again. That only makes it worse."

"Then tell me how to make it better."

"It's no use." He shook his head. "There's nothing you could say."

She touched her hand to his cheek. "Not even I love you?"

The words rocked him. He refused to let her see.

"No. I dinna want to hear that."

"Well, I want to say it. Now, when there are no obligations. No threats hanging over my head. No lies to protect. I love you, Logan. Somehow . . . It began before I knew you."

"That doesna make any sense."

"I know it doesn't." She smiled. "But it's true."

"No." He caught her face in his hands and held her tight. "It isna true, and you know it. I've had enough of falsehoods."

"I love you, Logan. That's not a lie."

He clenched his jaw. "Those words are always a lie."

Perhaps those words weren't false for everyone. But they were always a lie when spoken to him. Everyone who'd ever claimed to love him had deserted him. Disclaimed him. Left him for dead.

And she was no different. She'd given him a false demise on the battlefield, and when he'd forced his way back into her life, she'd found another way to worm out of his grasp.

Right this moment, her trunks were packed. She was planning to leave him in the morning.

And now she dared to chase after him and tell him this?

He bent his head and pressed his brow to hers. "Stop."

"You don't think I've tried stopping? For that matter, I tried mightily not to start in the first place. Neither strategy succeeded." Her fingertips grazed his jawline. "I can't help it. And I can't deny it any longer. I love you. Whether anything comes of it or not, I want you to know."

He would not let those words into his heart. He would not believe them.

But he would use them to his advantage, any way he could.

She kissed his mouth, so softly. Then his cheek. Then his temple.

"Remember the first night we made love?" she whispered, sliding her arms around his waist. "It was Beltane. Everyone was gathered around the bonfire, and we slipped away in secret."

"Aye." The word slipped out as a moan. He could feel himself giving in to the sweet warmth of her. "I remember."

"Remind me what happened next. Did we spread your plaid on the heather and make love beneath the stars?"

He shook his head, nuzzling her throat. "We almost did. It was tempting. But I wanted our first time to be in a proper bed."

"Oh, that's right. I recall it now."

She stared up at him, waiting.

Enough with teasing. He needed to know.

Logan made his voice grave. He framed her face in his hands and gave her a mild shake to be sure she was paying attention. "If you dinna want this, tell me now. I know you're curious. I know you have desires. And if a bit of exploration's all you're after, there's no shame in that. But that's not what will happen if we do this tonight."

Her lips parted, but she didn't speak.

"I mean to make you mine, *mo chridhe*. Touch all of you. Taste all of you. Learn you from the inside out. Once I've held you like that, I'm not going to let go. Ever."

And in response, she spoke a single word:

"Good."

Very well. He'd tried to warn her. He'd given her every chance to demur. She'd asked for this.

He did what he'd been threatening to do since the very first night. He picked her up and slung her over his shoulder like a sack of oats.

And carried his bride home.

To bed.

It might have seemed strange, Maddie supposed, for a woman who was currently slung over a Scotsman's shoulder with her hair and feet dangling in the night wind to claim that moment as any sort of triumph.

But victory was exactly what she felt.

At last, she was getting the man of her dreams. On her own terms. And unless her Highland lover meant to expose himself as a shameless liar . . .

Tonight was going to be verra, verra, *verra* good.

The castle was completely dark. Every fire had been extinguished. Moonlight got them as far as the courtyard, then Logan was forced to set her down. They gathered a candle and flint from the table in the entry hall and, after a bit of cursing and fumbling in the dark, managed to light it.

The small yellow light glowed like a promise.

It wasn't a spark carried home from the bonfire, but it was one they'd created themselves.

A new flame. A fresh start. Nothing in the past mattered any longer. There was only the future now.

And the future was theirs for the taking.

Maddie placed the candle in a holder, and together they climbed the stairs to her bedchamber.

Their bedchamber.

Her heart began to pound harder with every step. She closed the door behind them and turned the key in the lock.

Then she found herself pinned against the door.

He caged her there with his body, using one hand to wind her loosened hair around his fist, pulling it up and away. Then his mouth, hot and hungry, descended on her neck.

She gasped with the sweet shock of it. The firm tug on a thousand nerve endings. His tongue, running from her collarbone to her ear.

Her knees wobbled.

She braced her arm against the door.

She slumped forward there, helpless to move as he covered every inch of her neck with kisses and possessive sweeps of his tongue. The rasp of stubble scraped against her skin, adding a deliciously sharp contrast to the soft heat of his mouth.

Soon her whole body felt aflame. Beneath her bodice, her nipples pressed to hard points, craving touch. Craving his mouth. And his kisses kindled a low, hollow ache between her thighs.

She'd been biting her lip to keep from crying out. But when he reached to cup her breast, she couldn't hold back any longer. She abandoned that last shred of self-consciousness and moaned with pleasure.

The sound only seemed to encourage him. He responded with a low groan of his own.

His free arm slid around her waist, and he gathered her close. His erection pressed against the small of her back. Impressively hot and rigid, even through the layers of chemise, corset, frock, and heavy kilt.

He kissed her ear now, tracing the ridges with his tongue and catching the nub of her earlobe between his teeth. His thumb found her nipple, and he rubbed it back and forth. Just lightly teasing. The torture was exquisite.

"Logan. Please."

She tried to turn to face him. He put his hand on her waist, forbidding it.

"Not just yet."

"But . . . when?"

"Soon, *mo chridhe*. Soon."

His hands went to the closures of her frock. He fumbled and cursed as he yanked them free. His difficulty with the buttons let her know he wasn't quite as collected and in control as he would have her believe.

He was every bit as eager as she was. Perhaps even anxious.

Desperate.

When he'd loosed the hooks and buttons and laces sufficiently to allow her frock to slide to the waist, he spun her around to face him, pressing her to the door once again as he took her mouth in a possessive kiss. His hands tugged at her frock and her stays. She tried to help as best she could, pulling her arms free and then getting them out of the way by lacing her hands behind his neck.

He cupped her bared breast in one hand, lifting and kneading. She sifted her fingers through his soft, heavy hair as they kissed. He moaned against her mouth, and she tasted the lingering fire of whisky and his own unique, elusive sweetness. He kept that sweetness hidden from the world, but she knew how to draw it out.

She savored it.

Impatient, she began to tug at the fabric of his shirt, pulling it loose from the belted waist of his kilt and gathering it in rough handfuls. When she'd managed to work the hem high enough, he broke their kiss long enough for her to yank the garment over his head and toss it aside.

And when they kissed again, his bared chest met hers for the first time.

The sensation was bone-melting in its intensity.

All that skin on skin. Heat on heat. His solid muscles shaped her softness. The light hairs on his chest teased her nipples.

His heart pounded against hers.

"Lift your skirts," he muttered, sliding his tongue down her neck.

Merciful heavens.

Given her choice of any three words to hear from Logan's lips, Maddie probably would have chosen *I love you*. But she had to admit, *Lift your skirts* had an undeniable appeal.

Her softest, most secret parts quivered.

She obeyed, gathering the silk in rough handfuls and hiking it until the hem reached her knees.

His hands slid to her backside, and he lifted her off the ground and against the door, wedging his hips between her thighs and locking her stockinged legs around his waist.

She gave a little shriek of laughter.

Then his mouth found her nipple, and her laughter became a languid sigh.

The rough surface of the door scraped against her bare back, but she couldn't be bothered to care. His lips and tongue were working magic on her breasts, and the hard ridge of his arousal was just where she wanted it. He rolled his hips, and a pure, bright joy swept through her. She let her head fall to the side and clung to him, riding the waves of bliss.

After he'd treated each of her breasts to a through pleasuring, he gathered her to him and turned her away from the door, carrying her toward the bed.

"Be careful," she whispered, still gasping and giggling. "It's so dark. It would be a shame if you—"

Thunk.

He bashed his head against the overhanging part of the bedframe.

He cursed. Together they tumbled to the mattress. Maddie scrambled to assess his wounds.

She pushed the hair back from his brow, skimming her fingertips over his temple and crown. "Are you all right? Are you bleeding? Do we need to stop?"

He didn't answer right away.

She caressed his scalp again. "Logan?"

"I'm fine, *mo chridhe*. I'd have bashed my head like that days ago if I knew you'd touch me like this." He reached for her hand and brought it to his lips, kissing first the backs of her fingers.

Then her palm.

Then that sensitive bracelet of flesh at her wrist.

And from that moment on, everything between them was a little less frantic and a great deal more tender. As he moved above her, rolling the stockings down her legs and helping her free of her gown, she felt treasured. Precious.

Loved.

Once she was bared, he laid her flat on the bed and began to caress her everywhere. His palms swept over her breasts, her legs, her hips, her belly.

Her own fingers itched for their turn.

She wanted to touch him.

In all their previous encounters, Logan had been very much in control. He'd decided when and where to touch her. Or even when and where she should touch herself. This time, Maddie was determined to be an equal participant. Even if she felt timid or unsure, she wouldn't allow herself to be deterred. Not if she knew what she wanted, and she did.

She went straight for the kilt.

He helped her with the fastenings in front, and then the heavy pleats of plaid fell slack. Pushing the fabric aside, she reached eagerly for the man beneath.

And she didn't have to search long to find him.

His erection all but sprang into her hand, filling her grip with hard, heated flesh. She stroked up and down his length the way she'd watched him stroke himself that night, and he groaned with helpless pleasure. His skin was softer than she'd imagined it could be. Like ridged velvet. She circled her thumb around the broad, smooth crown, then stretched her fingertips to explore the thick root of his cock and the vulnerable sac beneath.

She was just beginning to enjoy herself, when Logan pulled her hand away.

"That'll have to be enough for now, *mo chridhe*. Or this will be over before it starts."

"But—"

"Later." He caught her hands in his and pushed back, pinning her arms against the mattress on either side of her head. "I canna risk unmanning myself. I've waited too long for this." He lavished kisses along her neck. "Days. Weeks. Years."

Holding her arms pinned to the mattress, he licked and kissed his way down the center of her body. When he reached her navel, he paused.

"I mean to taste you, *mo chridhe*. Try not to kick me in the head this time."

Despite the warning, her hips still bucked when he laid his tongue to her most intimate place.

Oh, he was good.

Verra . . . verra . . . *verra* good. Within moments, he had her writhing beneath him. He explored every fold and hollow with his tongue, circling her bud before sliding down to dip his tongue inside her.

"Logan, please. I'm too close to—"

He showed no signs of stopping. Or even acknowledging her pleas. To the contrary, he redoubled his efforts, nuzzling and licking her to a fierce, sudden climax.

"That's unfair," she pouted between labored breaths. "You wouldn't even let me touch you."

He released her arms and sat back on his haunches.

"It's better this way. The joining will go easier for you if you've already found your peak." He caressed her cheek. "I've no wish to hurt you."

As he settled himself between her thighs, she slid her hands up his bare arms, enjoying the contours of his strength.

"Ready?" he asked, positioning himself on his elbows.

"Yes."

Yes.

When he pushed inside her, it did hurt. Maddie had to bite her lip to keep from crying out. He nudged deeper in patient strokes, and she felt her body slowly stretching to accommodate his.

When at last he was fully seated within her, he remained motionless for a long moment. Just holding her, as she held him. Her body began to relax.

"Are you well?" he asked.

She nodded.

He carefully withdrew a fraction, then pushed back in, reaching a new depth within her. They both groaned.

"You're so tight," he murmured, sounding concerned.

"I think it's more that you're so big," she said. "But you don't need to worry. I'm fine."

He went slowly at first.

But slowly didn't last long. Soon a more urgent rhythm took hold as his thrusts increased in both speed and intensity.

The force of his passion took her breath away, but Maddie would be damned before she'd ask him to stop. She loved feeling just how much he wanted her, just how desperately his body needed hers to be complete.

He began to murmur words she didn't understand. Little sweet promises in Gaelic, or so she flattered herself to think. Even though she couldn't decipher their meaning, there was no mistaking the tone in his voice. It was one of raw emotion. She was certain she heard a few familiar phrases in the mix:

Maddie.

Mo chridhe.

Na tréig mi.

She wrapped her legs around his hips and clung to his shoulders, holding him as tight as she could.

Then he reached a point where there were no more words. He braced himself on one elbow and slipped the other arm beneath her waist, drawing her body tight against his. When he thrust, his cock reached a place so deep inside her that she felt him *everywhere*.

After a few final thrusts, he shuddered and groaned. He slumped atop her and buried his face in her neck. She put her arms around his shoulders, hugging him close.

They lay there together, just breathing.

Her heart had never been so full.

All too soon, she began to hear noises from the lower floors of the tower. The men and the servants were returning from the bonfire.

"Perhaps I should go down to meet them." She started to rise from bed.

"No, no. Where do you think you're going, Mrs. MacHasty?" He grabbed her arm and pulled.

She laughed as she tumbled back to the bed. "What did you call me?"

"I believe . . ." He rolled to face her and gazed at her wonderingly. "I called you my wife."

"Are we fully married this time?"

"Of course we're married."

She raised an eyebrow. "You're verra, verra sure?"

"We've just consummated the relationship, Maddie. I warned you, once I held you this way . . ." His eyes grew intense. "You can't ask me to let you go."

"Oh, Logan. I'm not asking that. I want to be your

wife. More than anything. I was only teasing when I asked if you were sure." She brushed the hair back from his brow. "I'm so sorry."

His stormy expression didn't clear.

She skimmed a touch down his bare chest, nestling close. "Believe me, there's nowhere I'd rather be than here. With you."

The men downstairs would have to fend for themselves.

She pressed a kiss to the underside of his jaw, then slid her tongue down his neck, willing the corded tendon there to relax.

It had been thoughtless of her to tease him that way, knowing what she knew now about his childhood. It might be months, even years, before those nightmares ceased and he stopped worrying she'd abandon him the moment he gave her the chance.

Tomorrow she would commence finding other ways to reassure him.

For tonight, she hoped kisses would make a good start.

Chapter Twenty-four

$\mathcal{I}$n the morning, Logan woke alone. He knew a moment of bleary-eyed, unreasoned panic—until he found a note on the pillow beside him.

My dearest Captain MacSleepy,

Forgive me. I didn't want to disturb your well-earned rest. When you wake, your breakfast will be waiting downstairs.

   Your loving wife

Wearing a shirt, loose trousers, and an unabashed grin, he entered the hall. His men sat assembled about the long table.

Logan cleared his throat. "Good morning."

All heads swiveled to face him. They regarded him in silence for a moment. And then, to a one, they rose to their feet and broke out in spontaneous applause.

"Huzzah."

"At last!"

"Take a bow, then."

Logan waved off the teasing, but he couldn't bring himself to put a stop to the merriment. He knew this was a landmark of sorts for them, too.

Lannair was truly home now. For all of them. That was something to celebrate.

He looked around the High Hall with a new perspective, noting any crack in the plaster that needed patching, any bit of paneling that had dulled with time. The men were well on the way to completing their own cottages. Starting today, Logan could turn his attention to making this castle a home.

He would have to do something about those steep stairs before any bairns came along.

The mere thought of fatherhood was dizzying, in all the best and worst ways.

"Took you long enough, but I expect it was worth the wait." Rabbie came forward and punched him on the shoulder. "Good work, Captain. And not a moment too soon. After last night, Callum has his eye on one of the village lasses. Now he can court her proper."

Callum's face colored. "I'm not courting any lasses."

"I saw how you looked at her all saft-eyed. I give it a week."

Logan had endured the ribbing with good humor, but he couldn't ignore the gnawing worry in his gut for long.

"Have you seen my wife?" he asked.

"Mrs. MacKenzie's in the kitchen." Munro threw him a wink before settling back to the plans.

The kitchen?

Bemused, Logan made his way down to the castle's ancient kitchen, with its lofty ceilings and massive hearth.

Even before he'd entered the room, a familiar scent assaulted him—a sharp, metallic tang. He rounded the doorway to find a scene that stopped him cold.

Maddie stood in the center of the room, wearing a woeful expression and an apron smeared with blood.

"Good God. Maddie, are you—"

"I'm fine!" she hastened to assure him. "None of it's mine. I'm fine."

"What the devil happened? Has someone been murdered?"

"No." With her wrist, she wiped her brow and then dislodged a stubborn lock of hair with a huff of breath. "I'm making haggis. Grant's helping."

She tilted her head toward the corner, where the big man sat chopping onions and mumbling to himself.

After a stunned pause, Logan broke out laughing. She was making haggis, of all things? It seemed the most adorable confession in the world.

"I know, it's the most absurd thing I've ever done. And when it comes to me, that's saying something. But I gave Cook and Becky the day off, after all their hard work yesterday. I found a recipe book, and I thought I could fill in, since my aunt left this morning."

"Aunt Thea left?"

She nodded. "The carriage was already readied and packed, so I asked her to go ahead. She's going to break the news of our marriage to my father and invite them all for a late-summer holiday. It's been far too long since we were all together, and now there's nothing to keep us apart. I can't wait for Emma and Henry to meet you."

Logan found himself eager for that to happen, too.

She smeared a red fingerprint on the page of the recipe book. "Do you have any idea what's *in* this?"

He nodded. "Sheep's heart, lungs, and liver, all stuffed in its stomach . . . plus oats, and a bit of gravy."

She gave him a blank look. "And yet you still eat it."

"As often as I can get it." He peered into the pot at the lumpy, misshapen haggis. "This doesna look half bad."

"Truly?"

"Let's have a look at your tatties, then."

She blushed and crossed her arms over her chest. "What? Now? Here?"

"Not those. Your tatties. The potatoes, *mo chridhe*."

"Oh." She bit her lip. "I did think it was a bit early in the day for all that."

He caught the back of her apron and gave her a wicked look. "Trust me, it's never too early in the day for all that."

As she reached for the potatoes, she fumbled one in her slippery fingers. It squirted out of her hands and nearly hit him in the head. Only his quick reflexes saved him.

"Oh! Sorry."

"Let's have you out of the kitchen before someone gets hurt." He unlaced the apron tied at the back of her waist and pulled it over her head. Then he picked up a towel, moistened it with water, and wiped her hands clean, one delicate finger at a time. "I canna fathom what possessed you to take this on this morning."

"Can't you?" She looked up at him with a baleful smile. "I was excited about being Mrs. MacKenzie. Eager to slip into the role. But I don't know that I'll ever make a proper Highland bride."

Logan cupped her cheek in his hand. He was on the verge of telling her she was the only wife he could ever want, proper Highland bride or no. But the words stuck in his throat just long enough for an explosive clatter to preempt them.

Bang.

Maddie gave a little cry of alarm and shrank close to him.

"Calm yourself, *mo chridhe*. It's only the haggis that's exploded."

"I made an exploding haggis? Oh, Lord."

He looked into the pot and tsked at the ruined pudding. "Before you put it in to boil, you need to give it a prick with a—"

A savage roar echoed through the vaulted kitchen. Logan dropped the pot lid and wheeled around.

Jesus.

Grant had risen from the seat where he'd been chopping onions. The explosion must have startled him. He looked more wild-eyed and terrified than Logan had seen him in months.

But one thing was different.

This time, Grant was holding Maddie. He had her wrapped in one arm, and with the other hand he held the kitchen knife to her throat.

"Where are we?" he asked. "What's happened? What's this place? Where are my bairns?"

Logan caught Maddie's eye.

"I'm all right," she said softly. "I'm not afraid. He doesn't want to hurt me. He's only confused."

Logan wished he could feel so certain of that. Between the explosion and the smell of blood hanging in the room, he could only imagine the hellish places Grant's mind might have taken him to, or what kind of enemy he might believe Maddie to be.

"Easy, Grant," he said. "You're home in Scotland. The war's over."

"No." He swung his head back and forth. "No, no, no. Dinna give me that tale, Captain. Not again. Day after day it's the same. We'll go to Ross-shire tomorrow, you tell me. Always tomorrow, never today."

Logan swallowed a curse. Of all the times for Grant to stitch together a few pieces of his shredded memory. "Easy, *mo charaid*. Let's just calm ourselves, and sit down to a nice glass of—"

"I want to know now!" Grant shouted, holding the blade's edge to Maddie's pale throat. "You tell me the truth, MacKenzie."

"First, let the lass go. She doesna know anything." Logan moved toward him, open hands raised. "I'll tell you the truth, but you must let her go."

Grant shook his head, keeping Maddie in a tight grip. "Where are they? I want my children. My family. I want the truth."

"Just tell him," Maddie whispered. "Please."

Logan steeled himself and looked his friend in the eye. "They're dead. They're all dead."

"That's a lie."

"No. We went there together, months ago. The

wee ones perished of typhus a good year back. What remained of the village had been evicted. The houses were all burned out, and the survivors had been sent to Canada. Their ship sank in rough seas. There's nothing left."

"No." Grant pressed the knife to Maddie's throat. "No, you're playing me false. I'd remember that."

"You saw their graves, *mo charaid*. To the side of the old kirk, beneath the rowan tree. I stood by your side as you wept and prayed for them."

Grant's face contorted with anguish. The big man sobbed, and his grip on Maddie went slack.

Logan made eye contact with her. "Go. *Now*."

She ducked under Grant's arm and escaped to the side of the room.

Before Grant could reach for her, Logan stepped in his way. "I'm the one you're angry with. Turn the knife on me."

The big man gave an inhuman howl and did just that, charging forward and swinging the kitchen blade in a wide arc. Logan ducked fast enough to put himself out of harm's way, but he heard the swish of steel pass all too close to his ear.

"Logan!" Maddie cried.

Then Grant changed direction, charging again. Logan scrambled backward over the table, putting a barrier between them. They circled round it as Grant chased and Logan stayed on retreat.

Logan kept his voice even. "Madeline, leave the room."

"No."

"I said *go*, Maddie."

"I'm not leaving you alone with him. Not like this." Out of the corner of his eye, Logan saw her reach for an oversized wooden spurtle and lift it like a cricket bat.

Then his attention swung back to Grant.

From the other side of the table, the battered soldier leveled the knife with a trembling hand. "What's happened to my mind, Captain? I canna hold onto the days. They slip through my fingers. The last thing I properly recall, we were on the battlefield."

"It was a mortar at Quatre-Bras."

"My head was ringing. It's still ringing. All the time, the ringing. The blood." He struck himself with an open palm to the temple. "I told you to leave me. You should have left me."

"I—"

"You should have left me to die. Then I'd be with them now, not stuck in this hell. Feeling them die again and again. This is your fault."

"I couldna leave you, *mo charaid*. We're brothers. Kin. *Muinntir*. We dinna leave one another behind."

Grant's voice became a roar. "I told you . . . to leave me. Why did you not leave me?"

With his free arm, Grant lifted the short end of the table and overturned it, rushing forward. Logan was swept up in the momentum and smashed against the stone wall. He felt the swift burn of the blade slashing his flesh, but he couldn't let it slow him down. Gathering his strength, he caught Grant by the shoulders and shoved him back.

The big man tripped over the upturned table leg, and together they tumbled to the floor. Logan had the advantage now. He straddled Grant's torso, pinning his arms at his side. Holding him still.

"Breathe, *mo charaid*. Just breathe."

He held his friend there, immobile, until a familiar cloudiness overtook his eyes.

And then, just as he had a thousand times since that mortar blast, Grant startled back to life.

"What's all this, Captain? Where are we?"

Logan almost choked on a wave of relief. "The war's over, Grant. We're home in Scotland. Safe."

"Oh. Well, that's bonny."

"Aye. So it is." Panting, Logan moved to the side. When he moved to stand, he winced at the pain in his chest. He'd likely broken a few ribs when Grant had smashed him against the wall.

He turned, seeking Maddie. There she was, holding the spurtle like a weapon. Fully prepared to bludgeon her favorite person on Logan's behalf.

Sweet lass.

"Be easy," he told her. "All's well now."

She lowered the spurtle, but her face remained pale and wary. "Logan, you should be seated."

"I'm fine. Just a bit shaken up." He winced. "I might have a broken rib or two. Nothing that willna mend."

"Logan, please. Sit down at once."

Her voice was so cold and serious.

Even Grant kept staring at him.

"What is it?" he asked. "Have I grown a second head?"

Then again, it wasn't his head that seemed to be holding them rapt but something several feet lower. He followed Maddie's gaze downward.

Ah. So that's what had her so concerned. Grant's knife was embedded in his thigh. To the hilt.

Strange, that. He had been so focused on the ache in his ribs that he hadn't even noticed.

He stared down at it, feeling like a detached observer of his own body. When he spoke, his voice sounded distant to his own ears. "I expect Munro will want a look at that."

He blinked. Twice.

And then the world went dark.

Chapter Twenty-five

*L*ogan!"

Maddie wasn't prepared to catch six feet and fourteen stone of Scotsman, but she did her best, lunging to reach his side before he could fall.

She helped him slide to the floor, all the while being mindful of the knife. She didn't want to jar it and injure him further.

Once he'd lain down on the floor, his head in her lap, she tried to better assess his injury. She pulled aside a fold of his kilt.

Oh, Lord.

The wound might have worried her less if it had been bleeding more. But this was no superficial slash. The entirety of the five-inch blade had been buried in his thigh.

To the hilt.

And if not for Logan, that same blade could have been buried in her throat.

"Logan. Logan, can you hear me?"

His eyelids fluttered. "*Mo chridhe*?"

"Yes. Yes, Logan. It's me." She pushed the hair from his brow. "Be still, my love. We're going to have you mended in no time."

Then his eyes rolled back in his head, and his grip on her hand went slack.

Oh, Lord. Oh, Lord.

She found his pulse with her fingertips. So long as that beat kept pounding, she could tell herself everything would be fine.

"What's happened?" Grant came to sit beside her, now oblivious to the mayhem he'd caused. "The captain's been hurt?"

"He'll be fine," Maddie said, needing to convince herself as much as she needed to convince him. "Don't worry, Grant. He'll be just fine."

"He's come through worse, the rogue." He smiled a bit, then looked up at her. "Who are you then?"

"I'm Madeline. The sweetheart who sent him letters, you recall? Now I'm his wife. I'm . . ." A hot tear spilled down her cheek. "I'm Mrs. MacKenzie."

She only wished Logan could hear her say it.

Grant looked from her to Logan and back. He chuckled and nudged Logan in the shoulder. "MacKenzie, you lucky bastard."

The other men came rushing in, no doubt drawn by the clamor of the table overturning.

"Help him, please," Maddie said, seeking out the field surgeon. "He's hurt."

Munro knelt at her side.

"I won't know how bad it is until I remove the knife. And I canna remove the knife until I know he'll stay immobile. He has a few cracked ribs. Too much thrashing about, and one of those broken ends could puncture his lung." He looked to Maddie. "Do you have any opiates in the house?"

She nodded. "I'm sure we do. My aunt has about twenty different elixirs and tonics and miracle remedies ordered from ladies' magazines. I'd wager they're all primarily laudanum."

"Go and get them, then."

She nodded and prepared to stand.

Logan's hand closed tight around a fistful of her skirt. "No," he murmured. "*Na tréig mi.*"

Her heart wrenched. "I can't leave him."

"I'll go retrieve the medicines," Rabbie said.

"In my aunt's dressing room," she said. "Two stairs up, fourth door down the western corridor."

"*Na treig mi,*" Logan rasped again. "Dinna leave me, Maddie."

"I won't." She took his hand in hers. "I'm right here."

He squeezed it tight. "You must swear it, *mo chridhe*. You're my heart. If you leave me, I'll die."

She pressed her hand to his cheek and looked into his eyes. "I won't leave you. You're not going to die. Munro is going to patch you up. I'm going to be right here while he does. Neither you nor I are going anywhere."

Rabbie returned with an armful of dark bottles. Munro uncapped and sniffed them, one by one. He handed a dark green vial to Maddie. "This should do."

She placed the bottle to Logan's lips. "Now drink this."

He did as she asked, choking down the bitter liquid with barely a grimace. His eyelids began to grow heavier at once.

"Munro." Logan turned his head from side to side, seeking the surgeon. "Munro, do you see this woman beside me?"

"Aye," Munro answered. "I see her."

"You see how bonny she is?"

Maddie blushed.

"Aye," the surgeon said, smiling. "I do."

"Well, we've been married for weeks now," Logan said, lifting his head groggily. "I've only bedded her the one night. And I'll be damned if that night will be the last. You had better mend me, Munro. I have a lot of pleasuring to do."

"Understood, Captain."

Maddie's face burned, but she couldn't help but laugh. She pressed a kiss to Logan's forehead.

"Maddie . . ." His voice grew thick. He sounded as though he were speaking to her from a dark, deep well. *"Mo chridhe,* I . . . I . . ."

"Hush," she told him, holding back tears. "I'll stay with you, Logan. Always. Just please promise you'll stay with me."

Logan came through the surgery easily enough—or so he later assumed, given that he could not remember it. It was the days afterward that threatened to dig him an early grave.

A fever set in the evening after Munro had removed the knife from his thigh.

The next few days were a blur of fitful sleep, racking chills, cool cloths swabbed over his body, weak broth offered to him on spoons . . .

And dreams.

His sleep was a riot of wild, vivid dreams. So many dreams that he suspected his mind was compensating for those lost years of darkness. He dreamed of people and places he'd long forgotten. He dreamed of battlefields and bedsport.

Most of all, he dreamed of Madeline. Her dark eyes and her slender fingers, and her sweet, essential taste.

When he finally woke, his fever broken and his mind at rest, she was right there beside him.

But the woman would *not* let him get out of bed.

For anything.

Sponge baths were not nearly so amusing as a man might think they'd be. Not even when administered by a beautiful woman.

On the third straight day of his invalid treatment, Logan rebelled. "I hope you know I despise every moment of this."

"I do know." She swabbed him under the arm with a soapy sponge. "That's why I'm enjoying it so much."

"I'm perfectly able to do for myself now. I'm well."

"Oh, no. I'm sentencing you to a full week of nursing in bed. If you do well with that, next Tuesday I might start letting you spoon your own parritch."

Logan grumbled in response.

"That's what you get for being heroic and saving my life."

She leaned forward over him, plumping his pillow. The pose gave him an unobstructed view down the valley of her cleavage.

"Be careful, lass. You're brushing close to danger."

She smiled. "You're no danger to me in this state."

"That sounded like a challenge."

"In all seriousness, Logan. You always work so hard taking care of everyone else. For a few days, I'm going to take care of you. And you will have to lie there and endure it."

Logan tried not to seem too churlish. It wasn't that he minded her presence, of course. He'd never known this kind of tenderness and attention. He simply despised the feeling of helplessness. He hated knowing that if someone charged through the door, he'd be powerless to stop it.

But he also had to admit to himself that there was a certain intoxicating pleasure to be found in surrender.

"You don't need to sit here all day," he said. "I know you probably have work to do. How are Rex and Fluffy?"

She set the sponge and basin aside. "Getting on very well indeed. She molted. They've mated and entered the tending phase."

"And . . . ?" he prompted. "Don't leave me in suspense. Which position *do* lobsters favor for their lovemaking?"

In response, she only smiled and shrugged.

Logan pushed himself up in bed, a realization settling on him. "You missed it. You missed the whole thing, didn't you? Because you were here with me."

"It's no matter. I'll just have to catch them next time. Fluffy will be ready to breed again in . . . oh, eighteen months or so."

Her response was light, but he knew this had to have come as a blow. He reached for her. "Maddie."

Before they could discuss it further, Munro entered the room to make an assessment of Logan's wound and bandages.

"You're out of the worst danger," he declared. "No strenuous activity for a month."

"A month?"

"A month. And if you mean to trouble me with complaints, I suggest you be grateful you're alive to complain."

"*Mo charaid.*" Logan reached to take the field surgeon's hand. "I owe you a debt for saving my life. It willna be forgotten. Thank you."

Munro nodded.

"That said, I hope you'll take this in the kindest possible way. Get out. I want to be alone with my wife."

The grizzled surgeon cracked a rare smile. "That I can do."

Once they were alone, Maddie settled on the bed next to him.

"Come here, then." He pulled her close, burying his face in her neck.

She resisted. "You just heard the man. That wound will take a month to heal. For the past several days, the both of us worked day and night to keep you alive. I'm not going to undo it all now."

"If I have to wait a month to hold you tight, I swear I'll die of wanting first."

She stroked a hand through his hair. "I suppose a gentle embrace might be acceptable."

He supposed he would take that.

She scooted her backside further onto the bed and cozied up to him, molding the curve of her body to his and laying her head on his chest. Her fingers stroked lightly on his collarbone, back and forth.

He pressed his nose to the top of her head and breathed deep.

She gave a soft laugh against his chest.

"What is it?"

"Oh, Logan. I hate to tell you this. But I think we're cuddling." She nuzzled into the linen of his shirt. "You're doing a wonderful job of it, too."

The little minx. Very well, she'd finally gotten her way.

They were cuddling.

And Logan rather liked it.

He loved it.

And it seemed she must truly love him. Or had succeeded in convincing herself that she did.

He slicked his hand down the tight braid of her hair. "You didna leave me."

"Not for a single hour."

He knew it. She'd been by his side through everything. The blood, the stitching, the cautery, the fever and racking chills. He'd felt her presence beside him, her arms holding him when he couldn't cease shaking on his own. Her faint scent of lavender and sweetness had reached him even in sleep.

And the dreams. He'd dreamed of her, day and night, and for the first time in his life there was nothing cold or dark or lonely about those fantasies. They were flooded with more color and light than a circus tent.

Her shoulders gave another slight quiver. Was she laughing at him again?

He heaved a teasing sigh, then regretted it. Even sighing hurt. "What have I done that's so humorous this time?"

She didn't answer. Because, just as softly as she'd started to laugh a few minutes earlier, she had begun to cry.

"I was so afraid."

"It's all right, *mo chridhe*. It's all right. I'm here now. I'm not going to leave you, either."

He tipped her lovely face to his.

And then he kissed her. How could he not?

If he tried to speak, he would have failed. There were no words for the emotions flooding his chest. His heart pounded in his chest so fiercely that he feared it would break his ribs again—this time from the inside. Or simply burst from being swollen with too much feeling.

Too much joy.

All that emotion had to go somewhere, or it would surely kill him. A kiss was the only answer.

She kissed him back, as though it meant her very life as well, sliding her fingers into his damp hair to hold him tight. Beneath the bed linens, sleeping parts of him began to stir and assert their vitality, making demands. *We're not dead yet,* they said.

"I want you," he whispered, tugging at the neckline of her frock and bending to kiss her neck. "Here. Now. Maddie, I need you."

I love you. God, I love you.

The thought moved through his mind, and Logan fought the instinct to drive it away. He didn't say it aloud—but he didn't chase it down and squash it like a bug, either. That alone felt like a victory.

He moved one hand to her breast, thumbing her nipple to a tight point and easing his fingers under the lacy neckline of her powder-blue frock to feel the delicate heat of her skin. A possessive growl rose in his chest.

"Logan . . ."

Despite her chiding tone, she let her head roll to the side, giving him more room to nibble at her earlobe.

"Let me have you, *mo chridhe*." He slid his hand inside her stays, cupping her breast. "We won't be disturbed."

"Logan." She pulled away with obvious regret. "Munro said no strenuous exercise. You know I can't ignore his orders. I care about you too much."

He let his head fall back against the pillow.

"So . . ." She walked her fingers up the center of his bandaged chest, until they reached his breastbone and her eyes lifted to his. " . . . we'll have to be very, very careful."

Yes. Holy God, yes.

"I can be careful. I can be so careful." Logan reached for her.

"Shhh." She held those two fingers against his solar plexus and pushed him, gently but firmly, back against the bed. "I'm the one who's going to be careful. Just let me do everything."

"You dinna have to do *everything*."

Her fingers pinned him to the mattress. "I'm going to do everything. And you must lie there and take it."

There was nothing in the world that came less naturally to Logan than reclining on a cloud-soft featherbed and allowing someone else to do everything. Much less the woman he'd come to treasure and protect.

But part of him liked the idea.

Liked it verra, verra much.

"I'm going to take care of you," she whispered in his left ear. She slipped her loosened frock downward, whispering in his right ear. "I'll give you everything you need."

Her breathy, sensual promise sent chills racing over his scalp and cascading down his spine. The unobstructed view of her breasts left his mouth dry with thirst.

He could only manage a word in response: "Hurry."

She gave him a slow, mischievous smile.

She lifted her breast with her hand and leaned forward, teasing the lavender-scented softness against his unshaven cheek. Logan turned his head, capturing her nipple. He drew the tight, luscious peak into his mouth, and she gave a breathy gasp that made his cock stir.

He licked and teased with abandon, loving the taste and softness of her. Even better were the little noises she made as he suckled her hard. Gasps and sighs and low, erotic moans.

"I . . . I'm supposed to be pleasing you."

He released her nipple just long enough to reply, "You are, lass. You are."

He ducked his head, nuzzling the underside of her breast and pushing it higher with his brow so that he could lick the sensitive curve beneath. Then he found her nipple once more and lavished it with long, slow passes of his tongue.

When he released her, she sat back. Her eyes had that glazed look of pleasure, and her cheeks were flushed pink.

She was lovely. So lovely, and so his. He'd done that.

"Keep very still," she said.

She gathered her skirts in one hand, settling between his legs. He bent his uninjured leg at the knee, pulling it to the side to give her more space. She drew the bed linens downward, exposing his entire body to the room's chilly air.

His eyes closed in anticipation of her touch.

But his anticipation went unfulfilled.

After a pause that seemed to last hours, he opened his eyes and glanced down at her. What was the matter now?

Apparently nothing was the matter. She was staring at the rude curve of his cock, artistic fascination plain on her face. The same way she might stare at the claw of a lobster or the wing of a butterfly.

She ran a light touch up his thigh. "May I sketch you sometime?"

"You can do whatever you please with me. As long as it's some *other* time." His voice was shaking. He made fists in the bed linens. "Lass, I'm dying here."

"Oh." She bit her lip with abashed regret. "Well, we can't have that."

At last, she touched him. Her fingertip made a long, slow pass up the underside of his shaft, circling the sensitive crown.

He cursed. His hips arched off the bed.

"Don't move like that," she said.

"Dinna tease like that," he growled.

She took pity on him. Her hand curled around his staff, catching him in a proper grip. With her first stroke, bright light flashed through his brain, blanking it. He fell back against the bed, staring up at the ceiling.

Yes. That. More. Faster. Please.

He squeezed his eyes shut to savor the sensation. Every sweet, slow stroke of her hand tugged him closer to release.

And then . . . a new sensation joined the mix. A cool, gentle flutter just at the tip of his cock. Almost like a breeze.

She was *licking* him. Swirling that shy, pink, clever tongue around the crown of his erection. Kissing and lightly tasting.

The feeling was intense. Sublime. Not nearly enough.

He endured perhaps a minute of this exploration before his thighs went rigid. He couldn't stand it anymore. With a trembling hand, he reached down to stroke her hair.

"Take me in your mouth."

The words were a risk. He might have scared her off entirely. She might have lifted her head, released his aching cock, and given him a lecture about how she wouldn't be ordered around.

To hedge his chances, he followed with a desperate "Please."

But even before he'd remembered his manners, she'd complied, bathing the head of his cock in wet, blissful heat. Pleasure engulfed him, and he moaned in helpless surrender.

"I love you."

The words just slipped out. He couldn't hold them back anymore.

He immediately cursed himself. Of all the idiot moments to say that for the first time. Now she'd stop for certain. She'd pull away with joyful tears in her eyes, and they'd have to sit up and discuss their feelings. Maybe even cuddle.

But she didn't stop. She just looked up at him, smiled a little around his cock, then took him deeper still.

He groaned again. "God, I love you so much."

She started out tentative. Understandable, this being her first time. But she didn't exactly require a great deal of skill. He was aching with need, and she was enthusiastic, if not experienced. Short of biting him, there was little she could have done that would not have felt good.

She was more than good. She was amazing.

He found himself rolling his pelvis, striving to push deeper every time her sweet, lush mouth sank down on him. He began to fear losing control and pushing her too far.

"Take me in you," he urged. "I need to feel you. Fill you."

Again, he didn't have to ask twice. She eagerly rose up and gathered her skirts to her waist, straddling him with caution. Logan reached between them to position himself, parting her folds with the head of his cock. She was wet. So wet. The knowledge that she'd found that oral attention just as arousing as he had . . . ?

He gave a strangled groan.

She sank down on him, and he slipped easily halfway. With a gentle rise and fall of her hips, she took him deeper by agonizing half-inch fractions. It was paradise and torture all at once.

At first, she was careful not to take him all the way, mindful of his wounded thigh. But after a few minutes, she braced her hands on his shoulders and set a rhythm that he could tell had less to do with his injuries and more to do with her own mounting need.

Good. He stared up at her, powerless to look away from the gentle bounce of her breasts and the evident pleasure on her face. She was the most arousing thing he'd ever seen.

Suddenly, her eyes flew open. Her gaze met his, pleading. "Logan, I . . . *Logan*."

He knew what she needed. Pushing his hand through the cloud of her skirts and petticoats, he reached down to where their bodies joined. Without breaking eye contact, he pressed his thumb to the swollen bud at the crest of her sex.

"That's it, *mo chridhe*. Let it happen. Come for me."

Her brow furrowed, and she bit her lip. She held his gaze for just a few more strokes before her eyes squeezed shut.

She came hard, convulsing around him and shaking with pleasure. Her climax commanded his. With a guttural cry, he surrendered to it, losing himself in sensation.

In the aftermath, he wanted to pull her down to him. Stay inside her and let her fall asleep against his pounding heartbeat. But she'd remembered his injuries and her nursing duties now, and she wasn't having any of that. She moved aside, nestling into the crook of his arms.

Well. That was fine, too.

"There's just one thing I still don't understand," she murmured. "Where on earth *are* those letters?"

Chapter Twenty-six

In an instant, Maddie felt Logan's body tense. His heart kicked into a faster rhythm.

"It's not what you think," he said.

"I hadn't formed any thoughts."

"I had those letters. I did. I received them all, read them all again and again."

"I know you did."

"And then after the last one, where you left me for dead . . ." He cursed under his breath. "I got so angry, I burned them all in the fire one night. All but one."

"So when you pulled one of those letters out of your pocket and read it to me . . ."

"I was reciting from memory. I knew them by heart. No matter how I tried to forget you, I never could get you out of my heart."

She hugged him gently. "Logan. That is the stupidest, sweetest thing I've ever heard."

"What can I say. I'm . . ."

"Squish. Pure squish."

"I was going to say I'm in love with you, but I suppose it isna much different."

He caught her hand in his, and their fingers laced together in a tight knot atop his chest.

"First rule of love: dinna panic."

"What's the second rule? I think we'd better skip to that."

She lifted her head and gave him a wicked smile. "No thrashing about."

Maddie had just craned her neck to give him a deep, passionate kiss, when a knock sounded at the door.

"Mrs. MacKenzie? Are you there?"

Logan kissed the top of her head. "I like hearing her call you that."

"So do I." Maddie propped her chin on his chest and smiled up at him. "I suppose I should go answer."

"Dinna bother." Logan lifted his voice. "Come in."

With a little shriek of alarm, Maddie moved to rise from the bed.

His arm tightened around her. "Stay right where you are. It's hardly the last time the servants will catch us in bed together. She might as well grow accustomed to it."

"I'm the one who'll need to grow accustomed to it." Maddie felt a blush creeping up her throat already. But she didn't move.

If Logan wanted her at his side, that was where she would stay.

Always.

When the maid entered, Maddie remained curled up at Logan's side. "What is it, Becky?"

To her credit, the maid took it in stride. "I . . . I'm sorry to disturb you, ma'am. But there's a caller for you."

"A caller?"

"Yes, Mrs. MacKenzie. And it's a man."

"A man?" Rising up on her elbow, Maddie exchanged a surprised glance with Logan. "Are you expecting someone?"

"Not unless you are."

"Did this gentleman give his name?" she asked Becky.

The maid shook her head. "I forgot to ask. Oh, Mrs. MacKenzie. He looks ever so—"

"Big?"

"No. Strange."

Now Maddie was completely at a loss. "Please show him into the parlor, Becky. And ask Cook to prepare some tea. I'll be down in a trice."

Once the maid left, Maddie gave Logan a bemused shrug. "I can't imagine who it might be."

"Do I need to be jealous?"

"Well, I must warn you, the last time I had an unexpected gentleman caller . . ." Smiling, she glanced down at their linked hands on his chest. "This happened."

"That's it." Logan released her hand and sat up in bed. "I'm going down there with you."

"Logan, I was only teasing. You should stay in bed. There's no need."

"I'm going down with you," he repeated in his most stern, commanding tone. He reached for his shirt and pulled it over his head, wincing as he worked one arm through the sleeve. "Just in case this unnamed strange gentleman tries something untoward."

"And if he did, what would you do about it? Bleed on the man?" She laughed.

He didn't.

He gave her a solemn look. It wasn't the look of an invalid but of a warrior. "I'd have to be dead in my grave before I stopped fighting for you, Madeline. Even then, I'd move six feet of earth to find a way."

Oh. Be still her heart.

"Very well, then."

What else could she do when he said such things? Maddie knew better than to try talking him out of it. If his mind was set on rising from his sickbed, there was no further benefit to arguing. And to be honest, she felt comforted to see him healthy and on his feet.

They went slowly. She buckled his *fèileadh beag* about his waist and helped him pull the shirt down over his bandaged torso. Despite his boyish protests that he could do it himself, she insisted he sit while she attacked his wild hair with a comb.

When he was presentable, they made their slow journey down the corridor, arm in arm.

The identity of the man in the parlor came as a true surprise.

"I'm Mr. Reginald Orkney," he announced.

Becky was right; the man looked every bit as out of place in her parlor at eleven o'clock in the morning as Maddie had felt in Lord Varleigh's ballroom. He was dressed in a tweed coat, dark-blue trousers, and thick-soled boots. When they entered the room, he launched from his chair, whipped the hat from his head, and greeted them with a deep bow.

"Good morning, Miss Gracechurch." He bowed again in Logan's direction. "Captain MacKenzie."

"Actually," she said, "it's now Captain and Mrs. MacKenzie."

"Is it, then? Well!" Mr. Orkney clapped his hands together in surprise. Unfortunately, the gesture flattened the hat he was still holding in one hand. He awkwardly tossed the thing to the floor and kicked it under a chair. "My felicitations to you both."

And then he showed no signs of saying anything further.

After a moment's silence, Madeline prompted, "Mr. Orkney, to what do we owe the pleasure of your visit?"

"Oh. Yes, that. I'm not sure the visit has a purpose now, strangely. You see, Miss Gracechurch—or Mrs. MacKenzie, I should say—I confess, I came hoping to engage you."

The tension in the room leapt to a new level.

"You came to propose?" Logan sounded wonderfully envious.

Mr. Orkney looked mildly terrified. "Not engage her as a wife," the man quickly amended. "Lovely as she might be, I have a wife of my own. Oh, dear. I seem to be making a muddle of things." He cleared his throat and began again. "Mrs. MacKenzie, I had come hoping to engage your services. As an illustrator."

Logan relaxed. "There's no reason you can't commission my wife's work. Even though we are newly wed, she intends to continue illustrating." He looked down at her. "Don't you?"

"Certainly," Maddie said.

"Well, that's excellent to hear," Mr. Orkney replied. "To deprive the world of such talent would be a true tragedy."

"But Mr. Orkney, are you certain you want to hire me? Perhaps you didn't yet receive my letter. There was a delay, of sorts, with the lobsters."

"Yes, yes. But that is of little consequence. This is a new project, you see. You may have noticed, I'm a different sort of naturalist from Lord Varleigh and his friends. I've no desire to trap the things and bring them home to England as effigies. I prefer to study and record my findings in the wild. My aim for this voyage is to record the native mollusks and crustaceans of Bermuda."

"Bermuda. My goodness. What an adventure."

"Yes. I had come here to ask if you, Miss Gracech— Mrs. MacKenzie, would be available to join the expedition as our illustrator."

Maddie couldn't speak for a moment.

He wanted her to join an expedition to *Bermuda*?

Mr. Orkney tugged on his ear. "It's quite short notice, I'm afraid. We hadn't planned on leaving until later this summer. But just last week we were offered passage on a ship that sails from Port Glasgow this Thursday next. I couldn't pass up the opportunity."

"Thursday next? So you're asking me to leave—"

"Immediately." He pulled an apologetic face. "I'm afraid so, yes. Once you have your things, we'd travel from here to Glasgow and use the remaining time to gather supplies for the voyage. You'd be welcome to bring a companion, should you desire one.

However, my wife will be undertaking the journey with me. I know she would be glad of female company."

When Maddie's head stopped spinning, she managed a reply. "It sounds like a most exciting opportunity, and I'm honored that you would think of me. But I'm a newlywed, as you see. My husband is recovering from an injury. I simply can't—"

Logan's hand tightened on her arm. "How long would she be gone?"

"About six months."

Logan nodded. "Will you give us a moment to discuss it?"

"But of course." The man bowed again, more deeply than ever.

Maddie followed Logan into the corridor, confused. What was there to discuss? He didn't need to talk her out of it, if that's what he meant. She'd already expressed her intent to decline with regrets.

He said, "I think you should go."

"What?"

"I think you should accompany Mr. Orkney on his expedition to Bermuda."

She couldn't believe this. "What about everything we said to each other on Beltane? Everything we shared in bed that night? If you've forgotten all that, surely you must remember twenty minutes ago."

His mouth quirked in a little smile. "Believe me, I'm not going to forget twenty minutes ago so long as I live. I still think you should go."

"I thought you wanted us to stay together. Always."

"What I *want* is to hold you tight and never let you out of my sight again. What I *want* is to spend every moment of every day with you and clutch you skin to skin for every moment of every night. I love you to the point of madness. But I am just rational enough to know that I want those things because I have difficulties with trust."

"And I understand it."

"I know you do, sweet lass that you are. That doesn't change that it's my problem to overcome." He took her by the shoulders. "This is a remarkable opportunity. An expedition to Bermuda. Illustrating from life, rather than these dead, dusty things they send you. A chance to travel and establish your career. It's what you've longed for."

"But . . . Logan, I don't want to—"

"You want to go." He laid the backs of his fingers to her cheek. "I've seen your studio, *mo chridhe*. That faded map with all those wee pins. You can't tell me you don't want to go."

"Part of me might," she admitted. "But all of me wants to be with you."

"I'm not going anywhere."

"What if I'm pregnant?"

"It's unlikely after so few times. When do you expect your courses?"

"Any day now."

"Then you'll probably know for certain before the ship sails. In the meantime, you might as well prepare. An opportunity like this won't arrive every day. Mr. Orkney could be your best chance to chase your dream."

"My dream?" She arched an eyebrow. "Since when do you put any credence in dreams?"

"Call it a recent development."

"If you ask me, *you're* afraid. You're so afraid I might think of leaving, you're pushing me away."

He shrugged. "You could be right. You say you love me, but I can't stop thinking . . . How can you be certain? I've known you for years. You haven't known me but a few weeks, and now you'll give up the chance of a lifetime? How do I know it's me you want? Perhaps you're still hiding behind the story."

"So now I'm the girl who cried kilt. Because I made up a Scottish officer once upon a time, you will never fully trust that I love you?"

"What I'm saying is this, Madeline. If you followed your dream and came back to me . . . ? I'd trust that."

She stared at him for a long moment.

They couldn't live this way, always doubting each other, always questioning whether their bond was a true love union or a convenient arrangement.

Was it their hearts that locked together like two pieces of a puzzle? Or merely their fears?

She loved him. She felt certain of it, even if he didn't. But unless she wanted to live out the rest of her life under the fog of his doubt, she had to convince him of that.

Maddie would go to the ends of the earth. To hell and back, if need be.

By contrast, Bermuda didn't seem so far.

"Let me ask you this way." Logan tipped her face to his. "If he'd come here and asked you two months ago, before I ever came into your life . . . what would you have said? I think we both know."

Maddie nodded to herself. She did know exactly how she would have answered.

And after she considered it that way, everything became clear.

Before she could give herself time to rethink it, she returned to the parlor. "Mr. Orkney, I can leave with you today."

Chapter Twenty-seven

*L*ogan did not take well to idleness.

It hadn't been a week since Maddie's departure with Mr. Orkney, and he was already out of his mind with boredom. And, of course, missing his wife like mad.

He didn't know how he was going to survive six months of this.

At least the men seemed to know he needed company. It was just like old times on campaign. They all sat around the fire of an evening, drinking whisky and talking of lost loves and their future lives.

Logan reached into his pocket and touched the corner of a folded paper. He'd found it tucked in his sporran the night after she'd left with Mr. Orkney. Just the sight of a creased paper with her handwriting had sent his mind tumbling into memories. His heart had given a familiar throb. Could it be another letter?

And then he'd opened it to find something so much better.

A sketch.

The little minx.

He wouldn't take it out in company, but he'd taken to carrying it with him always. The charcoal drawing all but glowed like an ember in his vest pocket, threatening to burn straight through the pocket lining.

He uncapped his flask to pour another whisky. Then he thought better of it and put the flask away. After scratching his chin, he decided he could do with a bath and a shave as well. If he wasn't careful, he'd be a raging drunk with a yard-long beard by the time Maddie returned.

And she *would* return to him.

He had to believe that, or he'd truly go mad.

Grant roused himself. "What's this, then? What's happened?"

Logan considered mumbling through his usual litany of reassurances: we're in Scotland, they'd go Ross-shire tomorrow, and so forth. But then he stopped himself.

Instead, he put his hand on his friend's shoulder. "You've suffered an injury, *mo charaid*. One that disrupted your memory. We're back from the war, safe.

Your family wasna so fortunate. But I'm here, and I'll always tell you the truth. Ask me whatever you wish."

But Grant surprised him. "I know where I am, Captain. And I'm starting to recover pieces of the rest. There's only one question I wanted to ask. Where's Madeline?"

No one could reply. If the rest were anything like Logan, they were wondering if they'd heard him wrong.

"Where's Madeline?" he repeated.

"She's . . . well, she left."

"Left? Why would she do that?"

"I told her to go." Logan scrubbed his face with one hand. "I sent her to Bermuda to draw sea creatures with a naturalist."

Grant was quiet for a moment, and then he spoke the words everyone—Logan included—seemed to be thinking. "You *stupid* bastard."

Logan raised his hands in defense. "What else could I do? She has talents. And dreams. I dinna want to stand in the way of them. She'll be back."

He had to cling to that thought. She would come back. She *would*.

Wouldn't she?

Callum scratched his head. "Well, I understand why you wanted her to go. But what I canna fathom is why you didna go with her."

Go with her.

Logan had to admit, the idea had never occurred to him. "I couldna go with her."

"Why not?"

"We've only just settled at Lannair. I'm the laird of the castle now. Someone needs to watch over the property. And you lads need me here." He looked around at the men. "Do you not?"

His only reply were the sounds of a clearing throat and someone's boot scuffing back and forth against the stone floor.

So. They didn't need him.

"I see," he said tightly.

"It isna that we *want* you gone," Callum said. "But we're grown men, the lot of us. We can fend for ourselves. The cottages are underway; the crops are in the ground. Even Grant is on the mend."

The words were meant to console him, but Logan felt hollow inside.

If Maddie's true dreams had been hidden in the margins of her letters, his own hopes had been hidden on the borders of his plans. It wasn't the land he'd wanted. It was family. Kinship.

Love.

This motley assortment of broken-down soldiers around him was the only family he'd ever known. He'd looked after them the way he would look after his own kin. If Maddie was gone and the men didn't need him . . . who was he anymore?

"I thought we were a brotherhood," he said. "A clan. *Muinntir.*"

"Aye, we are," Rabbie said. "And that's the thing about bonds of brotherhood, *mo charaid.* They stretch. For thousands of miles if need be. You can depend on us to hold the place together while you take your bride on a honeymoon."

A honeymoon.

What a notion. Logan hadn't even thought of it that way. Men with his origins didn't have holidays. Now it was all he could imagine. Sailing with Maddie through clear blue waters, watching the breezes stir her dark, unbound hair. Making love to her on sandy shores.

At last, they could really take that walk along the beach.

"What day is it?" he asked.

"Wednesday," Callum answered.

Logan rose to his feet and kicked his chair to the side. "Then there's time. I can catch the ship before it leaves."

The men snapped into action.

"That's the spirit," Rabbie said. "I'll ready your horse."

Callum brought him his coat, and Logan eased into it.

He brushed his hands down the red sleeves before spearing his fingers through his hair. He had no hose, no stock or cravat. There wasn't any time.

"How do I look?" he asked Callum as he jammed his left foot into a boot.

"Like something a wildcat dragged through gorse," Callum said.

Logan shrugged. Nothing to be done about it now. She would either take him as he was, or she wouldn't.

"Wait, wait." Munro blocked his way. "To have any chance of traveling to Glasgow by coach, you'd have to leave"—the field surgeon checked his pocket timepiece—"twelve hours ago. And as your doctor, I canna recommend you ride overland. Not with that recent injury."

Logan leveled a hard stare at the man. "Doctor or no—if you value your own health, you willna try to stop me."

"As I said, that's speaking as your doctor." Munro gave him a sly grin. "As your friend and brother, I say ride well and Godspeed."

Logan acknowledged him with a nod of gratitude.

"Chances are you'll still miss her, you know."

"I know. But I have to try. And if I'm too late . . ." He pushed his right foot into the other boot. "I suppose I'll write her some letters."

"Letters?" A familiar feminine voice rang through the hall. "Oh. I am sorry I'll miss those."

Maddie.

* * *

Oh, the expression on Logan's face when he turned around.

She would treasure it forever.

He looked red-eyed, as though he hadn't slept in days. He certainly hadn't shaved. The smell of whisky hung in the air. His shirt was unbuttoned and his hair was unkempt. He was a portrait of misery without her.

She loved it. And she'd never loved him more.

"You're here," he said, sounding bewildered.

"I'm here."

He drew closer. Slowly. As if he was afraid that if he moved too close, too fast, he might scare her away.

Maddie smiled. She wasn't going anywhere.

He stopped a few paces distant. Then simply stood there for a moment, letting his gaze roam every part of her.

"You look beautiful," he said, passing a hand over his face.

"You look terrible," she replied, smiling.

"Why are you here? The expedition was postponed?"

She shook her head.

"Called off?"

"No."

"You're not with—" His gaze dropped to her belly.

She smiled and shook her head. "Not that either."

"Then you changed your mind about sailing with him."

"Actually, I never went to Glasgow at all."

His brow darkened. "Did that Varleigh bastard—"

"Logan." She stepped forward and put a hand to his chest. Warm and solid as ever. It felt so good to touch him. So essential and right. "This would go much faster if you'd stop trying to guess and simply let me do the talking."

He opened his mouth to speak. Then shut it.

She took that as her cue.

"You asked me to think about what I would have answered had Mr. Orkney invited me to join his expedition two months ago. And I knew at once what my answer would have been. It would have been no. I would have been too intimidated, too fearful. I would have pinned myself to a specimen board and let my own wings shrivel to dust. The only reason I could even contemplate leaving . . . It was because of you."

"Then why are you back here?"

"Because you wanted me to chase my dream. And it wasn't in Glasgow or Bermuda," she explained. "I did what I should have done the night of the Beetle Ball. I apologized to Mr. Orkney and went to Edinburgh instead, where I took my portfolio to Mr. Dorning. He's the printer working on the encyclopedia, if you recall."

He nodded.

"You were right, Logan. I do have ambition. I do want to do something grand with my talents. But the encyclopedia was the commission I truly wanted from the first. So I showed Mr. Dorning my work and offered my services for his project."

His eyebrows lifted. "And . . . ?"

"And . . ." She smiled. "He gave me the post."

There was no holding him back any longer. He caught her in his arms and lifted her off her feet, swinging her around in a circle.

Maddie felt as though she were flying.

And even when he dropped her feet back down to earth, her heart kept on soaring.

"Your ribs," she said, suddenly remembering. "Be careful. Remember what Mr. Munro said about your lung."

"My lungs are fine. It's my heart that's about to burst. With pride. That's brilliant, *mo chridhe*." He turned to his men. "Lads, Mrs. MacKenzie here is going to illustrate an encyclopedia. Four whole volumes. Congratulate her."

The men offered their hearty congratulations, which Maddie was most glad to accept.

"Now bid her good-bye," he said.

"Good-bye?" Maddie looked up at him, confused.

"Aye." He pulled her close and growled into her ear. "Once I have you upstairs in our bed, they'll not see you for a fortnight or two."

Her face heated. "Oh."

He followed that promise with a searing kiss that tasted of whisky and sweetness. She kissed him back, sinking into the embrace fully. No safety net, no tether to grasp. From this moment forward, she wasn't holding anything back.

She refused to let him carry her from the room. But he whisked her away by the hand, leaving her breathless as they mounted the spiraling stairs. By the time they reached the bedchamber, she was dizzy with laughter and desire.

Together they fell onto the bed.

He pulled at her frock, working the buttons loose with one hand and pushing up her skirts with the other.

They made love in slow, cautious strokes. Partly in deference to his injured state, and partly just to savor the closeness. Neither of them wanted it to end too soon.

Afterward, he stayed inside her while she held him close.

"Did you really mean to keep me here a fortnight?" she whispered.

"Maybe two."

"I can't stay in bed forever, you know. There's work to be done. And I feel I need to warn you . . . soon my studio will be crawling with beetles, dragonflies, moths, and more."

She felt him shudder.

"Don't worry. Most of them will be dead."

He peered down at her. "*Most* of them?"

"And people almost never die of insect bites."

"*Almost* never."

She gave him a teasing nuzzle. "Breathe. Just breathe."

His brow pressed to hers. And for a moment, that's all they did: just breathe. Trade the same air back and forth, until there wasn't his breath or hers, but just theirs.

"I love you," he said.

"I love you, too."

"I missed you fierce, *mo chridhe*. I was a jackass to ever let you go."

"Oh, you were Captain MacJackass."

He smiled a little. Then his expression grew solemn. "I just didna want to hold you back from your dream."

"That's just it. You never could." She stared deep into those eyes, the same brilliant blue as wide Highland skies. "Logan, you *are* my dream. You always were. You have to know that. The deepest desire of my heart. And as wild a fantasy as I spun . . ." She laced her arms about his neck. " . . . the reality of us is so much better."

Epilogue

It took him a few months, but once he'd fully recovered from his injuries and the summer sunshine had warmed the air, Logan finally managed to whisk his wife away for a proper honeymoon.

He took her to the seaside. Nine years after they'd first "met" on the beach in Brighton.

Better late than never.

He found them a well-furnished cottage near Durness, situated near a wide, sandy crescent of beach with a perfect view of the pink-orange sunsets. It wasn't Brighton or Bermuda, but it was lovely and secluded and theirs.

Considering it was the first holiday he'd ever planned or taken in his life, Logan felt rather proud of his success.

Every afternoon, they walked along the shore together. Maddie collected shells and sketched them in her notebook. Logan gave her a gold wedding band he'd had engraved with both their initials. More than once, they made love on his green-and-blue tartan spread over white sands.

And they bid farewell to two dear friends.

"Fare-thee-well, Fluffy," Maddie whispered. "Take good care of her, Rex."

They released the lobsters into the ocean and bid them a good journey and best wishes for thousands of healthy offspring.

As they looked out over the blue water, Maddie reached for Logan's hand and laced her fingers in his. "Remember when you held our firstborn child in your arms?"

He pulled her close and kissed those sweet, soft lips. "I believe I do remember that. As I recall, it was about nine months from now."

She laughed. "More like six, I think."

"What?" Stunned, Logan lifted his head and looked down at her. "No. Already?"

She nodded.

"But . . ." He racked his memory for any evidence. "You havena been sick."

"I was at first, just a little bit. Aunt Thea gave me a tonic."

He dropped her hand, stepped back, and stared at her, rubbing a hand over his face.

God help him. He thought he might faint.

She bit her lip. "I confess, I thought you'd react with more enthusiasm."

"I'm not lacking for enthusiasm. I want to squeeze you tight and spin you around and lay you down and make love to you. But I'm suddenly terrified to do any of it." He swallowed hard. "You're with child. It's a delicate condition."

"Delicate?" She smiled. "Logan, the child I'm carrying is yours. I feel certain he or she can survive just about anything. Including love."

He reached to trace a gentle caress along her collarbone. "*Mo chridhe*. My own heart."

She took his hand and placed it on her belly. "There's another little heart inside here now. It's a bit of you and a bit of me, and a lot of someone we'll have to wait to know. But Logan"—her dark eyes tipped up to meet his—"this means we're a family."

His knees truly did buckle then.

He pulled her roughly to him, clutching her tight to hide his own overwhelming emotions. Later, he'd blame the redness in his eyes on wind-driven sand.

For now, he buried his face in her hair and murmured promises.

Thou art bone of my bone, flesh of my flesh.

The same words with which he'd vowed his life to Madeline, he whispered now to his unborn babe. This child would never know hunger, never feel cold. Never know the pain of fear and darkness. Not while Logan had breath in his lungs and life in his veins.

And as for love . . .

Even when his heart stopped beating, there would be no end to his love.

He held her there until the incoming tide lapped at their toes.

And then he swept his wife into his arms and took her home.